STOP ME IF YOU'VE HEARD THIS ONE

ALSO BY KRISTEN ARNETT

With Teeth

Mostly Dead Things

KRISTEN ARNETT

STOP ME IF YOU'VE HEARD THIS ONE

corsair

CORSAIR

First published in the United States in 2025 by Riverhead Books
First published in Great Britain in 2025 by Corsair

1 3 5 7 9 10 8 6 4 2

A CIP catalogue record for this book
is available from the British Library.

Hardback ISBN: 978-1-4721-5912-0
Trade Paperback ISBN: 978-1-4721-5969-4

Book design by Meighan Cavanaugh

Printed and bound in Great Britain by Clays Ltd, Elcograf S.p.A.

Papers used by Corsair are from well-managed forests
and other responsible sources.

Corsair
An imprint of
Little, Brown Book Group
Carmelite House
50 Victoria Embankment
London EC4Y 0DZ

The authorised representative
in the EEA is
Hachette Ireland
8 Castlecourt Centre, Dublin 15,
D15 XTP3, Ireland
(email: info@hbgi.ie)

An Hachette UK Company
www.hachette.co.uk

www.littlebrown.co.uk

for anyone who's ever been called
funny as an insult

Start every day off with a smile
and get it over with.

Attributed to W. C. Fields

COLD OPEN

ou can tell a joke one of two ways:

1. Open your mouth and say the damn thing.
2. Wait for someone else to try to tell it for you.

The second way is almost always funnier. People don't want to hear a punch line; they want to feel like they've beaten you to it. Pretend you're dumber than the audience, at least at first, and suddenly you've got them eating from the palm of your hand. The real gag is waiting behind the scenes, tucked neatly inside the fake-out. It's an actual diamond ring disguised as a gaudy cubic zirconia.

I'm telling this to the woman from the birthday party, but she's not listening. Her eyes have that faraway look, sleepy with desire. Lips part to reveal a slip of tongue and a back tooth gone inky with rot. I've got her up on the sink, underwear pulled down. She's jiggling her legs rapidly, knees knocking together because I'm taking too long. She's been after it ever since she opened the front door and found me waiting on her porch.

Listen, I've been busy. For the past two and a half hours, I've entertained her six-year-old son, Danny, and his entire first-grade class in a sprawling suburban Central Florida backyard. I've built zoo animals from stringy multihued balloons and pulled never-ending scarves from the ends of my belled sleeves. The bulbous yellow daisy on my lapel has shot water at the woman's husband, soaking the neck of his expensive Ralph Lauren polo. I've thrown a whipped cream pie into the moon of a child's upturned face and spritzed seltzer at an elderly schnauzer who took my rented pant leg between its tiny razor teeth and yanked until the hem unraveled.

"Come on," she says, voice breathy and impatient. "Hurry."

There's a swath of black hairs lining the top of her right ankle, a sprawl of red dots climbing the inside of her bare thigh from a shaving rash. She kicks free of her underwear and almost knees my nose off in her rush to get naked. I reach up to right it, smearing a lick of greasepaint on my gloved fingertips. I'll have to wash them with dish soap right when I get home or else they'll stain. I tell her this, but she doesn't care about that either.

"We've got ten minutes," she says, which means we've got less time than that.

I keep my clothes on because that's what she wants. The baggy polka-dot blazer, the orange-striped shirt and gold bow tie, the purple spangled suspenders, my oversize parachute pants with their lines of glittery silver thread outlining the sperm-shaped squiggles of bright neon green. My shiny red shoes are long enough to bang into the side of the toilet bowl as I wrench off her blouse. Buttons plink onto the black-and-white tiled floor.

"Finally." She wraps her legs around my waist, feet bouncing against my back as I slip off a glove with my teeth so I can slide my fingers in-

side her. She looks away from my bare hand, not wanting to see anything that's *not* CLOWN; she's paying for CLOWN and has wanted
CLOWN since she called the agency's number two months earlier to
plan her son's birthday party. She stares hungrily at my painted face:
the wide slick of paint that surrounds my mouth, the black and indigo
triangles that shape my eyes, the iconic red foam nose that holds my
overly hot breath inside its spongy interior. The wig I wear is powder
blue, curls springy and cute, like a deranged Shirley Temple who just
got back from Burning Man. Atop the wig sits a tiny rhinestone and
suede cowboy hat I picked up one afternoon at a pet shop, which is now
a staple of my clowning gear. I'm Bunko, a rodeo clown who's terrified
of horses. Goes over great with the kids.

"Do you have a dick?"

I stop thrusting and look down at her, finding us suddenly off-script.

"A dick?"

She licks her lips. Pink lipstick feathers at the corners of her mouth.
"Not a real dick. I know you're a female clown, I'm not dumb. I mean
like . . . a *dick* dick."

"A dick," I repeat, because our time together is nearing its inevitable
conclusion and neither of us has gotten off. There's sudden shrieking
inside the house, the bang of sneakers against the expensive maple
floorboards, the groan of furniture as bodies ricochet against the walls.
Soon her husband will do the thing that all husbands do when faced
with a crew of screaming children: he will search for his missing wife.

"Also, I'm not trying to be a jerk or anything, but could you use the
clown voice? I mean, I'm paying for the experience, you know?"

Shifting back into Bunko is easy enough. I grin down at her and
widen my eyes dramatically.

"Let's see what I've got up my sleeve," I say, high-pitched and giggly,
the tone I've worked to perfect since I took up clowning eight years
earlier. "I bet Bunko's got something just for you."

I've got nothing like that in my clowning kit. All my dildos are at home, squirreled away inside my nightstand. But if I've learned anything from clowning, it's that there's always a way to turn nothing into something. I've entertained an entire backyard full of people with nothing but a wooden spoon and a cast-iron pan as accompaniment, drumming the theme from *The Brady Bunch* while simultaneously dancing a jig. I've landed a somersault on a Slip 'N Slide while juggling three Coke cans and somehow managed not to break my neck. If I can't MacGyver myself a dick out of thin air, then I need to find a new profession.

Clowning is an excuse to make everyday life wildly, luxuriously absurd. I create a drumroll sound effect with my tongue, wriggling my fingers expectantly before delving inside the interior pocket of my coat. I rummage in there for a moment, allowing the expectation to build, and then suddenly produce a magic wand.

Her eyes widen. "Ooh."

It's collapsible. I'd used it earlier at the party, tapping the brim of Bunko's undersized cowboy hat to summon a rubber snake, exclaiming in alarm when the wand broke into pieces and the reptile suddenly "escaped." It gets a laugh every time, that stupid wand, and I hold it out in front of me now like I might actually create some real magic.

As she tentatively takes it in her hands, I let it collapse. The woman screams with joy, legs immediately spreading as I command the wand erect again. It's not nearly as wide as a dildo, but it's not the size of the wand that matters, it's the motion of the potion that counts, and the woman seems thrilled with what I've produced. I prod it inside her as she stares up at my makeup-caked face, hands knotted in the sides of my bright blue wig, grunts spilling from between her closed lips as I hurry, hurry, hurry. We're definitely running out of time. It sounds like there's a stampede heading toward the bathroom, so many little bodies needing to purge their bladders and bowels after swilling cups of overly sugary lemonade and consuming a towering Publix layer cake that must have cost the woman a small fortune. People with money never think about what birthdays cost. No expense is spared for a kid who will barely remember the day; there is no other choice than to have a party because the alternative—no party, no gifts—is unthinkable for the upper middle class. They'll never have to waffle over a bank account in the teenage digits, deciding which birthday dreams get to live and which must crawl away and die.

I should have charged more.

She cranes upward and presses her face to mine, tongue slipping inside my mouth as she comes. I wrench backward and push her away, sure my makeup is ruined, and it must be, because some of it now coats the right side of her face in a Picasso-style swirl. Sudden banging on the bathroom door. The wand has collapsed again, slithering out of her body. I shove it back in my pocket as she yanks her underwear on, blonde hair mussed and frizzy from repeatedly rubbing against a stack of bright yellow hand towels.

"Hurry," she says, but this time it's said with a trace of genuine fear as she works to scrub the greasepaint stains from her chin with a wad of damp toilet paper.

I clear my throat, but she won't look at me. My usefulness has reached its inevitable conclusion upon delivery of her orgasm; the clown must go back in the box. If I put out my hand and tried to touch her shoulder just now, she'd swat me off like a cloud of gnats.

More shouting. It's the husband. He's agitated, demanding a response from his wife. "Marcia, are you okay? Marcia, answer me!" She looks more like a Samantha, I think, then pocket the thought for later as I climb inside the oversize tub and clear the windowsill of bath products. I shove the frame open and use the soap dish as a stepping stool, bottles of Pantene Pro-V and floral-fragranced shower gel falling to the floor as I heft myself onto the lip, shower curtain wrapped around my scissoring legs.

"Shit," I say, because the thick loop of wire that keeps my pants extended has caught on the edge of the frame. The lock on the door has proved ineffective in the face of the husband's outrage; there's a loud crack as the cheap fiberboard breaks. Pieces of MDF clatter onto the tile floor as he bursts into the bathroom.

One more solid push and my pants finally tear. Someone grabs my leg and yanks off one of my oversize shoes as I slither through the opening. I fall forward into the blazingly hot Florida afternoon, landing face-first in a thatch of bougainvillea. My blazer snags on the thorns as I roll free, knocking into a pair of black garbage bins.

It's always the jokes that go off the rails that work best, I think, as my own shoe flies from the open window and whacks me hard in the neck. The beauty of it stuns me for a moment, and I stand in the sunshine and watch the shoe roll down the hill and land in a nearby flower bed, squashing a clutch of fuchsia peonies.

"You fucking clown!" The husband yells it again, in case I missed it the first time. "You goddamn *fucking clown*!"

He chucks a shampoo bottle at my head. I duck and it smacks into the side of the garbage bin, Pantene spurting from the broken lid. I take off down the street at a gallop, abandoning my clown kit in the middle of the couple's living room. It's full of stuff I need for work, a hundred fifty dollars' worth of makeup and gear, and as I'm running for my life, I realize that the man isn't wrong. The punch line is sitting right there.

I am a literal fucking clown.

AQUARIUM SELECT III

The hot older lady with the baby bearded dragon is at Darcy's register. I know this because Darcy is clicking the talk button on her walkie-talkie and repeatedly whispering the word "fire-breather" into the mic. It sounds like the opening to an especially bad EDM track. Jamming the button alone is usually enough to pique my interest; it's our signal that something special is happening so we should drop what we're doing and pay attention. For an exotic pet store, "special" happens way less often than you'd think.

The headset buzzes, and then there's a brusque, no-nonsense voice in my ear. "Stop messing around."

Darcy clicks back in, all mock professionalism. "Yes, sir, Mister Manager."

Work is boring, but at least it's predictable. The paycheck is fine for part-time work that barely requires rubbing two brain cells together. It gives you time to think about anything other than what you're getting paid to do. That's what Darcy and I tell each other when the days begin to stretch out in front of us like chewing gum that's had all the flavor gnawed from it. Boring is better than stressed-out. We're financing our creative careers.

Clowning ain't cheap, I think. I mentally pour one out for my kit, abandoned last week in that woman's living room.

"I need restock on aisle four. Filter socks and media baskets."

If we don't respond, he'll yell at us again. On a boring day that would be fine by me—it gives me something to do, and he's funny when he's pissed. In fact, several of my clown identities have taken on very specific uptight Mister Manager vibes: peacocked chest, veins in my neck protruding as I grind my teeth. But since I want to check out the woman at the register, I take one for the team and answer him.

"Right away, Mister Manager."

"Knock that crap off," he says. "I'm tired of it."

Mister Manager's real name is Roy Mangia, but Darcy and I have been calling him Mister Manager ever since the third week of work, when I heard him accidentally announce it as his last name over the intercom. He's a forty-something dude with a roachy patchwork beard who eats the same overly mustardy tuna sandwich every day for lunch. The guy drives a teal-green Mazda Miata with a rack for his incredibly expensive racing bike dangling from the back. He's the poster boy for masculine midlife crises.

Instead of heading to aisle four so I can do my actual job, I slip past the tower of glowing blue tanks that line the wall of the shop and power walk to the register. There she is: the MILF of my dreams. She holds out the lizard for Darcy's inspection. She's been coming in at least once a week after buying it from our coworker, Wendall, who neglected to tell her that baby bearded dragons are essentially the French bulldogs of the reptile world: allergic to nearly everything, expensive as hell, and almost always on the verge of death.

"He's shivering. See? His neck is all pale."

Darcy hums noncommittally. Her mohawk is especially tall today, nearly grazing the bottom of a long banner advertising Ocean's Blend supplements. Darcy Dinh likes a theme, and she generally sticks to aquatic colors when it comes to her hair: blues, greens, purples. This week, she's gone for a mix of all three. If she stood in front of the store, she'd blend in chameleon-like against the paint. The exterior was painted by a muralist ten years earlier. It features bloated whales and scraggly, bug-eyed seagulls on a background of murky, phosphorescent foam. Some days, when I arrive for a shift, it feels as though I'm entering a rip-off SeaWorld. It's a part of the scenery for me at this point. My eyes scan past the paint and over the aisles of piled-up junk. Wobbling stacks of glass tanks? Check. Bags of fluorescent gravel? Check. Gigantic wall mural that features what might be a demonic mermaid? Check.

Wendall is standing next to the entrance, pretending to clean the window. The rag in his hand moves in circles about five inches from the actual glass. His face is bent over his phone, and it's giving his skin a greenish, unattractive tint. It used to be that Darcy and I would have yelled at him by now for leaving us with all the work, but lately she's been giving him a pass. Making fun of a coworker is a team sport, and she's dropping the ball.

"Cherry?" Darcy waves me over. "Can I get your help with this?"

The woman turns to me and holds the lizard out for my inspection. I stare at it like I know what I'm doing and declare that it needs a better heat lamp. Despite four years working at Aquarium Select III, I know almost nothing about reptile care.

"He's cold," I say, because even I feel frozen inside the tundra that is our shop. Mister Manager keeps the temperature akin to that of a walk-in freezer. He claims it's good for circulation, but really he's just trying to prevent us from curling up in dusty, hidden corners of the store and napping when business is slow. It's a miracle that the animals haven't all died in this latest ice age.

I lead the woman to aisle two, where we keep the reptile habitats and various supplies, supplements, and equipment. Most of this stuff has been sitting on the shelf for years; we don't have much turnover because people prefer to buy their pet stuff online. The boxes are coated in a fine layer of grime. I can feel Darcy's eyes boring a hole into my back. I don't have to see her to know that she's thrusting her hips in a pornographic gesture that would get her suspended if our boss caught her. When I turn around, I see that Wendall has wandered over from his "cleaning" project and is busy showing Darcy something from his notepad.

Seven clicks in a row over my headset as I put my arm around the woman's shoulders and guide her around the corner.

"I'm going to take the walkies away from you."

"Yes, please," Darcy replies, high-pitched and saccharine. "Thank you, Mister Manager."

"Screw you both."

Wendall's not included in this lambasting because he is never around. I'm not sure he even has a walkie-talkie, much less an earpiece. It's a point of contention between myself and Mister Manager because I'm of the opinion that since Wendall takes two-hour bathroom breaks and three-hour lunches, he's technically the worst employee at Aquarium Select III, yet we're the ones getting chewed out over a little harmless fun. Wendall is a slam poet who is never *not* high. On shift he's either spaced-out or droning on and on about black holes, so it makes sense that he wouldn't care about stocking shelves. Darcy used to hate it too, but now she laughs when she sees him scratching down goofy little phrases in his notepad, like he thinks he's going to be the next Kerouac. But I'm not fooled. The guy's a secret menace. Whenever he does anything job related, it just turns into more work for everyone else. Take restocks, for instance. He puts everything on the wrong shelf, then throws up his hands in despair when confronted with the error. Usually, it's me or Darcy who's tasked with fixing it, the age-old tale of women having to take care of a helpless man. Except he's not helpless; he's just lazy. Or maybe, a little malicious. It's like how my older brother, Dwight, used to load the dishwasher poorly so that our mother would stop asking him to do it.

I bet she wishes she could yell at him about the dishwasher now, I think. We could take turns really laying into him in person instead of dealing with all the jumbled detritus of his memory piled up in our heads.

"Which light are you using?"

"This one," the woman says, picking up a box. "Is it no good?"

She has stowed the bearded lizard inside her neon-pink fanny pack. I can see his tiny face mashed against the mesh front pocket as he wriggles around frantically, searching for a way out. I pretend to examine the light, but mostly I'm staring at the incredible amount of cleavage spilling from her Lycra workout top.

"It's possible you need a different bulb for it," I say, because that sounds sensible enough to be actual advice. "Something warmer."

Along with the Lycra top, she's wearing a pair of pink-and-yellow spandex leggings and fluffy white leg warmers. Her hair is what a box of dye might call "spicy cinnamon," and there's approximately two pounds of makeup on her face. I don't know what it is about women who could be my mother that gets me off, but I am a sucker for anyone over the age of fifty who looks like they are about to lead a very rigorous step aerobics class. Possibly it's due to the fact that I'm looking for someone to take care of me since my own mom forgot to call me on my last birthday, but even I've got my limits; I'm not going to ogle this woman's tits while reminiscing about my unhappy childhood.

Aquarium Select III stocks only three different types of heating bulbs, so we take our time poring over the packaging—the woman because she's genuinely interested in saving her lizard's life, and me because her skin smells like a mixture of cotton candy and dryer sheets.

"I'm not sure," she says, frowning so hard it looks like it hurts. "What do you think?" Her lipstick is a slick of bright red, a color that's entirely reminiscent of the clown paint I wear for work events. I wonder if it's the same brand I use when I'm out of the good stuff.

I could lie and make something up, some bullshit about faulty heating elements and Florida humidity, but my heart's not in it. It's thinking about the clown paint that did it; my kit with all my best stuff abandoned in some woman's living room because I was too much of a coward to go back for it. There's not enough in my bank account to buy more. I'll have to use the cheap, shitty stuff that makes my face break out until I save up enough for the good greasepaint again. There's an audition in a couple of weeks I've been gearing up for—an opportunity to get in on a traveling children's showcase that tours from Gainesville down to St. Petersburg—and if I prep my set list wisely enough, I could be good to go on gigs for the entire summer. I could network with half the clowns in Florida and land even more full-time work. But no gear means no audition means no money. Twenty-eight years old and broke with a chin full of acne isn't exactly a persona I want to lean into.

"I'm actually not sure either." I slide the box back onto the shelf. "It could be any of these."

The woman sighs deeply. "I don't want him to die. My husband left three months ago, and Bradley is the only thing getting me through it."

"Bradley's a great name for a bearded lizard. It makes him sound like he's got a 401(k)."

I awkwardly pat her shoulder as her lip quivers and her eyes leak trails of bright blue mascara.

"Your name's Cherry?" She sniffles hard. "That's exotic."

"Not really." My name is actually Cheryl, but nobody except my mother has called me that since I moved out at eighteen. Cherry is a good time, a person who owns a muscle car and drinks straight gin and parties 'til three in the morning. Cheryl is the name of the person who does taxes for a living and drives a sensible, buff-colored sedan. Cheryl is Nancy's letdown of a daughter, Dwight's disappointing younger sister who was never as funny or as cool or as smart as he was. But Cherry belongs only to herself, and she's beyond fine with that.

"I'm LeeAnn. Boring name for a boring old broad."

"I don't think you're boring," I say, poking at the lizard that's squashed inside her fanny pack. It has stopped moving, which probably isn't a good sign. "I think you're a very cool reptile broad."

She's crying again. Instead of prolonging her misery, I lead her to the back of the store, where Mister Manager is directing a trainee named Austin on how to painstakingly scrub stains from the sides of the turtle enclosures. They're coated with a thick layer of sickly green algae from the bacteria that drifts off their shit and from rotten chunks of uneaten food.

"No, like *this*." There are large sweat stains darkening both of his armpits. "Up down, up down. You gotta get a real rhythm going or you're gonna miss spots."

I clear my throat. Austin the trainee looks at me with puzzled recognition. He has a real baby face: chapped pink cheeks, bare hint of stubble over his puffy pink lips. Can't be older than seventeen. I probably clowned at a birthday party he attended; it's happened before.

"Mister Manager, this customer needs some of your expertise."

He stops windmilling his arms long enough to scowl at me. "We're busy, Cherry."

"LeeAnn here is having a problem with her bearded dragon." I lean forward conspiratorially and shout-whisper as loud as my voice will let me. "One she bought here. From Wendall. With the protection plan. Ninety-day refund guaranteed in cases of animal loss."

He straightens up and smiles at her. "Right. Let's get you sorted."

I leave them to figure it out.

Back at the register, Wendall has disappeared. Darcy is painting her chewed-up fingernails with a bottle of gummy Wite-Out that has probably been sitting in the supply drawer for at least ten years.

"You fuck her?" Darcy asks.

"I wish." I hop up onto the counter and let her paint stripes of Wite-Out in my short black hair. I need a haircut. It's getting too long in the back, threatening to turn into a mullet, but I can't be bothered to pay someone to cut it properly when I know I'm just going to be shoving it under a wig. At times I wonder if it would be cheaper all around to just dye my own hair like Darcy does; then I could perm it and walk around all day like I've been electrocuted.

"Do you think Bunko would've fucked her?"

"Probably." My black jeans are frayed at the hem and dragging on the floor, picking up dirt and lint. I put my foot up on my lap and yank at the threads until they come off in my fingers. "Look, pubes."

"Don't change the subject." She yanks on my hair, and I yelp. Darcy's short, but she's strong. She plays drums for a local punk band called RHINOPLASTIZE, and her arms have the kind of muscles that could choke a man to death without her even breaking a sweat.

"I'm not going to fuck that old lady," I say. "She's too nice."

"What does nice have to do with anything?"

I let her paint a stripe of Wite-Out down the center of my nose. "Too nice for me."

Someone walks through the double doors at the front and squints blindly in the dank, purplish light. We can't keep anything too bright in the store because it upsets the aquatic pH balance of the fish tanks, according to Mister Manager, but it seems like it has less to do with any of that and more to do with the fact that you can't tell the store is a pigpen if no one can actually see the tumbleweeds of dust rolling around on the scuffed linoleum floors.

The guy stops at the register across from us. "Y'all got Science Diet?"

"What's that?" Darcy blows on my nose so the paint will dry faster. Her breath smells like the Sour Patch Kids she ate for lunch. "Like Lean Cuisine?"

He looks at her in disbelief. "No, it's dog food. How can you work at a pet store and not know that?"

She stares back. "You're saying you want to eat dog food?"

"*What?*"

"Try five blocks over at our partner store, Aquarium Select II," I say, interrupting before the interaction can turn into something that requires disciplinary action. Darcy might think it's fun to get fired, but unlike her, I need this job. Her need for constant conflict occasionally makes me want to strangle her.

When he leaves, Darcy throws the bottle of Wite-Out at the closing door. It ricochets off the glass and bounces into a coral display. "What kind of moron goes to an aquarium shop looking for dog food."

"What kind of aquarium shop sells bird feeders?"

It's true that our selection makes no sense from an aquarium perspective. While Aquarium Select II and Aquarium Select III both offer a variety of fish, dozens of tanks, assorted filters, corals, crustaceans, reptiles, and a wide range of aquatic plants, they also stock items that have nothing to do with aquariums, including cat toys, Weedwackers, mole repellent, potted orchids, and fireplace implements. There is no Aquarium Select I.

"None of this matters." Darcy closes out her register with a bang and then gives it the finger. "This job is a negative, a zero. It's a time suck. What matters is the stuff out *there*."

I act like we haven't had this conversation at least two dozen times over the course of the last week. "Out where?"

She jabs her thumb in the direction of the front door. "There. Where shit is alive."

"Okay, Dr. Frankenstein." She's not wrong, but recently I'm finding it hard to stay motivated. Aside from the upcoming showcase, the agency can't approve any bookings until I rectify my gear situation, and there's no quick way to refit a kit, especially if you're broke. The pants I ripped were a rental, which means that even though I stitched them up the best I could, I still owe money for the repair. It's a tremendous bummer to realize that I'll have to work at least ten more mind-numbing shifts at Aquarium Select III before I can afford to pay for all of it.

"We should quit," Darcy says for the fortieth time. "Start making art."

"I am making art."

"You know what I mean."

I do and I don't. It's not the same for Darcy, which is a reality she conveniently forgets. If Darcy quits this job, she's got a financial safety net ready and willing to catch her. There will be other jobs, other opportunities. If I quit, I've got my car to live in and a twenty-five-dollar Dunkin' gift card for groceries. The two of us have very different ideas when it comes to how to achieve our dreams. And recently, our discussions about how to get there have gone from talking to stepping carefully around a minefield full of arguments.

Mercifully, she changes the subject. "Are you coming to my show tonight?"

"I can't," I say. "I've got a date."

Darcy doesn't like this. Her nose wrinkles, mouth twisting like she's tasted something rotten. "Bring her. Unless she's a piece of shit who doesn't like good music."

Our friendship is predicated on the fact that we both pour all our real energy into our respective creative passions. We hang out, we fuck around at work, and we discuss our plans for the future. RHINO-PLASTIZE is a whole separate problem. Darcy has it in her head that her band could suddenly take off, like maybe the record label people might stumble into a decrepit house show in the middle of Central Florida and point directly at her, as if she were the next John Bonham. It's that kind of fantasy thinking that keeps us both constantly hustling—her with music, me with clowning. Neither of us has time to date. It's one thing to hook up with women; it's quite another to admit that at some point I might end up with a girlfriend. That would ruin everything.

Easier to turn it all into a joke, I think, and quickly pivot to clown mode. "I don't like bringing new women around my friends until I'm sure they can behave themselves."

"So, what you're saying is you're a misogynist?"

I gather my backpack from where I'd stashed it earlier beneath the counter. "I wasn't talking about the women behaving. I was talking about you."

"Fuck off," she says, and barks out a laugh. "You're such an asshole."

Darcy's got a great sense of humor. And by that I mean that I can tell the same joke fifteen times and she'll still listen to it, even if she does roll her eyes and call me a moron.

"I'm taking off," I yell to the back of the store, and when Mister Manager comes on the walkie-talkie to tell me I still have twenty minutes left of my shift, I pull the plug from my ear and toss the whole thing to Darcy.

"Bye, bitch!" She chucks the walkie under the counter. "Hope you get laid!"

Outside in the late-afternoon sun, I stretch my arms and let my skin bake before climbing into my car. After spending six hours chilling in an icebox, the heat is intoxicating. I remove the shade from my windshield and stash it in the back before running my hands along the oxblood leather seats, fingers tapping along the shiny chrome of the dash, a breathy woman's voice rasping out sexy lyrics from the custom speakers, bass throbbing beneath me.

Cheryl might drive a sensible sedan and stay far away from drama, but Cherry has a candy-apple-red Pontiac Firebird, and she's not afraid of anybody's blowhard husband. Cherry's got an audition in a few weeks. Cherry's going to ace it.

"Let's go get your gear back," I say to my reflection in the rearview mirror before blowing myself a kiss.

ORANGE YOU GLAD

I t's not all good.

I mean, I adore being a clown, regardless of anyone else's feelings about it. But there are times when it wears me down to a flat-out nub. Makes me wish, at least for a moment, that my heart had picked anything else to love.

First, there's the issue of money. Clowning is cost prohibitive for people like me who live paycheck to paycheck. Like most creative arts gigs, you start off doing stuff for free, hoping to get picked up by an agency. And once you start getting paid for clowning jobs, you're lucky if you manage to rake in enough to cover the time you took off from your actual job. Plus, there's the matter of your agency's cut, which can sometimes be as large as 20 percent. I've never met somebody well-off who decided they wanted to get into clowning. Stand-up comedy, sure. That's all focused on the self. It's the *I*, not the *you*.

Most clowns, myself included, are struggling to pay off one bill just to have four more crop up in its place like someone poured water on a

Gremlin, or they're retirees who genuinely love kids and want to spend their golden years feeling like they finally gave something back to society. I enjoy that stuff too, don't get me wrong—if you hate kids, you'd be better off driving Lyfts than donning the greasepaint—but it's deeper than that. When I clown, I become something bigger than myself. And hey, I know what it's like to have to work harder for what I want than anyone else. I'm a queer person living in Florida, aren't I?

To clown, you need lots of *things*: clothes and makeup and props and, above all else, you need time. Large, uninterrupted swaths of it. That's when you can plot and plan and polish your craft. Try out those pratfalls without anyone watching. Perfect your gags. That way when you get out onstage, all the audience sees is your persona. No visible seams.

Of course, there's the other obvious clowning hardship: you're universally despised.

Grown men will cry out for Mommy when they see me walk down the street. Kids often run screaming. They do this because they're frightened by the lore that's been built around my profession. To them, I'm the boogeyman: something that crawls out of their closet in the middle of the night, intent on devouring them whole. Many of the things I love about clowning—the swagger of it, the slyness, the bold colors and absurd shapes my body makes—are, for some, the exact behaviors that fuel their worst nightmares.

You need very thick skin. Clowning requires a kind of steeliness that I associate with my coming-out process: the knowledge that there will always be people in life who will hate you for who and what you love. There are women who won't date me once they find out what I do for a living. I've lost friends over it. My own mother nearly disowned me the first time she caught me in full clown gear. I had wanted to surprise her with how good I had gotten, to show off my act. Tumbling, juggling, magic tricks. Dwight had already seen me perform back when I was first starting out. He'd liked it fine, he'd said, but it wasn't exactly his thing. That I understood—my big brother was never going to be the kind of guy who'd admit that I was funnier than him. But my mother, that was different. I'd wanted her approval. The look on her face, I'll never forget; it was as if I were the most revolting thing she'd ever seen. Like she couldn't believe she'd given birth to something so foul.

"Cheryl," she'd said, after several agonizing seconds had passed, "What do you want me to say?"

That was the first and last time I ever performed in front of my mother.

But you get used to it. Much like you hone tricks for your act, you devise the necessary skills to remove yourself from sticky situations. You learn to spot trouble before it happens and therefore avoid it entirely. Eight years into clowning, I can easily recognize the guy who might deck me if I get too close. Men get violent when confronted by the things that scare them. I watch their fists. Are they balled up, knuckles white? If so, I keep to the opposite side of the room. I twist my act, like I'm turning the wheel of a car, and completely change direction. I'll tell jokes they already know. No surprises.

Orange you glad I didn't say banana?

When it comes to moving through the world in this particular suit of flesh, I have to be careful. I don't get to make the same kind of jokes my brother would make. I can't prank people and expect not to get punched. If I'm not careful, if I don't watch what I'm doing, I could get hurt.

I'm remembering being chased out a window when I pull up to the woman's house. My heart is thumping like it wants me to let it out, free it from the prison of my rib cage so it can take off down the street and away from this terrible decision. It's smarter than me, I think. If I were paying attention, I'd recall that not even a week earlier, a man tried to brain me with a shampoo bottle at this very house after he caught me fucking his wife in their bathroom.

The neighborhood is one that looks like all the others in this partic-ular area of Central Florida: an expanse of perfectly manicured lawns with expensive sprinkler systems that are undoubtedly depleting all the water from our state's limited aquifers. The woman's house is painted buttercup yellow with perfectly clean white trim and large windows bracketing the front door. There's a hand-painted mailbox beside the curb that features a twined pair of pink flamingos in dark sunglasses and wacky striped bow ties; THE WALLACES is scrawled above them in bright green calligraphic script.

For a moment I consider parking on the street because my car has been leaking coolant, and their driveway is made up of a patchwork of dun-colored bricks that I know must have cost a small fortune—but the need for a quick getaway overrules my worries. Why should I care about what these people think? It's not like we'll meet up at their coun-try club or chat over dirty martinis at Hillstone; it's doubtful they'll ever set foot in the dingy, grunged-out bars where Darcy and I spend our weekends, bumming drinks off drunk tourists. They live in the kind of neighborhood that has made it impossible for anyone from Orlando to own a home, transplants from up North who've decided to help gen-trify the parts of Central Florida that used to belong to the locals. My mother owns a house, sure, but it took her years of scrimping and saving to manage that, and it was before the housing crisis began in earnest. Unless you work in finance or real estate or were born with money, your odds of owning property in Central Florida are remarkably slim. Dwight never owned a home. I doubt I will either.

I pull in behind a shiny black Range Rover and make my way up the walk. When I ring the bell, the chime inside plays the opening notes to the University of Florida fight song. I completed only three se-mesters of community college, but the reason I know the Gators fight song is because I used to date a woman who was really into football. I finger comb my hair, and my elbow connects with the tray of a hummingbird feeder. Syrupy water slicks around my elbow and trails down my wrist.

The woman who eventually answers the door is not *the* woman but looks significantly like her, only older. Must be her mother, I think, and my mommy issues flare to sudden bright light.

"Is Marcia home?" I ask. "Could I speak to her, please?"

She stares at me awhile longer, no real expression on her face, and I find myself squirming under her scrutiny. She's my height but for some reason appears taller. Blue eyes stabbing into me like she knows I've done something awful.

It's intensely erotic.

"Marcia," she suddenly yells. "Someone at the door."

She disappears down the hall, leaving me alone. I try to wipe the liquid from my arm, but my fingers stick in the tackiness of the drying sugar. It's like someone chewing Bubble Yum decided to spit on me.

"Can I help you?" Marcia says.

She doesn't recognize me, but that's understandable. She's only ever seen me dressed in full clown gear, and this afternoon I've shown up in my work clothes with no wig and my face completely naked, not even a lick of tinted ChapStick to give my mouth some color. She's wearing a pair of lavender joggers, and her short blonde hair is pulled back into a barely contained ponytail that sprouts from the back of her head like pineapple leaves.

"Hey," I say, suddenly shy. Sometimes that happens when I meet someone without the added layer of protection provided by my clown ensemble. It's as though all my confidence comes from the greasepaint. "I was hoping I could pick up my stuff."

"Stuff?"

"That I left here." When her expression doesn't change, I continue in a hurry. "An olive-colored duffel bag with brown leather handles? I stashed it behind the sectional sofa in the living room."

She drinks me in, and there it is, the sudden knowledge that I'm the person who had a magic wand up her pussy. Disappointment clouds her features. "Oh. Hi."

"Hi." I kick at the front mat, which reads WELCOME, YOU, and the grammar is so weird and bad it makes me want to turn and leave. "I need my stuff. For work."

"Right." She turns around halfway to see if anyone is behind her in the hall, then leans in close—much closer than expected. Her breath is hot and scented with traces of wintergreen-flavored gum. "Check the garbage, out back. My husband tossed it. You know . . . *after.*"

Looking at her now is a miserable experience. There's disgust in her eyes, sure, but there's also pity. This woman with her expensive car and her homeowners association and her neat little family of three and her good-looking mother. It doesn't matter that I did an incredible job entertaining her guests with my clown work (I'd juggled lit candles, for Chrissake, thrown actual fire) and possibly did an even better job fucking her. To this woman, I'm simply a minor inconvenience.

I turn on my heel and walk stiffly around the side of the house, all the way to the back garden with its rosebushes and flowering citrus trees. You're doing this for the audition, I tell myself. You're doing this because you're always willing to get your hands dirty in order to achieve your dreams. Opening the garbage cans produces some of the most unholy, stomach-churning smells I've ever encountered, odors akin to sour milk and formaldehyde and rancid pork. One of the bags splits open as I shove it aside, unearthing what looks to be the remains of a seafood boil, busted crab legs and shrimp shells and gray, mealy potatoes and gnawed corncobs nestled in a damp newspaper wrapping. At the very bottom of the bin, I finally find it: the faded duffel bag that holds my most treasured possessions.

Crowing with delight, I yank it free, unearthing the remaining Hefty bag, which rolls down onto the freshly mown grass and ejects wadded toilet paper and several used tampon applicators. My bag stinks to high heaven, but it's still the sweetest sight I've ever seen.

I set it on the ground and unzip the top. The relief I feel is palpable; I'm giddy in a way that's nearly post-orgasmic. I've conquered my cowardice, and I'm reaping the benefits of facing my fears. Here, I think, is my reward.

Everything is there, my creative life stuffed in a single bag: pants and shirts and ties, my miniature accordion, the ventriloquist's dummy I'd named Velma after getting stoned and watching too much *Scooby-Doo*, bike horns and kazoos and glitter bombs and extra wigs and a bag of red noses and Hacky Sacks for juggling and spare packs of balloons. But I keep digging, suddenly frantic, because I've realized that the most important thing isn't here. My makeup kit is missing. The expensive greasepaint that I'd spent six months saving up for, in order to perfect the visage of Bunko: a clown cowboy whose dream is to compete in the rodeo, but he's never going to make it, is he? Not with that debilitating horse phobia.

And I know exactly where I'll find that missing kit. Marcia, you sneaky bitch, I think, as I march around the side of the house, this time forgoing the doorbell with its goofy college football chime, and instead banging the side of my fist repeatedly against the wood.

When she opens the door, I'm ready for her.

"If you don't give me my shit back, I am going to come inside your house." I widen my eyes and smile my wild Bunko grin. My voice goes up an octave, turns giggly. I pull one of the red noses from my kit and jam it onto my face. "And I'm going to stay here, rolling *allllll* around on your sofa, until your husband gets home."

Marcia puffs up, ready to scream at me, but then we both hear a voice. It's her son, calling for her from inside the house. She immediately deflates.

"Can't I keep it?" she whispers. She clasps her hands under her chin, like a child reciting a bedtime prayer. "Please. I just . . . I'm begging you."

And I can see that she really does want the makeup. Wants it badly enough that she's willing to hide it from her husband, who is exactly the kind of guy I'd avoid at a gig: a dude who'd punch me not just because I'd fucked his wife, but because I'm a clown and I scare him. I'm queer, but she's not. All she'd seen was the clown, and she'd wanted that. Nothing to do with gender. Everything to do with performance.

"I can't afford to replace it," I say. "And I need it for work."

Her face lights up. "I can pay you."

The thought of going back out and having to buy the stuff makes me pause again. "It's expensive."

"That's fine, I've got the money. Wait here."

Of course she has the money. These people always have the money, don't they?

She disappears down the hall. I take off the clown nose and stuff it back in my bag. There's a food smell wafting from the open doorway, air redolent with sautéed onions and butter and garlic. My stomach growls, loudly, and I slap a hand to it, as if I might be able to shove the offending noise back inside my body. I haven't had anything to eat since my breakfast coffee, though Darcy is always quick to inform me that coffee does not actually constitute a meal. She's one to talk; she never fixes anything for herself, content to live at home with her mother, who packs her some of the most incredible lunch spreads I've ever seen. Back when I regularly saw my mother, I was lucky if she'd reheat me leftovers scrounged from the back of the fridge.

The woman reappears, clutching her pocketbook.

"Smells good in there," I say. "You guys cooking dinner?"

She dismisses the question with a wave of her hand, unfolding her billfold to reveal a wad of cash. "How much?"

Incredible that a person could simply say "how much" and not worry about the amount effectively bankrupting them. I could say any number, but I figure I should keep it close enough to the actual price that she won't realize that I'm gouging her. "Two fifty."

"Fine." The fat stack of cash in her hands is obscene. As she's filling my open palm with crisp twenty-dollar bills, she assesses me again, taking in the dusty work polo, sweeping her gaze down my wrinkled, ill-fitting jeans, which house a fair amount of hip but sadly not all that much ass. I suddenly remember the Wite-Out Darcy put in my hair. I must look like a skunk.

"Aquarium Select III?" she asks. "What's that?"

"Oh." I hold out my shirt and look down at the embroidered logo. It's gone fuzzy from repeated washings. "That's where I work."

I can see that she regrets ever letting me touch her. I'm not a kinky, horny clown, fucking her in a bathroom. I'm a random dirtbag who works part-time at an aquarium shop for only slightly better than minimum wage. She stares forlornly at my face: my slender blade of a nose, my dark eyes with their even darker circles beneath them, my thin slash of a mouth with the barely-there chapped lips. She's judged me, and the verdict is in: nothing all that great.

"You've got some white shit in your hair." She slips the last bill into my hand. "Thought you should know."

The rejection hurts worse than I'd thought it would, even though the woman's not really my type. How can there be such a gap between the people who have nothing and the people who have something? Sometimes, like now, the divide feels like an entire gulf, wider than Florida itself. I laugh, and it doesn't sound all that funny. It feels a little like I'm drowning.

When she goes to put the rest of her money away, I clear my throat and wiggle my fingers.

"Restocking fee," I announce. "That'll be an extra hundred."

Her mouth screws up in distaste, but she doesn't argue; she just counts out the extra twenties and hands them over. I let myself focus on the money, and it helps numb the sting of her dismissal. When she's done, the door is unceremoniously slammed in my face.

I shove the wad of cash in my pocket—$350, more than enough for greasepaint and even enough to buy some stuff I'd put off acquiring because it was too expensive, plus easy admission to the audition and money for gas and lodging on the overnight drive out to Tampa—and I toss my gear kit in the trunk. As I climb back into the front seat, the woman's husband pulls up. He rolls down the tinted window of his Lexus and peers in at me.

"Nice car," he says. "Seventy-nine Firebird?"

"Seventy-seven."

He whistles, long and low. "Love that paint job too. American muscle. A real classic."

Truthfully, the man reminds me of my older brother. Dwight had the same kind of bulky block head perfect for a crew cut, tailor-made for the army. Pouch at his waist threatening to turn into something serious from consuming too much alcohol. But unlike this man, Dwight's been dead for five years. He'll never have to worry about a beer gut again.

The man's got his hand on the window frame, and his gold wedding band glints in the late-afternoon sunlight. I nod congenially, and he gives me a brief wave before exiting the car, hauling his black leather briefcase behind him. Tasteful gray suit and a crisp white shirt with a loosened tie dangling around his thick neck. Lawyer, maybe. Or something that has to do with finance. He doesn't give me a second thought, this stranger idling in his driveway. He looked only at the car.

As I reverse, I take in the neighborhood: speed posted twenty miles per hour, a bright yellow DRIVE LIKE YOUR KIDS LIVE HERE double-sided sign propped at the edge of a violently green lawn. Zero traffic or pedestrians in sight. I rev my engine and back directly into that god-awful flamingo mailbox.

Carefully, of course. Wouldn't want to scratch the paint.

SAND WITCHES

irthday party clown, though admittedly retro, has never officially gone out of style.

The bulk of my gigs are set primarily in public parks or fenced back-yards, hamming it up for a group of kids who'd much rather be watching YouTube videos. That's the thing about performing: to hold people's attention, you have to be more interesting than what's on their iPhones. You also have to realize that you will *never* be as good as what's available on the broad expanse of the World Wide Web. Games, chats, social media, porn; the bar to compete is set impossibly high. But if you give it your best, you'll find that you can keep *some* people's attention for *some* of the time. Not everyone is going to be your audience. Once that's straightened out in your head, things become a lot easier.

I've performed at all the usual spots. Bar and bat mitzvahs, public libraries, elementary schools, state fairs. I've done family reunions and barbecues and church bake sales and winter carnivals. These gigs don't pay great, but they pay enough to get you through to the next one. Most of the time, that's how you find your next stop: word of mouth. Someone's mother will approach you at the end of the party and book you for her own kid's birthday. A school administrator will see you perform in front of a class and ask you about rates for private events. They feed into each other; it's *The Human Centipede* but for the gig economy.

Perhaps all this talk of "work" has convinced you that I'm not good at my job. But, baby, I'm the best. There's a reason why I've kept up a steady stream of gigs in a steadily declining economy. Nobody gives better clown than me. In Orlando—and the clown community at large—Bunko is a hot commodity. The problem? Going rates for clowns are at basement lows.

What I want most of all is a solid timeline of how I get from barely-making-it clown to established performer in the Orlando community. My scattered brain at one point even put together a spreadsheet, a dry Excel document that lives on my ancient computer, outlining how I might find the right birthday party that would rocket me into a local clown collective, which would end up with me starring in my own traveling Florida showcase. But for now, it stays numbered cells in a digital form. So much of artistic practice means being in the right place at the right time. It can sometimes feel like it's all about luck, and I can say with assurance that I've never been a person anyone has described as blessed.

Because no matter how good you are, the work inevitably runs out. I can't clown 24 hours a day, 7 days a week, 365 days a year, which is maybe what I'd need to do if I wanted to quit my job and still make rent.

Occasionally, there are dry spells. Certain times of year pay less than others. Maybe you book a bunch of holiday gigs, but once January rolls around, there's nothing out there. Your kit lies dusty on the floor of your bedroom as you wait for the phone to ring.

That's when you get creative. And this is what I mean when I say I'm good. I create my own luck.

During early slow months, I begin contacting local businesses, offering to work their corporate retreats. Dressed as Bunko, I run workshops on how laughter can prevent stress in busy office environments. I did seasonal shifts at nearby haunted houses and corn mazes, though doing those gigs made me question whether clowning was even worth it. Attendees screamed at me, and the drunk ones sometimes threw beer bottles. When times became really desperate, I even called a dungeon master and offered up a version of my services. For three nights, I stood in the far corner of a converted basement and blew up balloons shaped like genitalia. I made over five hundred bucks that weekend. And the participants *actually* tipped!

Funny, right?

These are the stories I usually whip out on first dates. But the woman I'm sitting across from at this family-owned Italian restaurant doesn't look interested. She's avoiding eye contact, sitting tight-lipped. Being a clown means that I'm constantly assessing people's body language. And right now, hers is very much giving "get me the hell out of here."

She has a right to be pissed.

I'm late. *Really* late. After getting my kit back from Marcia's, I needed a shower to remove the funk of garbage from my body. When I arrived, I found my date already seated and clutching a menu.

"Sorry I'm late."

Eyebrow raise. "You could have called."

I look at my watch and wince. "Ten minutes."

"Twenty."

"Traffic was a nightmare," I say, sliding into the chair directly across from her.

I chose the restaurant because it has all the romantic prerequisites: soft music, flickering candles, white tablecloths, and Italian food. Servers in actual black bow ties. Plus, it looks a lot more extravagant than it actually is. Nothing on the menu is going to bankrupt me if she leaves me stranded with the check.

She's drinking from an overly full glass of red. After every sip she pauses, puckering her lips. Finally, she pushes the glass away entirely. When the waiter arrives to take our order, she tells him that the wine tastes old.

"I'd like a new glass," she says. "From a *fresh* bottle."

I wasn't aware that was a real thing, but then again, I don't go to nice restaurants all that often. When you're cutting back on expenses, one of the first things you lose is eating out. I generally subsist on a diet of black coffee and whatever food remains in my fridge from the previous week's grocery trip. Sometimes Darcy's mom sends me home with care packages: leftovers from their family meals that provide most of my nutrients. I constantly feel as though I'm on the verge of contracting scurvy from a lack of vitamin C, which should be impossible since I live in Florida with yearlong access to citrus.

Speaking of fruit, I decide to ask her about the wine because I'm curious. "I thought wine was supposed to be old? Fermented grapes, right?"

"That's not what I meant." She declines to elaborate further.

I had wanted to make a good impression, but as usual I've done the opposite. For the life of me, I can't remember how to make small talk. She smiles at me and waits. Crickets.

Once the waiter comes back with a fresh glass for her to try, she takes a sip and nods her approval. He leaves us again and silence descends, blanketing the table and nearly smothering me. I'm dying to crack a joke but force myself to sit still, wadding my fists in my napkin.

"So, the food's good here?" she finally asks. "You mentioned this place was one of your favorites."

Truthfully, I've been to Marco's Italian Eatery only once, and that was because another date brought me here and told me it was *her* favorite spot. I look around, suddenly sure I'll spot that woman—who I ghosted after a mediocre fingering session in her downtown apartment—but thankfully I don't see her. Anyway, the restaurant feels classy, which inevitably makes me seem more sophisticated than I actually am. I've only ever ordered one thing here, and it's the fettuccine Alfredo, because it's the cheapest option on the menu. But I don't tell her that.

"Yes," I say. "It's nice."

"Okay. Great."

I can tell she's trying, but my responses aren't giving her a lot to work with. I'm nervous, I can admit that. For multiple reasons, I really need this date to go well.

I stare at her from across the table and compare her in-person face to the pictures she'd selected for the dating app. Her hair is wavy and dark and streaked with chunks of gray. Eyes large and heavily done with thick eyeliner. Her lipstick is so deep a red that it's almost black, and when she sips her wine, the kiss remains behind on the rim, as if her mouth is still drinking. Black sweater and skinny black jeans and black heeled boots that she uses to tap at the table leg when she's bored, which she obviously is, because she's kicking it nonstop. Lots of chunky silver jewelry including a ring on her index finger that resembles a hunk of meteorite. Yes, she is just as good-looking as her photos, I think, and I wonder what she thinks about me.

My dating app pictures all feature animals. Puppies, kittens, even a baby alligator that I held at the local mini golf course. Not fish, though. That's a little too straight-guy coded.

"So . . . Margot," I say. "You look like a Margot."

She tilts her head. "What does that mean?"

"Some people's names don't match their personalities." I think about the woman, Marcia, and how she could have been named almost anything else. I'm still stuck on Samantha; all that blonde hair, she could be a namesake of that infamous TV suburban witch, no problem. "But you really are a Margot. Very cool and Parisian."

"I was actually born in Italy," she replies dryly, eyeballing the tacky wicker-wrapped wine bottle with a candle jammed in its mouth. I immediately wish I'd picked any other type of restaurant.

"Oh, cool." My beer is half full, and I'm trying to conserve it so I don't run out of things to do with my hands. "That's where some of the great clowns are from. Italy. You know, like Pagliacci?"

"The character's real name is Canio." When I stare blankly at her, she sighs deeply and rubs her temples. It's not lost on me that the gesture reminds me of my mom. "From the opera," she says. "His stage name is Pagliacci."

I decide I don't care about saving my beer any longer and drink most of it in several large gulps. "Sure, okay. I was just trying to make a joke. Like that meme that got popular?" Now it's her turn to stare at me blankly. I continue on, as if she cares about the joke at all, which she obviously does not. "But doctor, *I'm* Pagliacci!"

"I'm unfamiliar with the joke."

The server arrives with our food. The fettuccine Alfredo for me, while she has ordered something called seafood Portofino. It features a slew of open-mouthed mussels in a creamy garlic broth. The smell immediately reminds me of the carcasses I unearthed in the woman's trash can mere hours earlier, and I have to work hard to suppress my gag reflex.

Margot's staring at me as I try to choke down a single bite of my food. Some of the Alfredo sauce drips off my fork and dots the front of my shirt. I scoop it off with my finger and pop it into my mouth, sucking off the residue.

"How old did you say you were again?"

My profile on the app claimed that I was thirty-nine because that was the age I'd picked when I created it. The reasoning behind this was simple. Older women tend to date people closer to their own age. If I said that I was thirty-nine, it meant that someone who was forty-nine might ostensibly swipe right on me. The fact that I was twenty-eight didn't generally factor into matters because there was almost never a second date.

"How old am I?"

"Yes." She stares at me patiently, unblinking.

Here's what I knew about Margot: She was fifty-two. She was happily child-free and had a master's in business management. Her family owned a glassmaking business, and their work was often displayed in fine art galleries across the country. She owned a slender black cat named Zelda that featured in many of her online photos. The line under her profile picture claimed that she "preferred dry wines and sweet women." But aside from all of that, the most interesting thing about her was her work. Margot was Margot the Magnificent, one of the most well-respected magicians in the greater Orlando area.

This was why I was so nervous. Because Margot *was* magnificent. I knew this from experience; I'd already seen her in action.

Last year, I'd attended a performance showcase downtown that featured old and new talent: plenty of clowns, jugglers, circus and animal handlers, tumblers, and contortionists, as well as quite a number of magicians. I'd been sitting in front of the main-stage shell next to Lake Eola, enjoying the steady parade of performances. It was a Saturday in early May, no rain, the sun lodged like a blinding, burning coal overhead, but the air was still miraculously cool for near summer and mostly free of humidity. Sunscreen had dripped into the corner of my eye; I kept swiping at it until the elderly man to my right eventually offered me a tissue, sure that I was crying. I'd brought a notebook and was scribbling down notes, things I could take away from all of it to fine-tune my own act. But then Margot strode onstage in her tall black hat and her silk-lined cloak and I forgot about the problem with my eye and gave up the notebook entirely.

It wasn't just that she was good at her job. Every trick took on mythological importance. The vanishing, the reappearance, the summoning. Even the floppy-eared rabbit obeyed. She was *compelling*: so commanding a presence that the audience couldn't keep their eyes off her. Her voice was deep and melodic. Nobody dared to breathe. We were mesmerized by what she could make us believe.

That was why when I saw her profile pop up on the dating app, I knew that I had to speak to her in person. A year and a half ago, she'd separated from her wife, and it was causing friction. Portia had been her magician's assistant, featuring prominently in all her bigger showcases: disappearing acts, the hewn woman, even water submersion. Margot was taking on fewer gigs as a result, and it was clear that this bothered her. It was present in the stress lines on her face, downturned lips, and bruised skin beneath her eyes. For people like us, when we're not making art, we can never truly be happy.

"How old are you?" she repeats, leaning forward. "How old are you *really*?"

Her voice is low, intimate. The purr of it designed to produce magic out of thin air.

There's no point in continuing the lie. My cheeks flush, and I'm glad that she can't see me in the dim glow of the candlelight. "Twenty-eight."

She leans back again in her seat, resigned. "That's what I thought."

I feel compelled to explain myself so I might save the date. "I'm sorry. I know that's weird. Like, such a dumb lie, right? But the thing is, I don't like dating women my own age. And it's not about maturity or anything like that. It's bigger. There's something lacking when it comes to discussing creative fulfillment. I can't talk about my dreams with them. Younger women just . . . They don't interest me."

Instead of answering right away, she takes a few more bites of her food. She swipes at her lips with a napkin. "This is not very good." She says it almost like an apology.

"Oh." I feel bad, even though I wasn't the one who cooked any of it. "I'm sorry about that."

"I know, I'm terrible. It's a curse to be so picky. It's just that I'm particular about the freshness of my seafood."

"Sure," I say, even though the last time I had shrimp it came frozen and breaded in a bag featuring a fisherman sporting a yellow slicker. "I feel the same way."

She tilts her head. "Explain what you mean by creative fulfillment."

The tables around us have steadily filled. People are sloughing off their workdays and slipping into conversations that feel a little more comfortable. A bottle of champagne is uncorked with a sudden pop, busy hum from the kitchen as a server sweeps past with a tray of steaming food, the clink of silverware scraping against plates. I am scrambling for words, rooting around in my brain to find the right answer—one that won't make me sound like someone who doesn't know what she wants, because that's my biggest fear when it comes to my clowning. That regardless of the time I've put in and the work I've done, I'm still a person who is floundering. Margot's been at this a long time; she's a true professional, a queer woman in performance. She could guide me in the right direction, maybe even put in a good word for me at the audition I have in less than two weeks.

And look at her, I think, taking in the beautiful way that the candlelight reflects off her dark hair, the way her long, graceful fingers hold the stem of her wineglass. She's perfect.

I decide to be careful with how I voice my feelings. "I guess I want to be with someone who is just as passionate about their art as I am."

"Art."

"Yes, art." The couple next to us are sharing an order of bruschetta. They giggle as pieces of diced tomato fall onto the tablecloth, feeding each other bits with their fingers. I wish that was the vibe at our table. Instead, I feel a little like I'm being interrogated. Intimacy isn't my strong suit.

"I work part-time to pay the bills, sure, but what I'm really interested in is focusing on my long-term goals," I say. "You know, my career."

"And what career is that?"

"Are you serious?"

"Almost always."

I can't tell if she's fucking with me. My online dating profile talks all about my clowning ambitions. I learned right away that if I didn't, there was the strong chance that people would freak out. Once a woman dumped an entire glass of iced tea on my lap because I told her that I thought Ronald McDonald was kind of sexy.

We hadn't talked about it before our date, but I just assumed she'd seen the pictures on the app.

"My dream," I say, "is to be a professional clown. Full-time, sustainable work. I want to make art that matters."

"Art that matters," she parrots. "Professional clown."

Again, her face is a blank page. I could write anything into it. Maybe that's her magician's trick.

"I want to command an audience. I want to make people laugh."

"All right. So, tell me a joke."

I stare at her. "What, right now?"

"Yes. Right now."

"That isn't exactly how clowning works," I say, because I wonder if she's confusing me with a stand-up comedian. "But okay. Sure."

We sit in silence again as I try to come up with something. The first thing my brain lights on is a joke that's been one of my favorites since elementary school. Better than nothing, I think, and launch straight into it.

"Why was the beach spooky?"

"I don't know. Why?"

"Because of all the sand witches there."

Her head tilts questioningly. "Why wouldn't you start with 'Why can't you be hungry at the beach?'? Then you could say it's because of all the sandwiches there. Then it makes sense, because it's food."

I'm sweating again, and this time it's not from running late or the Florida heat. She's my captive audience, my future mentor and future fuck, and I'm bombing. "That's one way to tell it."

"That's the better way."

Only someone with no sense of humor would think there's only one good way to tell a joke, but I don't tell her that.

The conversation has veered wildly off course. I decide to steer things back to the safer port of her own work. "I just want to be taken seriously. Like you, right? You're a professional magician. You hone your craft; you want to be respected for your work."

"Respect is important, yes."

"Exactly!" I smile at her and pray that there's nothing stuck in my teeth. "You get it. I mean, your ex understood that, right?"

She pauses with her wineglass halfway to her lips. "Do you know Portia?"

I've gone too far. There's no reason that I should know anything about her ex unless I've been lightly stalking her online for the past few months. Which I have, it's true, but that's nothing she needs to know about. "No. I mean, I just know that your wife was part of your act. So obviously she would understand how important your work is to you."

"I don't talk about my ex-wife on first dates."

"Sorry. I'm not trying to pry." I shred my bread to bits and drag a hunk of it through the lake of Alfredo sauce congealing on my plate. "All I'm saying is that I want to be in a relationship with someone who's just as invested in my dreams."

A chill descends upon the table. Part of it is from the air-conditioning kicking on overhead, but there is another part of me that feels the cold might actually be emanating off the woman across from me. Her body language has turned frigid: arms crossed over her chest, shoulders hunched inward. It's as if we're passengers on the *Titanic*, and Margot has gotten the last life raft, leaving me behind to freeze to death.

Freezing to death inevitably makes me think of Leonardo DiCaprio. Nineties Leo was a lesbian icon, I think. So many closeted gay women thought they wanted to be with him before discovering that they actually wanted to *be* him. Now look at him, refusing to date anyone over the age of twenty-five. Couldn't be me.

"I think we should get the check," she says. "It's late."

It can't be past eight o'clock, but I readily agree.

She pays for both our dinners—insists on it, waves my hand away as if it were a bothersome pest as she throws down her credit card, which turns me on more than it should—and after my leftovers are boxed, we walk outside into the damp Florida evening.

"Where did you park?" she asks. "I'll escort you."

It would be a sweet gesture, if the date hadn't already died. I point toward my Firebird, sitting lonely at the back of the lot beneath a fluorescent streetlamp. The thing about owning a car you love is that you quickly learn to park it far away from where other automobiles might scratch or dent it, but you also need high visibility so that no one will be tempted to steal its overpriced parts.

"This is yours?" She runs her fingertips over the slick width of the hood, stopping to casually fondle the chrome-edged driver's side mirror. "It's stunning."

"It was my brother's, actually. He put a lot of work into it."

"You must be very close with your brother for him to let you drive this beautiful work of art."

I go ahead and say the part I usually step around on dates, because I figure it doesn't matter; this one has already flatlined. "He passed away a few years ago. So, the car's mine now."

Her eyes soften. She places her hand gently on my shoulder. "I'm very sorry to hear that."

"We weren't all that close." Except we had been, once, hadn't we? He was eight years older, and he hadn't been a mean big brother; no, he'd watched out for me, for the most part. Taught me how to drive stick and yelled at me only when I stalled out in the middle of the highway, cars spilling around us like we'd dammed up the road with his rusted-out Altima. Showed me the good music, the stuff kids my age hadn't known about yet, so I could parade it out in front of my peers, acting like I'd discovered it all on my own. Back then, yes, it had been good. We hadn't been friends, but we had been close.

But he'd never gotten to see Bunko, the persona I created after years of honing my act. And now I'll never know what he might have thought of my art.

"Loss is still loss, even if we insist it isn't," she says.

She's squeezing the meat of my shoulder, rubbing at the muscle with the ball of her thumb. I realize that I am on the verge of tears. It's time to fire off a joke and make my exit before the night gets any worse.

"I haven't lost him," I say, clown's grin tugging my lips upward. "I know exactly where he is. Down the road at Glen Haven Memorial Park."

"Quiet," she says, but it doesn't sound mean, just authoritative. Suddenly, she's pressed her mouth to mine. I'm so dumbfounded by this turn of events that for a moment I just stand there, unmoving, as she kisses me. Then I remember that I have a body, and I wind my arms around her neck as she grips my waist.

She tastes sharp and sour, like wine, but it's not a bad thing. About a foot shorter than me, but she feels sturdier, wiry and compact and solid. We kiss like that for a few more minutes before she steps back and ends things, smoothing my hair away from my face.

"It was nice meeting you," she says. "I hope you have a wonderful life."

And then she walks back across the parking lot and climbs into a sleek black sedan.

Shakily, I unlock the door to my own car and sit down in the driver's seat, pressing my forehead against the steering wheel until I feel the embroidery of the thread embedding itself in my skin.

There's a yellow Post-it note stuck to my dashboard. I put it there almost five years ago, after an especially hard week of work, a week when everything that could possibly go wrong had gone horribly, terribly awry. My brother dead. No money, no real relationship, no gigs in sight.

WHAT DO YOU WANT TO BE REMEMBERED FOR?

I want to be remembered for making someone laugh. For them to really fucking feel it, right in their guts.

Even if they don't want to.

GETTING YOUR ACT TOGETHER

Because I must forever press my fingers against the bruise of my heart, I sit in the parking lot of the restaurant for the next hour and click through articles on my phone about my dead brother.

There aren't that many, but I'm a slow reader, and sometimes my eyes skip ahead when I encounter any references to my mother or myself. Then I force myself to go back and start all over again.

Our father isn't mentioned in these articles because our father is in fact two different sperm donors. Like me, my mother is a lesbian. She had my brother with a former partner, her college roommate, who my grandparents always referred to as "Nancy's good friend Patricia" when they were still alive. After the two of them split, my mother kept Dwight and then had me with a different donor, this time all on her own.

People are leaving the restaurant in dribs and drabs, heading for their cars. The couple who shared the romantic plate of bruschetta have their arms slung around each other's waists as they walk, horniness clouding their features. At least someone's getting laid tonight, I think to myself, and go back to my phone.

There are articles about my brother because, before he died, he was gaining notoriety for a series of flashy real estate ads. He'd used all of his savings (and borrowed a not insignificant amount from my mother's retirement fund) to buy airtime for these ads during Orlando Magic basketball games. They were shot cheaply, on what looked like a camcorder unearthed from a time capsule circa 1995, and they featured my brother seated behind a wide wooden desk with a model ship set jauntily on the corner. In these ads, he reiterated that the houses he sold were not haunted or possessed by demons. The risk of these goofy ads paid off. After making several big sales, he produced a secondary series of ads (with a much larger budget) in which he took a crew of "paranormal investigators" (played by my brother's high school buddies Lance and Derrick) through a series of homes in which phenomena like flickering lights, slamming doors, and creaking floors were deemed "definitely *not* poltergeist activity." These second ads were an even bigger hit. I thought they were fine—not exactly my cup of tea, but a good gimmick. He became something of a local celebrity; people stopped him at gas stations and grocery stores to pose for pictures. Dwight was able to expand his real estate business, and there was talk about his opening a second office in South Florida. He never asked my advice, and I never offered. A third series of ads had been planned but was never executed. The weekend before they were supposed to be shot, Dwight had gone out to New Smyrna Beach for some early-morning surfing before the arrival of a tropical storm. Flung out in the massive riptides, my brother drowned.

An auspicious way to lose such a large personality. I always imagined him going out in a blaze of glory: perhaps skydiving from a plane with a faulty parachute jammed on his broad back, or breaking into the large-cat enclosure at the Sanford zoo with a fanny pack stuffed full of frozen steaks. He was glib and he was goofy, and the way he washed up on the shell-studded shore—wan and bloated with seawater—was too quiet for his outsize self. I often wonder if his ghost wishes he could do it all over again, this time involving a great white shark or a cruise ship propeller.

Though they're available on YouTube, I don't watch the ads. It's one thing to read about who he was and who he might have been, if given the chance, but it's quite another to see his actual face—eternally youthful, while mine continues to grow and shift and age. He was thirty when he died, which means that in only two years, I'll have out-lived him.

I'm looking at the photo of him that accompanies the article. It's black-and-white, small and grainy. It barely looks like a person—more like what a computer might generate when tasked with creating a white human male between the ages of twenty-two and thirty-five. And I lied when I told Margot that I could just go visit him at Glen Haven; I haven't been out there since the funeral. As pranky as he was, Dwight would have found nothing funny about that staid, suburban cemetery with its whitewashed granite headstones and bundles of fake daisies plopped in cheap glass vases. My brother might be somewhere out in the ether, but he's definitely not there.

It's a special kind of pain to know that your mother wishes that you were the child who died. There are only two of us left in the Hendricks family, and our relationship isn't what you would call solid. Even before the clowning incident, my mother and I had never been close. Dwight always claimed we were too much alike, but I think the real problem is that I'm not *enough* like her. The lesbian daughter of a lesbian mother, I should have been her twin. We look alike, both dark-haired and swarthy and thin-lipped, but she's overly stern and I can never be serious, especially not with her, and that means our conversations dry up before they get started. I stop by every couple of weeks for dinner, and I show up on Christmas morning and sometimes Thanksgiving. Neither of us has all that much to say to the other. For most of our lives, Dwight was the one who did all the talking.

Part of that was because he couldn't stand for me to get any of the attention. Even before I was Bunko, he was the real clown.

That's enough wallowing, I think, and stab my key into the ignition. I could go home to my squat, dank, one-bedroom duplex, or I could catch the end of Darcy's show. I'm tired and sad and I'm still remarkably horny, but I figure if I show up for her gig, Darcy will forgive me for choosing a date over our friendship. So I make what should be a fifteen-minute drive magically turn into a ten-minute one by simply ignoring the speed limit.

It's possible that most people wouldn't recognize the venue as a pub, let alone a bar, because it's located inside what used to be someone's house. A one-story ranch with a double carport built smack-dab in the center of a large corner lot. The home's front yard is wildly overgrown, choked with weeds that won't get whacked until the city comes by and puts up a notice; then someone will pony up enough dough to hire a guy with a riding lawn mower who razes it all in under seven minutes.

All that juicy weeded stuff crowding the swampy front yard means there is a prolific number of mosquitoes. I swat at them absentmindedly, eyes stuck on the porch lights. By the time I reach the house, bass thumps so hard that I can feel it in the street through the soles of my shoes. The sagging front porch is packed with bodies. I push past a mob of people clutching plastic cups filled with undoubtedly shitty vodka in order to slip through the front door.

Though the exterior still very much resembles a classic 1950s Central Florida home, the inside has been completely gutted. The house, previously owned by the Delacourts (the mailbox still gets mailers with their names printed on them, which the bar puts out as coasters), has been converted to an open room. It still boasts the original terrazzo floors, sound bouncing around the place like a box to the ears. The kitchen has become the bar, fitted with retro appliances—double-wide copper-colored fridge and a matching stovetop, though the oven has been converted into a liquor cabinet—and buckets of ice and bottles of beer litter the beige Formica countertops. The bartenders, a married couple who own the place, won't serve you unless they recognize your face.

People call it the Pussy Palace because of all the queer people who hang out there and also because of the pink tile work in the home's solitary bathroom. It's one of the few truly queer spots in Central Florida, though it's not called that officially. It's just ours. We DIY our own places here because if we don't, we wouldn't have any. I grab a beer from the husband, Gino, and we nod at each other instead of saying hello because the music is so loud there's no possible way a human voice could be heard over it.

Darcy's mohawk stands at attention, but that's all I can see of her from behind the massive drum kit that takes up the back of the stage. The lead singer, a woman named Chelsea Bitter (whose actual name is Chelsea Butterman; I know this because we went to school together and kids used to riff off it all the time, like "Hey, better lay off the butter, man"), is screaming into the microphone about wanting to abolish capitalism. She has written several songs on this topic, and in my opinion they all sound exactly the same. Chelsea's father owns several large car dealerships in Central Florida, and she drove a brand-new Range Rover her senior year of high school. I have to wonder if her problems with capitalism are actually daddy issues.

There is no pit at the Pussy Palace because Gino and his wife, Diane, have expressly forbidden it. They're both in their sixties and don't want to deal with any broken bones or concussions. You can still feel the energy of it, though; the thrum of movement bleeds through the restless bodies in the room. Whenever someone does try to start moshing, Gino—who is six-foot-four and built like the Hulk—physically removes them from the house. They are never welcome back.

I post up against the wall and wait for Darcy to finish. The truth is that she's way too gifted a drummer to be part of this hack band. The bassist constantly loses the beat, the guitarist cares more about his day job than he does about learning new music, and the lead singer is a talentless control freak who won't let Darcy anywhere near the lyrics. She could do a lot better than backing a so-so middling punk act in Orlando, and I think everyone in the band knows that except for Darcy. That's part of her own self-sabotaging: unable to see that RHINO-PLASTIZE is actually a roadblock that prevents her from choosing projects that would put her on the path to real satisfaction.

Lately it feels like we fight all the time. Just last week, Darcy had gotten upset because of some joke I'd made about straight people with money. I hadn't meant *her*, and I told her that, but she still ignored me the rest of our shift and instead chose to hang out with Wendall—*Wendall!*—who I'm sure spent the entire four hours talking about the poetic quality of nebula or whatever other space crap he'd jotted in his notebook.

Darcy rolls out a long drum solo at the end of the set. Everyone in the crowd whistles and cheers as she plays; they are absolutely loving it. Chelsea Bitter takes it all in stoically, as if the applause should be for her alone, and after thanking the audience she storms off in an obvious funk.

I grab another beer from Gino because Darcy will be busy for a while. She has to gather up her entire kit and then help pack the amps and gear into the back of her bassist's van. She's the smallest one in the act, but she's undoubtedly the strongest. Loading everything would take three times longer if she weren't available to be their workhorse.

"Hey. I know you."

The woman next to me looks like she's part of the group that has gathered a few feet away. They've all got on similar outfits—what people call the old Orlando scene look: stretched-out white V-neck shirts and cutoff black jean shorts, greasy hair sloppily pulled back with hair bands they all sport on their wrists like bracelets, chapped bare lips, and lots of dark eye makeup. The kind of grungy try-hard attire that always makes me wonder if someone else is paying their rent.

"I'm Cherry," I say, but she's not smiling.

"I know you."

"Okay. You know me."

There's something about her face that looks familiar, but I'm drawing a blank. She's significantly younger than me, so I couldn't have gone out with her, but it's possible that I've seen her at one of Darcy's shows or even at one of my own gigs. That seems the most likely.

"Did I work a party for your family?" I ask.

"You fucked my mom," she says, and that's when I finally place her.

Tamara Oller had been an on-again but mostly off-again hookup of mine the previous spring. Neither of us made very much money, and we quickly bonded over that. She had three kids and wasn't out; neither of us was looking for a relationship. The sex was fine, nothing great. Just a way to pass the time. But the real nail in the coffin had been the fact that she had a huge problem with clowns. Not just in a "they weird me out" kind of way either; it was a serious phobia. When she'd seen a picture of me in full clown makeup, she kicked me out of her house. We haven't spoken since.

"How is Tamara?" I ask, not because I'm interested, but because I can't understand why her daughter knows about any of it. Tamara had been adamant that things between us remain a secret.

If I'm honest, that was one of the hottest parts about our time together. All that sneaking around, finding little pockets of time when no one was home or her kids were asleep. It added a thrill to the proceedings, some excitement to what would have otherwise felt like fairly blasé sex.

"Aren't you ashamed?"

"About what?" I reply, because there are millions of things I should be ashamed of; the list is infinite. Also, I find it hard to believe that any one of these Orlando scene girls would have a problem with queerness. It's built into the infrastructure of Central Florida. All those theme parks mean tons of gay people, workers and performers alike. Young people don't necessarily move out of town as soon as they graduate, at least not like before. More often than not, we're all sticking around, trying to make a go of it because it's our place too. There might not be as many gay bars in town as there used to be, but there are always spaces that hold us, cater to us in the wink-wink way we've perfected in Florida, building our own havens.

"Ashamed of what?" I repeat.

"She was married!" she yells.

I'm fairly certain Tamara was separated at the time, because she'd talked about being scared to come out to her kids in the wake of the divorce, but it doesn't seem like her daughter cares. "I'm sorry you're upset, but I didn't do anything wrong," I say.

"And she told me about your weird . . . perversion."

I'm trying to think of what sex act Tamara could have named that would make me sound like a pervert. Our time together had been fairly tame. We hadn't done much more than finger and eat each other out, aside from a truly embarrassing attempt with the strap-on that ended with me inserting it into a very different hole than the one originally intended.

All I can do is shrug. I genuinely cannot remember.

"You're a clown."

It's not what I was expecting, so I laugh. It's a loud, braying laugh, the kind I make when I'm genuinely tickled by something, and it snags the attention of her friends. They swivel as a unit to stare at us. I can see that Tamara's daughter hasn't anticipated my response. It's possible she thought I'd feel humiliated by the announcement, that hearing the word "clown" spoken aloud would cause me to blush with embarrassment.

She leans away, as if my laughter might infect her.

"You think that's funny?" she asks. "Really?"

"Sure."

"A grown woman obsessed with clowns? You find that amusing?"

"First of all," I say, "I am not obsessed with clowns. I *am* a clown. That's a totally different thing."

"No, it's not."

"Actually, it is." I could rattle off facts for her, describe the time and care I've put into a career I love more than almost anything else in the world, but it's pointless arguing with someone who's already decided they know exactly who you are.

Darcy is making her way across the room. The woman's friends immediately swarm her, unaware that Darcy loathes being congratulated for her talent. When she'd first joined RHINOPLASTIZE, she'd worn a white T-shirt over her head so no one could see her perform. "Then they're forced to focus on the drumming instead of the drummer," she'd said, as if that made a lick of sense. "Ghost Drummer," the local alt-weekly dubbed her, and it had stuck. The music is all that matters to Darcy, not anyone gushing over her, though she has a rabid fan base. Once again, I'm forced to wonder if Darcy, with her incredible skills and talent, could be living her dream if she'd just manage to shake off the deadweight of a lackluster band that's only holding her back.

"I like being a clown," I say. "There's nothing perverted about it."

"You're disgusting." The woman's voice rises at the end, and it comes with a little spit attached to it. The last time I was spit on was under much more erotic circumstances; there's a notable difference in tone, I have to admit.

"Beat it," Darcy tells the crowd of women, parting them with her arms. She hands me another beer, even though I haven't finished the one I'm holding. "Who's disgusting?"

"Me," I say. Tamara's daughter isn't sure what to do now that the drummer from the band she came to see is chatting with me.

"Oh, for sure, you're vile." Darcy sprays down the top of her head with an oversize water bottle. Her mohawk, powered by an unholy amount of wax and what I'm 99 percent sure is rubber cement, valiantly withstands the assault. "It's fucking hot in here. Are they so cheap that they can't afford air-conditioning?"

"Maybe you're hot because you spent the last hour clubbing some sticks against a tub."

She squirts the front of my shirt with the last dregs of her water. "Funny. I thought you had a date?"

"Ended early."

"Probably because you wore that cheesy button-down. You look like a middle school boy who's about to take a girl out to the movies while his mom drives them in the family minivan."

The woman's eyes ping-pong between us. After a few seconds, she can't take it anymore.

"You ruined my mother's life," she says. "You did that."

"Oh, I doubt it." Darcy swipes the drips from her face with the raggedy edge of her T-shirt. "I bet your mother's life was already pretty bad to begin with."

The woman looks revolted. She leaves abruptly without saying another word to either of us, heading off with her group of friends.

"You got to stop sleeping with people's moms," Darcy says. "Get your shit together. For real."

"Never."

"Now it's affecting my livelihood."

"What livelihood?" I ask. "How much did you guys make tonight, two free drink tickets?"

"One free drink ticket."

"Holy shit, you're rich!"

Most of the crowd has cleared out. The only people left are Pussy Palace regulars. Gino puts on Warren Zevon and lowers the lights until all that's illuminating the house are the pink twinkle bulbs draped across the ceiling. Our collective mood shifts from amped energy to chill basement vibes. It feels a lot like being a teenager and hanging out with kids who are just a few years older but much, much cooler.

"So, for real, the date sucked?" Darcy asks.

It did not, but I'm not sure if it was good either. I know it's not a great way to start off a relationship, regardless—thinking about Margot as a possible mentor; someone who might be able to show me the secret back doors into the performance world, those bouncer-fronted spaces that take one look at me and shake their heads like they're trying to knock me loose from their brains; someone who might save me the trouble of figuring out how to get hired all on my own. I'm still thinking about it, letting Margot and her wine mouth percolate in my head. She'd told me to have a nice life, which if taken at face value meant well-wishes, but it did not mean a second date. The kissing, however, gave me hope.

"It wasn't all bad," I admit, because that feels accurate enough. "She paid for dinner."

"Nice." Darcy chucks the empty water bottle at her bassist, a guy named Alex who has a question mark shaved into the side of his head. It bounces off his skull, but he keeps walking like nothing happened. "You want to spend the night?"

"Okay."

"You can't fuck my mom, though," she says. "I mean it."

"I can try."

I finish one of my beers and dump the empty bottle in an old newspaper box that's been repurposed as a recycling bin. The day has been long, but I'm the good kind of tired, lazy from all the pasta and beer.

"Let's get you drunk first," Darcy says, and I readily agree.

SLAPSTICK

Clowning is all about optimism. The absurd depends on the bright shine of unlimited possibility.

I roll over and force myself to stare at the sunlight that's slipping through the corner of the blinds. That way, when I close my eyes again, my lids are on fire. Colors are important to my work too. Imagine a clown: What do you see? There's the white canvas of our faces, but it's essentially a palette for bold, liquid color. Red nose. Brilliant spatters of paint around the mouth and eyes. And the clothes! All our patterns are vivid and startling. Clowns are a feast for the senses.

Darcy's room usually smells like lavender and rose petals, dusty bouquets of ancient flowers like dead potpourri, but now there's something else in the air. Breakfast aromas drift upstairs—toast just on the cusp of burnt, bacon, and coffee—and this morning I decide that my feeling of optimism is rooted in the idea that the domestic could be a good thing. A reminder for myself: not everyone parents like my mother.

I dig around the side of the mattress for my phone and find it shoved down the crack of the bed. Margot and I had already transitioned from chatting in the app to trading phone numbers. Our previous texts had been before meeting at the restaurant. Simple logistics: time of arrival, location. Except now I see that I sent messages to her after our dinner, one at 12:48 a.m. and the other at 2:13 a.m. The first is normal enough. I say I enjoyed meeting her. I say dinner was a real pleasure.

The second message is less formal. It doesn't make a lot of sense outside my drunk brain, a mind so powerfully fogged by alcohol that it apparently thought "why u hot" would be an appropriate message to send someone who was absolutely sleeping and who already blew me off. My shame is further amplified by the fact that Margot has read receipts turned on; she has seen this message and very wisely declined to answer my question.

Though I am reeling from embarrassment, there is something positive to be found in my incoming texts: my agency has a last-minute job to send my way, if I can get over to the Seminole County roller rink by late afternoon. This is great for my upcoming audition because they're always looking for someone who has the most recent work on their CV. It's a lot like cuts of meat: the fresher, the better. I tell them I'll take it.

"I'm hungover," Darcy announces. "My body is in crisis."

"You don't drink."

"I think I got *your* hangover."

She has her head stuffed under an enormous pile of heart-shaped pillows meant to resemble Valentine's Day candy. They're embroidered with sayings like ONLY U and MEANT 2B and CALL ME. Her room is incredibly frilly. The furniture—her trundle bed, the glass-topped vanity with its heart-shaped mirror, her dresser with its cut-crystal knobs—is made from white wicker. The walls are painted pale rose and hold framed posters of pastel-hued ballerinas pirouetting, lacing their shoes, facing the barre en pointe.

When asked about all the traditionally girly shit, she immediately goes on the defensive. She unironically likes Precious Moments figurines and has never ingested a drop of alcohol in her life, and one time she beat up a guy in a parking lot because he told her that her hair sucked. She's unapologetically interested in the things that she loves; something I can't often say for myself, a person who loves clowning but hides it from her family because she can't stand the idea that her own mother might look at her with disgust. A phrase I often hear from Darcy: Who says punk can't be pink?

Her mother's house is located on a historic street in Sanford, which is about a thirty-minute drive from work. I always ask Darcy why she doesn't just move in with me so she'd be a hell of a lot closer to the downtown venues her band plays at, but she says her mom would get lonely. That's probably true, but I'm also aware that because she lives with her mother, she doesn't pay rent. Darcy has the entire top floor of their three-story house plus her own bathroom. If she moved in with me, we'd probably have to share my duplex because the cost of living has spiked so outrageously in Orlando. Aquarium Select III pays just enough that you can fend off the creditors, but barely. I try not to get defensive about money with Darcy—we're best friends, and one of the top ways you can alienate someone you care about is to drag finances into the relationship—but there are times when I'm sobbing over a maxed-out credit card bill that I wish she had just a little less; that way we could talk about things more often without all the finance walls firmly erected between us.

I know it's not our only problem, but it's currently the biggest one in the room.

"Come on," I say, because the sun has been up for hours and I've got a gig on the other side of town. "Your mom made food."

"Cool it with the mom shit."

"Get up and make me."

I slip into my jeans from the night before, which feel scummy on my bare legs after sleeping in the cloudy dream that is Darcy's high thread count sheets. My hair is a wreck, greasy with pale patches of scalp bleeding through the tangled strands, but I'll be wearing a wig, so I tell myself it doesn't really matter. I scrub some toothpaste onto my teeth using my finger as the brush. Then I wash my hands and face, and by then I'm done waiting for Darcy to crawl from her nest of sheets.

There's a door on the opposite side of the Jack-and-Jill bathroom that leads to a substantially smaller room where Darcy stores her drum kit. I head in there and locate the handle that's set inside the crown molding, pushing open the door that leads to the hidden back stairwell.

When Darcy had shown it to me, I'd been awestruck. The secret placement of the entrance had reminded me of a Hitchcock film.

"Do you think people used this to hide valuables or weapons?" I'd asked, the ancient wood creaking beneath my feet, holding the footsteps of people long dead. "Have you ever heard phantom tapping or strange knocking?"

She'd looked at me with pity and not a small amount of secondhand embarrassment. "It was for the help. You know, servants' quarters? That way the rich people that built this place wouldn't have to see them coming and going. God, you're so white trash."

And yes, that had been dumb of me, but I have to admit, I still love the mystery of those hidden stairs. The house has a dumbwaiter too, but Darcy says she got to use it only once. The first day they'd moved into the place, Darcy had put all her Barbies inside it and pushed the button to send them on an adventure. The dumbwaiter had stopped working halfway down, leaving the Barbies trapped behind the walls. I like to imagine them back there like tiny, beautiful vampires, waiting for the day that some unsuspecting soul unleashes their evil on the world.

When I slide open the back door to the kitchen, there's Darcy's mom. She has her hair up in a loose twist and is wearing a white linen jumpsuit with buttons all down the front. If I tried to wear something like that, I'd look like an escapee from some kind of institution, but on her it looks classy and chic. She's setting wet, barely cooked slabs of bacon on a stack of paper towels.

I grimace. "Those aren't for me, right?"

"For Darcy. I'll cook ours longer."

"She'll wind up with trichinosis."

Darcy's mom keeps slapping down the meat. "Well, that's her choice."

I pour myself a coffee and sit down at the counter. I like Darcy's mom a lot. Much like her daughter, Brenda Dinh never lets anyone else's opinion color her own unique perspective. She's never been married because she claims that the idea of it bums her out. She exclusively drives minivans because she enjoys the cargo space, and she keeps her Christmas decorations up all year long. Her original name was Nguyet, but she renamed herself after Brenda Walsh from *Beverly Hills, 90210*, whom she claims was "wildly misunderstood" by audiences. She's much taller than her daughter, taller than most women I know, and she runs a pool-cleaning business that uses all-natural green ingredients. All the suburban moms love her.

And she's incredibly hot. If she weren't Darcy's mom, I already would've made a pass at her.

"What stinks?" She wrinkles her nose. "Cigarettes?"

"Sorry, I'm still in last night's pants."

She briskly washes her hands and takes down a bottle from the shelf over the sink. "Stand up."

I comply. She proceeds to spritz me down from the crown of my head to the tops of my bare feet, then has me turn around and does my entire backside, focusing mostly on my jeans. By the time she's done, I'm completely drenched. Normally, I'd feel weird about someone dousing me with God-knows-what, but it's nice to be mothered sometimes. It makes the shriveled lump inside my chest that some might call a heart threaten to swell with affection.

"There," she says, and recaps the bottle. I take a sip of my coffee and nearly gag. There's a sheen of oil floating along the top of the mug. I quietly pour out the remainder and get myself a fresh cup.

"Jesus Christ." Darcy comes in, waving her hand in front of her face. "Essential oils and pork for breakfast?"

We carry our plates to the porch and sit together at the long wooden table. The garden used to be manicured but has since been left to run wild: potato vines and sago palms and rosebushes twined together in knots of brilliant green. It's monarch season; black-and-orange spotted butterflies dance along the ropes of weedy yellow flowers that line the back fence. Darcy tells her mother all about last night's gig while I eat everything on my plate, then help myself to the leftover crusts of Darcy's toast.

I observe the two of them like a scientist collecting field notes. Darcy details the highs and lows of the performance, complains about her bandmates, and lists her ideas for next time. Her mother doesn't interrupt to give advice. She's completely invested in what her daughter has to say. Another way for me to press the bruise, forcing myself to watch the dynamics of a healthy parent–child relationship. I try to imagine my own mother listening this intently as I discuss one of my gigs, and the thought alone spoils my appetite. Dwight used to charm her; he could do something clownlike, minus the greasepaint, and have her laughing at herself in under thirty seconds.

It was different with Dwight. He was the clear favorite, and he knew it. If anyone else had tried those dumb pranks on her, my mother would have had the offender's head on a pike, but since it was her precious baby boy, she never did anything but lightly scold and laugh. Men get passes that women often don't. Even when Dwight was only mildly funny, he still elicited more laughs than I did on my best day.

"Thanks for breakfast," I say, because there's only so much wholesome behavior I can take. "I've got to get going."

"Don't forget your fettucine in the fridge," Darcy says. "The one good thing you got out of that date."

Brenda's eyes light up. "A date! Tell me about it."

"Nothing to tell," I say, gathering all the plates, focusing on the egg yolk that's running over my thumb. "One and done."

"What, you don't want to admit that you tried to booty-call her last night?"

I grit my teeth, caught. "It was a booty *text*, actually."

"What's a booty text?" Brenda asks. "Is that like a sexy picture?"

"I've got to go," I repeat, heading inside as Darcy proceeds to describe the difference. I clean off the countertops and drop our dishes in the sink before grabbing my leftovers from the fridge. Rather than heading straight home to my dingy duplex, I sit in my sunbaked car and take in the quiet normalcy of the neighborhood. There's a father who's watching from the driveway as his kids ride bikes on the sidewalk out front. The girl has training wheels, but the boy is wobbling along without them, riding what looks like his first two-wheeler. I have a sudden flash of Dwight. I superimpose his face on the boy next door and feel time pull out and stretch, fragile as blown glass.

I don't wait to see if the kid falls. I chuck my fettucine in the back seat and make the long drive home.

Once there, I grab the surplus of mail that's spilling from the box out front. The disturbance sends the mated pair of geckos that live beneath it scrambling down the wall and into the dead potted succulent that's been there since I moved in. My front door always sticks because of the humidity, so I have to slam against it with my hip, which now has a permanent bruise from smacking it against the wood on a daily basis. I throw the mail on my dining room table, where it will sit for at least the next four months before I throw it all away, unopened, which is the way I've learned to "handle bills." Then I take a shower and get ready for my gig.

It's another birthday party, but this time it's for a fifteen-year-old girl. That is unusual—normally my birthday fares are almost exclusively the ten-and-under crowd—but the new age group is a good thing. It could help me expand my repertoire, and it'll look impressive for my audition in a couple of weeks. I sit down on my bedroom floor and use the mirror attached to the back of the door to apply my makeup. I do this naked, aside from my underwear, because that way my blousy, oversize clown clothes won't drag through all the greasepaint.

I once sent someone a nude this way. She responded fifteen minutes later with a thumbs-up emoji, but then I never heard from her again.

My phone rings from its position on the floor next to me. I look down at the screen and see that it's my mother calling. She is a person who texts; she never calls. I'm worried that someone has died, though I'm not sure who because all our relatives are either already dead or dead to us for being homophobic assholes.

"Hello?" I say, putting the phone on speaker. I've already painted my face into a mask of pure white. Next, I begin my color routine by drawing the thick looping line of red around my lips. "This is Cherry."

"Cheryl, it's your mother."

Several more dollops of red greasepaint on the brush, evening out both sides of my mouth. "Mother, this is *Cherry*."

Silence for a few moments as she digests this. This allows me to finish up with the red paint and dip a clean applicator into the blue I'll use to outline the triangle around my right eye. I wink at myself; try to get my spirits in check. Chatting with my mother and getting into clown headspace aren't exactly compatible activities.

"I'd like you to come for dinner next weekend."

My ass hurts from sitting on the bare floor with nothing to cushion it. I wedge a dirty T-shirt under me and keep painting.

"Okay, sure." My mother, an extreme introvert, has never been a fan of talking on the phone. Not one for pleasantries, she always gets right into it. "Any particular reason?"

"Just wanted to catch up."

There's another pause as I wait for her to tell me what this is all actually about. I dip my brush into the blue again, sliding the applicator up the side of my temple.

"There will be someone else dining with us. I'm . . . dating them."

The brush slips sideways, dabbing a streak of blue up my forehead and into my hairline.

"Shit," I say, grabbing a clean cotton round to try to repair the damage.

"Cheryl? Are you there?"

"Yes." I'm wiping at the mess, but it's not coming off; it's mixing into the white paint until it resembles a giant bruise. "Dinner, got it. Just text me the details."

"What's wrong? Are you alright?"

"I have to go," I say, and hang up the phone.

I spend the next ten minutes fixing the mess I've made. My mother has not dated anyone seriously since her ex, Patricia, and that was nearly thirty years ago. I almost wonder if it's Patricia again—that classic friends-to-lovers-to-friends-to-lovers lesbian pipeline—but Patricia remarried right after their separation, and those two have kids and now grandkids of their own. Still, the fact that my mother is introducing me to a new person means that it's serious. My mother doesn't date; she U-Hauls.

How can I turn this into a bit, I wonder. That's how my brain always chooses to process trauma or grief or anxiety. How can I turn this into something easier to digest? A bite-size joke would be infinitely more consumable. Maybe my mother has finally decided to adopt a pet. Her new "dating partner" is actually a butch tuxedo tom named Mitsi.

By the time my clothes are on—minus the shoes; you cannot drive in those oversize boats unless you want to die in a fiery wreck—I've moved mostly past the weird phone call with my mother and am feeling a bit more like myself.

I adjust my wig in the mirror and tug on the brim of my miniature cowboy hat, setting it tipped at a jaunty angle over the pile of mustard-yellow curls. Then I lock up the house; it's time to make the twenty-minute drive to the roller rink, gliding by all the Central Florida haunts that wallpaper the borders of my life. It rained the previous night, and the oak trees have shed their clothes. Bushy rafts of Spanish moss dangle from a power line, skins of it hanging like abandoned pantyhose. Two teenagers clutching skateboards use their free hands to yank the excess that's draped over the top of a stop sign. They hurl the wads at each other, shrieking as the remnants of last night's rain shake off like glitter in all that sunshine, and I smile as I remember how fun it can be to be young and have a body and use it well.

Truthfully, I haven't been to a roller rink since I was in middle school, and even then I don't remember skating, only standing around drinking fountain sodas while I watched girls giggle and hold hands with boys on the rink.

It appears that they rented the place out for the party. The rink is decorated with spiderwebs and black silk fabric, skulls and skeletons and vampires; what looks like every possible prop from a going-out-of-business sale at Spirit Halloween. I find the mother next to the snack table. She's a petite woman in a cardigan set wearing an actual pearl necklace with matching earrings. She's setting out a sheet cake decorated with a zombie devouring a mess of brains straight from a human skull.

"Good, you're here." She leads me to a nearby bench and thrusts a pair of skates at me. "Put these on."

"Oh, I don't skate." I pull my oversize clown shoes from my bag. "Just these bad boys."

She stares at me, perplexed. "You absolutely have to skate. It's non-negotiable."

"Your teenage daughter wants to see a clown skate?" I suppose it's possible. People are into all kinds of weird shit.

"Didn't the agency tell you? You're supposed to chase the kids."

"Chase them?" I look out onto the rink and see a slew of teenagers dressed like they've raided a Hot Topic. It's a bevy of baby goths, black lipstick and fake blood dripping down their necks.

"You can do scary, right? You're a clown." She taps my hat with the tip of her finger. "What's with the cowboy gear?"

"Haunted rodeo," I say, already tugging on the skates. Despite the fact that I hate scary clown associations—Thanks a lot, Stephen King—I shut my yap and pretend everything is fine. I need the gig; every time I bail on something, the agency puts me on a DO NOT CONTACT list for at least two months as punishment. "Going to go round up the cattle."

"Great." She claps her hands. "Brianne is going to just *die*."

Once again, a mom who cares more about what her daughter likes than freaking out over how freaky it is that she's into getting run down by a stranger in greasepaint. I get the skates laced and stand up, wobbling as my knees lock. I feel too tall. I'm not sure what to do with my arms. If it's this hard to skate across the carpet, I can't imagine how it will be once I reach the oil slick of the rink. I head toward the entrance with my hands extended. The girl I'm assuming is Brianne has on a black sash, designed to look like it might go on an undead prom queen, and it reads BIRTHDAY GHOUL in red glitter. Her smile is enormous, teeth colored by all the fake blood, and as I step off the carpet and onto the rink, the entire group of teenagers takes off shrieking.

"I can do this," I tell myself, knowing that I probably can't and really shouldn't try. "No problem."

I'm afraid of crashing into someone and am therefore unable to move faster than a crablike crawl across the rink's slick surface. What I really want to do is clutch on to the side wall and sort of yank myself along, but I get the feeling that won't get me paid, so I suck it up and try to hurry. Almost immediately my legs slip out from under me. My butt hits the rink first, hard, quickly followed by the back of my skull. It's the kind of pratfall that usually requires a banana peel; it's that good. The place explodes with laughter.

Despite the throbbing in my head and in my tailbone, part of me—the sick, validation-obsessed part—is actually pleased. I mean, hey, busting ass in front of a room full of strangers? That's just good slap-stick. I crawl forward, not letting any of the pain I feel in my ass show on my face, gurgling out a laugh that sounds like a cross between the Pillsbury Doughboy and a demonic Easter Bunny. I grab for random legs as the teens glide past, gloved fingers curled into claws. I surreptitiously skid my fingertips along the red paint that lines my mouth and let it drag down onto my teeth. The next time the birthday girl rips past on her skates, I growl at her, showing off a bloody, cannibalistic grin. She shrieks in faux terror and gathers her friends, circling again and again.

I spend the next hour chasing the teenagers around the rink, falling repeatedly, hoping I don't wind up with a concussion or any broken bones. The kind of health insurance I have is a duct-taped first-aid kit lodged under my leaky bathroom sink.

At the end of the party, I leave with a check for $150 and a body so bruised I think it will be a miracle if I can walk upright the next day. I sit in my car and eat the remainder of my fettucine Alfredo, which has been baking in the back seat of the Firebird all day. I don't have a fork so I use my fingers, slurping at the noodles like an animal, praying I don't wind up with food poisoning.

Just like Mom used to make, I think, remembering the time she served us leftovers that had the green tinge of mold darkening their edges. "Just scrape it off," she'd said, when I'd pointed out that we were about to be poisoned.

Sometimes it's funny to consider the fact that if I were a mother, I'd probably be just like her. Not funny *haha*, though; more like funny *yikes*.

There's a stash of fast-food napkins in my glove box, which I use to wipe at my hands before I touch my phone. I've got a few texts from Darcy and two from my mother, who confirms our dinner. There's also one from Margot.

She's replied to my incoherent "why u hot" with a message of her own:

"you are"

I swipe at my lips with the stack of dirty napkins, but I can't manage to wipe the grin off my face.

AQUARIUM SELECT IV

To ward off boredom at my part-time job, especially when Darcy's not around, I like to compile lists of facts. This activity serves as a distraction from the inexorable creep of time, as I wait for my upcoming audition and wonder if any of my dreams will ever come to fruition or if I'll be stuck restocking dusty shelves for the rest of my natural life. The lists comprise two specific categories that I consider crucial to clowning:

Things that are FUNNY and things that are NOT FUNNY.

The selection process is more complicated than you might think. Consider this: A person's best ideas and their worst ideas live in their head simultaneously. The good and the bad are like prizes stuffed in a gumball machine. Those ideas can sit there for years, all mixed together, waiting for someone to eject them into the world. When you finally put in that quarter and turn the dial, out comes something, but you can't guarantee it's going to be a good idea or even a smart one.

When I make these dueling lists of FUNNY and NOT FUNNY, I distill what makes the brain tick down to its most basic elements. Jokes have a finite shelf life, and comedy exists on a timeline. It can morph and expand, but it can also fold in on itself. Consider pop culture, movies, or television shows with catchphrases that start out as hilarious but after a period of time become an annoying din that a person must learn to tolerate instead of enjoy. A laugh passed between friends might retain a certain zest long after it was shared, but mostly it's the nostalgia of the moment that flavors it and not the joke itself. You aren't remembering the humor of the gag, you're remembering the good feeling you shared with that person. It's the funny that comes after the funny, the tinge of comedy left behind in the glass, like humorous residue.

Things that start off NOT FUNNY can quite easily shift to FUNNY too. Sometimes all it takes is time.

For instance, take my job at Aquarium Select III. When I pulled into the lot that morning and saw the store, I stopped for a moment and considered the basic facts. There's the same hideous mural out front with its deformed whales and monstrous sea creatures and dank, chipped paint, the same obnoxious boss inside waiting to yell at me, the same plethora of jumbled tank detritus for sale. All the regular things that usually fill my day with horror suddenly take on a new light when I consider the addition of an unknown factor: the customer. People who wander into the store are the changeable variable in this jokey mathematic equation; how they interact with the space and how I choose to interact with them can become a brand-new joke every time I punch in the formula.

Sitting there in the lot, dreading my day and staring at the ocean mural from hell, I came to a decision. Because of the upcoming audition and because I think my mental health deserves it, I'm going to start numbering my days at Aquarium Select III. Every time I arrive for a shift, it will be a variation of the same joke. How many ways can I tell it and still glean humor from the bit? Today is Aquarium Select IV, I think, and pray that I can keep the FUNNY from becoming NOT FUNNY again.

"Can I take a peek at your inverts?" someone says from behind me.

I whirl around. "Excuse me?"

The man is older than me but not by a lot. He's got on a suit that's wearing him instead of the other way around, navy blue with white pinstripes that might be considered nice by Sears standards fifteen years ago. His hair is gelled up and away from his face in a style that was wildly popular in early-aughts boy bands.

"Your inverts," he repeats. "Can I see them?"

Normally, a guy being a pervert would be something I would unequivocally file under NOT FUNNY, but today I decide to make it FUNNY for myself by yelling at him. "Hey, asshole. I don't know what your problem is, but I don't make enough money at this job to put up with creeps."

"Whoa!" He backs up abruptly, knocking into a tall rack of ceramic turtles. They're hand-painted in a variety of aggressive hues: neon orange and magenta and lemon yellow. Mister Manager is dating the guy who creates them. As far as I know, we've never sold one. Today, staring at a particular turtle that has flippers attached to its back like some kind of Teenage Mutant Ninja rip-off, I find them FUNNY.

"What does your wife think about you hassling women who make minimum wage?"

"What?"

"Take your 'inverts' garbage someplace else," I reply. "I'm not in the mood."

He's got his hands up like I'm about to physically attack him. "I just wanted to ask about your hermit crabs. I saw them on your website?"

Now I'm the one who's confused. "Hermit crabs?"

"I swear. It's for my daughter." He attempts a smile. His teeth, which are short and dark, the kind of teeth that have seen way too much black coffee in their lifetime, wink out at me. "Invertebrates. You know, inverts?"

"Shit." Now that he's said it for the third time, the name sounds vaguely familiar. Definitely part of all that employee training I've relegated to the recycling bin at the back of my brain. "Yeah. Okay, sure. I think we still have one left? I can show you."

We head to the back of the store where we keep all the short-term fare that usually moves fast, the occasional hamster or corn snake or poison dart frog. In the far corner, I spot the terrarium that holds the hermit crabs. The one that's left is small and shy, half buried in the silica play sand. The bin smells like a mixture of mildew and peanut butter. Someone has slathered the entire front wall of the case with it. Bits of gunky apple sit clumped in the bottom. NOT FUNNY, I think, wondering how long the crab has been left there to rot.

"Do you need info on these?" I ask, handing him the terrarium. "Because I can get my manager. I'm not incredibly familiar with, uh, inverts."

"No, my daughter has done a lot of that research. It feels like I know everything about them now, she can't stop talking about them." He laughs and it puts me at ease. He likes his kid, which isn't FUNNY or NOT FUNNY, but instead is just genuinely sweet. He's here because he supports her. He cares about what his daughter likes.

"I know it's kind of . . . dirty," I admit. "I feel bad that this one is so scrawny. Are you sure you don't want to wait for a new shipment?"

"I can take him, I think." He holds up the case and peers inside. "It looks like he could use a new home."

"Thank you," I say, which embarrasses me further. For some reason I feel like it's my messy home the guy has walked into, and instead of making fun of me for the unwashed dishes and the overflowing garbage, he's gracefully ignoring it. The situation has officially gone back to FUNNY again. I laugh, but it comes out sounding like a wet cough.

Luckily for me, the guy doesn't seem to notice. "Katrina will love it," he says.

We walk back up to the front, and he pays for everything; I charge only half price for the hermit crab because I feel 75 percent certain that it will die before the week is out. NOT FUNNY.

"You look really familiar," he says as I pass him his receipt. "Do we know each other?"

I really don't want to tell him that he looks like every White Business Dad of a certain age. Their faces blur together. FUNNY. "I don't think so."

"Are you sure? Because I could swear . . ." He peers at me a moment longer and then suddenly slaps his hand down on the counter, scaring the shit out of me and the hermit crab, which rolls backward and into his shell so quickly that I worry we might have cut his already short life expectancy by at least half. "You're Dwight's sister!"

I don't say anything, but I'm sure I look surprised.

"Yeah, Dwight," he repeats. "We were on crew together, back in high school."

The rat that runs my brain roots through the file cabinets that hold my memories. It's true that my brother was on the crew team, but that was a long time ago. I don't remember most of his friends because I was eight years younger than him, and high school teens don't really give two shits about hanging out with little kids. The guy who knows my dead brother tells me that his name is John. He holds out his hand and I shake it limply, still reeling from the cataclysmic shift from FUNNY back to NOT FUNNY. Guy Named John who knew my dead brother. And from the way that he's talking about Dwight, he doesn't know that my brother is dead. That's a whole other level of VERY NOT FUNNY.

"Man! Dwight's little sister. Small world." He smiles. "That guy is hands down the funniest dude I've ever met."

"Yeah," I say. "Funny."

Guy Named John is on a roll now; I can tell because he has stopped seeing me and has become laser focused on the past. It's a look that people get when they're so fixated on remembering their youth that they forget about anyone else in the room. He's back in high school, young again, not middle-aged with an expanding paunch, standing in a failing pet store, purchasing an ailing hermit crab.

"There was this one time?" He interrupts himself laughing and has to take a beat to recover. "Oh God. Dwight pranked our rival school by wrapping a ton of Saran Wrap around their boats. Those guys were so pissed; they spent like two hours trying to get it all off. I think we had to forfeit because of it, but goddamn I don't think I ever laughed so hard."

FUNNY, even if the remembering makes it sad. I can't remember the specific occasion he's talking about, but I'm sure it happened. My brother loved pranks. He was the quintessential class clown; everyone was his target. My mother, me, kids at school, his coworkers, his girl-friends, even total strangers. That he got away with this behavior is a testament to how much everyone loved him. And that he was a straight white man. Even as a clown, genderless as we appear, I can't get away with shit like that.

"Tell him John Mancini says hey, okay?"

"I will," I say, pretending I'll do exactly that. That he's alive and waiting for this conversation. "It was nice seeing you."

He leaves with the dying hermit crab. I stand there watching the door close behind him, enveloped by the blue gloom of the shop, bub-bling tanks with their hundreds of fish swimming in endless circles, the overpowering scent of bundled hay, stocked for guinea pigs and ham-sters, that no one will ever, ever buy. NOT FUNNY. In the midst of all that, I try to imagine calling up my brother and telling him about my interaction with Guy Named John. I tell Dwight all about the invert-pervert stuff, the dying hermit crab, the fact that I let this man believe that he was still alive.

Good one, Dwight would say, and he would mean it. Because all my brother would want to be remembered for is what that guy said about him with genuine affection: hands down the funniest dude that he's ever met.

It's FUNNY, but it's also NOT FUNNY. My brother saw me clown only on a bare handful of occasions, and at that point, I was still refining my act. There's no way for me to know what he'd think of me now. My phone buzzes, set in front of me on the counter though it's supposed to be stowed in the staff lounge. Mister Manager has told me this at least fifteen times in the past three weeks, and I'm sure he'll tell me again before the day is out. The message is from Margot, who has responded to my request for another date with "not this week."

Not a yes, but not a no either. I decide to take the response optimistically, like it's a glass half full of good wine. Keep my hopes up.

"Put that phone away."

I click the response button on my walkie-talkie. "Yes, sir, Mister Manager."

"Quit it with that crap. I mean it."

FUNNY. "Whatever you say, Mister Manager."

He might not have understood my clowning, but Dwight would love the Mister Manager bit, I think, and suddenly I'm on the verge of tears. NOT FUNNY. I turn down the volume on my walkie and abandon my post at the checkout counter, skirting boxes of shrink-wrapped coral and bulk containers of fish protein powders. Then I slip into the staff lounge, where I can breathe in the dark and give my brain a rest.

Wendall's at the round table at the center of the room with his feet kicked up on the only other plastic chair. He has his earbuds plugged in, head drooping and nodding, long dishwater-colored hair hanging half in his face. There's a mostly full container of spicy seafood ramen on the table next to him. It's got the remnants of an egg sitting yolky-yellow on the top.

Aggravated at finding him there on his third break of the day when I need to be alone, I shove his feet off the other chair. He sits up with a surprised jolt. His face? FUNNY.

"That's Darcy's ramen," I say. "Not yours."

"What?" The music coming from his earbuds is loud enough for me to hear it over the fluorescents that are buzzing monotonously in the fixture overhead.

"You heard me."

"Huh?"

"You can't just steal people's food. There are only, like, six of us who work here. People will know it was you."

"I didn't steal anything."

I have to resist the urge to smack him. NOT FUNNY. "You're telling me you brought that to work with you?"

He looks down into the ramen as if he's just seeing it for the first time. "No, I didn't."

"So, you took it."

"No."

Talking with Wendall always feels like trying to have a coherent conversation with someone who's in a completely separate timeline; either forty-five minutes early or twenty-five minutes late to the discussion you're already having without them. The absurdity of it should be FUNNY, but it annoys me enough that it becomes NOT FUNNY. "That's Darcy's," I repeat.

"Yes."

"So, you stole it."

He shakes his head and looks like he might cry. That makes two of us, I think, before pushing the thought roughly away. NOT FUNNY.

"She gave it to me." He pushes the ramen across the table and away from him with trembling hands. "But if you think she's going to be mad, I'll put it back."

"Wendall, you can't put it back once you've already cooked it."

"I'll buy her a new one."

The conversation has reached a point of such futility that my mind has completely left my body. I'm sliding through the ceiling, floating up into the cloudless blue Florida sky. All I wanted was to stop thinking about my dead brother, and I guess that I've mostly succeeded because I'm stuck arguing with a person who cannot tell me whether or not he stole my best friend's food. FUNNY, I guess.

"Jesus Christ, never mind." I sit down in the chair opposite him and slam my walkie-talkie on the table. "Forget it."

Wendall pops his earbuds back in and returns to scribbling in his notebook. I can see the term "solar flare" scrawled across the top of the page in thick black ink, and I'm grateful that he's not reading me his slam poetry. Idly I wonder if I could turn our interaction into a bit but ultimately decide against it. It's all a little too "Who's on First?" for me. NOT FUNNY.

Darcy's been spending way too much time with him, I think, eye-balling his giant white hands that have never known a day's hard work. The other afternoon she told some joke that she'd thought I'd like, something about a frog's ass, which I have to admit was a funny premise. When I asked where she'd heard it, she told me she'd stolen it from Wendall. Obnoxious. Now I can't use the joke at all.

Instead of stealing some of Darcy's food from the refrigerator—it's different when I do it, FUNNY—I go on my phone and continue my slow creep through Margot's social media. I've spent a good amount of time poking through her professional Instagram account (her personal one is locked, and I don't feel confident enough yet to request access), and I've looked at all the photos on her professional website. Because I am who I am and I've had a terrible day, I decide I may as well take a peek at her ex-wife's social media and just get it over with.

Portia is blonde and tall and Nordic. She looks like she could be one of the hot, busty women who holds a briefcase on *Deal or No Deal*. Her most recent posts include pictures of a nice meal at a fancy local restaurant and several images of a fluffy, crusty-eyed Pekingese she calls Baby. She's been dating someone seriously, but she isn't featured in any of her pictures. No new girlfriend soft launch yet, I guess. I continue scrolling, moving backward in time in my quest to find the good stuff, and after a few moments, there they are: pictures of Margot. Here she is, eating a bowl of pasta with red sauce, perfect meatball perched precariously on top. There's the two of them holding hands on the beach, backlit by a peachy Florida sunset. As I scroll, the pictures become more intimate as their relationship improves. The two of them get younger, lines erasing from their faces as the quality of the images becomes grainier. Finally, toward the beginning of the account, I land on a picture of the two of them onstage. They're both holding large bouquets of flowers. Margot has her arm wrapped tightly around Portia's red-sequined waist. They're kissing. Margot's cape flares out behind her. OUR FIRST SHOW reads the caption, and when hastily I click to view the comments, wanting to see if Margot posted a reply, my thumb slips. I accidentally Like the photo.

NOT FUNNY. "Shit," I say. "Shit. Shit!"

Though I immediately Unlike it, Portia will still receive a notification. She'll see that someone—a stranger—has Liked a not-so-recent photo. She will click through to investigate. She will see my picture and my name. She might ask Margot about it. I swear some more. Wendall looks at me now with very real fear on his face.

"Here." He shoves the cup of ramen at me and leaves the breakroom in a hurry.

FUNNY, I think.

The soup congeals on the table in front of me as I attempt to clean up the mess I've just made. I'll change my username to something innocuous. A business. Then I'll lock the account. I need a new user picture that's not my face. I Google "shoe repair shops" and find an image of an old boot, then upload it.

The whole process takes less than three minutes. When I'm done, I sit with my heart pounding in my throat hard enough to make me want to vomit. NOT FUNNY. I stare at the laminated poster taped to the wall, next to the microwave, and go through the steps of how to perform the Heimlich maneuver.

"For a Single Individual, You Can Perform the Maneuver by Slamming Your Midsection Against Something Firm, Like a Countertop."

FUNNY, I think, and my throat opens up.

Someone's calling for me on the walkie-talkie. Wendall might be off break again, but he's so unreliable that even Mister Manager won't put him on the service desk. If Darcy were here, she and I would have commiserated over it: the fact that a guy who can't be trusted to count out correct change gets treated better than the two women who essentially run the store. I finally pick up after he yells my name again, just to inform him I'm on my break, and then I turn the walkie off and continue staring at my phone.

The picture I Liked was from nearly ten years ago.

NOT FUNNY. Embarrassed all over again, I eat the rest of Wendall's cold ramen and slurp down the untouched egg. On Margot's professional page, there is an updated list of events indicating when and where you can find her act, and I see that she is going to be performing at the downtown library tonight for a fundraising gala. The cost per ticket is $125. Normally, I would never spend that kind of money, but I still have the wad of cash Marcia handed me two weeks ago, and that means my circumstances have changed. There's enough money for me to get all new applicators and greasepaint (the good kind, not the stuff that leaks down my forehead and gets in my eyes when I sweat) and still afford to attend the gala. I try not to think about what "attend the gala" means. If anything, it might be considered "light stalking." I'll have to wear something nice. I'll have to see if I own anything nice.

I might have to buy something nice.

Part of me knows that by purchasing the ticket, I won't be able to afford the cost of my upcoming audition. The smart part, the thoughtful part, the part of me that's been working tirelessly at a job that I hate just so I can make it to the next stage in my ambitions. If I pay for this gala ticket, I won't be able to afford the gas it will take to get downtown to tryouts. I won't be able to afford a motel room for the night either. Is it worth it to me to throw away something that might be a sure thing for my career by betting on a dark horse like Margot, who won't even regularly text me back?

I'm feeling lucky, I think, and I impulsively press buy.

Mister Manager spends the next ten minutes berating me for taking a break without asking. I understand that this is a trademark of capitalism. The idea that workers are all little infants, underlings with soft, meager brains who are supposed to follow every single rule of the genius manager. He even wants us to ask before we use the restroom. I'm not going to do that, ever, and no amount of yelling from a man who has a customized license plate for his Miata that reads MI8T8 is going to convince me otherwise.

Darcy arrives for her shift in the middle of Mister Manager's rant, standing directly behind him as he drones on and on about responsibility. She does this thing that's incredibly FUNNY, this mimicking action where she perfectly mimes his body movements. She even mouths the words along with him, almost as if she's reading from a script. I try not to laugh. It's a trick that I'd love to incorporate into my own act someday, but I'm not nearly as good at it. It's like Darcy can get right inside his head; she can predict what he's going to do or say before anything even happens. I try never to think about Mister Manager, so maybe that's my first problem.

Once he finally leaves, I turn to Darcy. "I'm clocking out early."

"Good for you." Her mohawk is mostly sea green today, the purple all leached out. "Take tomorrow off too."

As I gather my stuff, I tell her about Wendall sneaking her food. "He left it on the table after I yelled at him, so I ate the rest. Hope I don't wind up with some wasting illness that makes me, like, completely incompetent at my job."

Instead of laughing, she busies herself putting on her headset. It takes a long time with her mohawk; she usually has to wedge it between two of the front spikes. "Huh. Okay."

"What?"

She rolls her eyes and slides open the cash drawer to count the money. "I told him he could. You know, if he was hungry."

Now I'm the one who's surprised. It's neither FUNNY nor NOT FUNNY. It's just weird. "Why the hell would you do that?"

"I've got more than enough."

"That's not the point." The point is that Wendall doesn't do any work. The point is that we're always having to cover for him, do his job for him, get yelled at when he messes up. The point is that even though he fucks up all the time, he still gets paid just as much as the two of us. But I don't have to say any of that to her, because Darcy already knows.

"Listen," she says. "I don't think anyone should work if they don't want to. Fuck capitalism."

"I mean, I agree, but c'mon . . . it's *Wendall.*"

Darcy doesn't answer. I leave it alone because trying to pry into Darcy's head when she doesn't want to talk is akin to getting your fingers slammed in a car door. No matter what, it's going to sting and you're not going to get anything from the experience except a lingering bruise and very hurt feelings.

I wave goodbye and leave through the front door without telling Mister Manager. Then I park my ass in the front seat of my car and take a screenshot of the gala ticket. I text the image to Margot.

"Maybe I'll see you tonight," I write.

It doesn't take long for her to respond.

"Maybe," she replies.

And that's enough. For now.

GET YOURSELF A DUMMY

Sometimes it's hard to take off the clown.

Okay, so I'm Bunko. I've slathered on the greasepaint and slid into my too-big shoes and popped on the bright red nose and donned my party-colored wig. I've got my stash of gadgets and magic tricks and party favors. Here's my miniature rhinestoned cowboy hat, jaunty as a wink. Snap on my white gloves. Gut busted, padded rear end, powdered and neoned and grinning.

I've described the costume, not the clown. The costume is purely physical. The clown is a persona that takes years to craft, if not decades. You develop it gradually, through trial and error, and by the time you're done, the clown is inside you for good. At any given moment, mine sits waiting inside the cramped clown car of my skeleton, pushing impatiently at the door of my rib cage, wanting out so it can really start fooling around. The clown doesn't care if I'm on a date or attending a funeral. The clown is my id, greedy and impatient and uncaring of the mess it might make in its quest to get off a good joke.

Any asshole off the street can slap on a polka-dot tie and juggle some oranges and claim to be something they're not. To be a real clown, you must accept that it changes you into something hard and occasionally cruel. Jokes aren't always sweet. Take, for example, the court jester. A role meant to entertain only the king, the jester finds ways to make his ruler laugh, often at the expense of others—but always at the expense of himself. In order to perfect my art, I must let it swallow me whole. The part that is my authentic self shrinks down so that the clown can grow in its place.

I lose myself. That's the price I pay for art.

To clown well, you must embrace the light smile and the dark heart. One of the best teachers I've had in these matters is a local who supplies my gear. I go out to Miri Gonzales's place to score the good grease-paint, the professional-grade makeup she doles out alongside practical advice. She might be seventy-eight years old, but she still knows all the best acts in town and sells the best gear hands down. It's true that you can buy most clown stuff online for a fraction of the price, but if you're serious about clowning, you know that small business is best. I'd rather pay people I know for their expertise, people who take my art seriously, instead of throwing my money at a corporation that only wants to drive the competition out of business.

Miri's house is out in the middle of nowhere. It's a drive that gets more scenic once you turn off the highway, slip out past the choked smash of suburbs with their matching pastel paint jobs and double-wide garages, and finally encounter the spread of old homes and swampy land that make up rural Central Florida. I've been to Miri's so many times that I don't need to look up the address, but if you were driving out that way looking for it, once you saw the house you'd know you'd arrived. The driveway is painted in a variety of multicolored checkered squares (and repainted again every six months, because this is Florida, and the pounding rain and the relentless sun mean that everything colorful and beautiful must inevitably fade), resembling a funny tie. The front door is bright red, the windows at either side outlined with triangles of shockingly blue paint.

Miri's house is a clown.

I park out front, taking in the purple-and-gold polka-dot curtains and the blue plastic daisies waving at me from their silver pots, which are shaped like a bunch of helium balloons. There's a red, white, and blue neon sign hanging over the front door that looks remarkably like Bozo the Clown. If the light is on, that means she's home. If it's off, then she's gone for the day and business is closed, which either means she's out drinking or she's off playing bingo. Lots of people, myself included, have told her it's a bad idea to advertise the fact that she's not home—basically guaranteeing that some idiot might try to rob her, an elderly woman who lives alone in a house filled with valuables—but Miri owns a very large pit bull named Priscilla Presley and claims that anyone who'd wrangle with her dog deserves whatever they manage to steal.

Today, the light is on. I've booked three more gigs in the next two weeks so I'd like to stock up on makeup and take a look at what else she has available. Some of it is her own vintage objets d'art from her time in the circus. Since I'm in a hurry, I know that I better get inside quick because a visit with Miri always lasts at least an hour.

Priscilla starts barking before I even reach the porch. Miri lets me in, and once her pit bull sees it's me, he nudges me hard with his gray block head, then goes back to nesting in his oversize pillowy bed beside the front door.

"Cherry Baby." Miri waves me into the living room. "I got some good stuff for you today."

And I know that she does, because everything Miri owns is good. Her home has a smell reminiscent of an antiques store—the vanilla and musk of old books, sun-warmed rugs, and stale coffee. It's an intoxicating odor of things from long ago, an homage to heydays past. There are intricate, hand-embroidered costumes displayed on the wall in glass cases, clowning kits that hold the remnants of ancient greasepaint pots stored in copper containers gone green with age, cracked bowling pins, dusty leather satchels full of yellowed silk gloves, and mounds of moth-eaten ties. Curio cabinets stuffed with porcelain knickknacks, clown babies and clowns in outdated makeup, clowns single and clowns paired. Then there's her couch, the brilliant jewel of her home: bright red vinyl, white piping and trim, coated in a variety of unknown stains. It's not really a sofa at all; it's the back half of what used to be a clown car. "My ex-husband made that for me," she tells people proudly, before admitting that the couch is the only reason that he got to keep his dick. She caught him cheating on her with one of the trapeze artists, and that was the end of their marriage.

"Tea service?" Miri asks, hand on her kettle. "One shot or two?"

I tell her that I'm in kind of a rush, so I can't get day drunk. For Miri, "tea service" means drinking whiskey from fancy porcelain cups. She's a party girl, that one. Goes harder than me even on my wildest day.

I sit down on a patchwork recliner that's been covered with the slippery fabric of a multicolored parachute. Miri is across from me on the clown car couch. She's got her long gray hair twisted up into dueling knots that sit at either side of her head. The only makeup she wears is bright purple eyeshadow and a slick of bloodred lipstick.

"Bitch, I don't got all day," she says. "Spill."

"Bitch, all you've got is time." I can see that I've got her there; she nods complacently. People don't visit Miri as often as they used to, not with all the cheaper online options available and the local clowning community steadily dwindling. People are more interested in taking gigs out at the theme parks where there is more job security and a steadier paycheck.

"What did you do?" she asks.

"Technically, I didn't do anything," I say, already leaning into the joke. "I'm not going to the audition."

She takes a dainty sip of her whiskey. The cup has a kitten in clown makeup painted on its side. It rattles as she places it back on its dish.

"So, what are you even here for?"

"What do you mean? I need new makeup."

She shakes her head. "You're not serious. If you were serious, I'd give you the good shit. But you're not, apparently. Not if you're skipping an opportunity that good."

"I *am* serious."

She finishes her cup and pours some more. "Kid's driving me to drink."

"There was something I needed the money for first."

"Hmm." She doesn't look like she believes me, but the whiskey softens her up, makes her more liable to give me the benefit of the doubt.

"I promise," I insist. "You know that I wouldn't fuck around when it comes to work."

She sighs heavily and finishes her whiskey in one long swig. "Fine. Come on." Miri wrenches up her kimono as she hoists herself back off the couch. She's wearing men's tube socks that nearly reach the tops of her wrinkled kneecaps. I follow her down the hall toward her office. The space doesn't have central air, but there's a window unit plugged into the wall. It puffs away fretfully, loud as a freight train, lending the space a whiff of icy, chemical-scented condensation.

"I need all new shit." I head over to the right wall and begin digging through one of the clear bins that holds tubes of white base coat. "Some lady with a fetish bought all my stuff."

"Hope she overpaid."

"It definitely cost her."

Miri hands me a plastic grocery bin from her stack—every time she goes to Publix she steals one—and leans against the wall as I go through what's available. I restock everything I sold to Marcia and grab a slew of new items, including a wide array of rainbow glitter that I can use on my face as well as on the audience. It's especially satisfying to pelt glitter at anyone who heckles you in a cruel way; it takes forever to get rid of the stuff, truly the hellish gift that keeps on giving.

"What's in the bag?" she asks. "Suit need hemming?"

"It's Velma."

I set the grocery bin on the floor between my feet and pull the ventriloquist's dummy from my backpack. I'm not a natural hand at ventriloquism, so she's not a regular part of my act, but I keep her around just in case. Velma's got a short brown bob. She wears chunky black glasses and a white-and-blue sailor suit. The outfit is coming apart at the seams, the sleeves drooping, and her left shoulder has slid out of its socket. She's not as old as the other dummies peppering the shelves of Miri's back room, but Velma isn't new either. Living inside a bag, jumbled around with a heap of other clowning gear like she's in a wash cycle, has left her in need of some serious TLC.

I can tell by the way Miri yanks the doll from my arms that she's unhappy. "Cherry Baby, you have to take better care of your friends."

"I know."

"I can't keep fixing the same mistakes, over and over again."

"I *know*."

She frowns. "Bitch, don't get mad at me. You're ruining things all on your own."

I can't argue with that. I follow her back out of the room, lugging the grocery basket full of makeup as she swaddles Velma, leaning down into her painted face and cooing at her like a doting grandmother. We head into the second bedroom, which serves as a makeshift sewing studio. Miri sits down with Velma on her lap and paws through a selection of fabrics on the table in front of her. She shows them to the doll, nodding her head occasionally, then throwing pieces out when she claims that "the vibes are off."

"This one?" She holds the swatch of green canvas to Velma's cheek. "No. Too sallow."

Back when I first met Miri, I quickly learned that the best way to learn anything from her was to simply shut up and watch. Miri Gonzales has been clowning longer than I've been alive, and she has the know-how to prove it. Her methods might be unusual, but they haven't steered me wrong yet. And one thing she's certain of is that all dolls have souls. How we treat them determines how we come back in another life. "I don't want to come back as something no one loves," she told me once, and that thought continues to haunt me.

"Now this will look good, I think." She holds up a piece of striped silk. "Yes. This will do very nicely."

She sets Velma on the tabletop beside her and begins to undress her to inspect the rest of the damage. It's not just her shoulder that's wrecked; the elbow has also popped out of its socket. "Saints preserve us, look at this arm." She swivels around and glares at me. "You let her go like this for *how* long?"

It could have been a week; it could have a been a month. "A couple of days, tops."

"Jesus knows when you lie, and so do we."

Velma stares up at me, brown eyes owlish behind her glasses. Miri cradles her round wooden head in her hand.

"Sorry, Miri."

"And?"

"Sorry, Velma. I'll do better."

Miri huffs. "You better, or you're going to come back as one of those pissing dolls that wets itself."

She lays the dummy on her back while she swatches the fabric with a few spools of thread. Then she holds it up for my inspection. "It's really nice," I say, because it is. The pattern is delicate, a cream background with a smattering of thin pastel vertical stripes. Baby pink and soft coral and slips of shiny gold thread.

"Of course it's nice! Like I would own anything shitty."

That reminds me, I still have to go buy fancy clothes. "I wish I had something that good. I got a weird not-date tonight."

She swivels around to face me. "Not-date? What does that mean?"

"Just trying to make someone fall in love with me," I say, because even though I'm joking, I'm kind of being serious. I pause for dramatic effect. "Margot the Magnificent."

Her eyes widen, lifting the thick purple eyeshadow nearly to her eyebrows. "Oh shit. You *are* working on something big."

"I think I can get her to mentor me."

"*Mentor*, is that what you kids are calling it these days?"

I crack a grin. "Mentoring with benefits."

She nods stoically. "That would be a hot number to catch."

"But I don't have an outfit. At least not anything nice enough for a gala? Whatever the hell a gala is."

Miri raises a finger and digs through a mound of clothes piled on top of a padded rocking chair. After a few minutes, she finally unearths something near the bottom of the pile. She flaps it out in front of her like a bedsheet, cursing at the wrinkles, and I see that it's a jumpsuit made from the same fabric swatch she'd chosen for the dummy.

"Here." She thrusts it at me, then instantly snatches it back. "Wait, I have to steam it first."

"What is it?"

"What the hell does it look like?" she says, shaking it in my direction so that the legs flap around like wind socks. "It's a fancy outfit. You can't get someone like Margot looking like . . ." She gestures at my body. "*That*."

There's a bar attached to the wall filled with empty plastic dress hangers. She slips the jumpsuit onto one of them and flips the switch on the steamer, quickly erasing all the wrinkles. As she moves across the torso, I can see that it's a genuinely nice piece of clothing. It's vintage and looks like it probably cost a boatload.

"I can't afford that," I say. "It's too expensive."

"Would you shut up? I'm trying to do something nice." She steams one cap sleeve, then does the other. "And who said anything about charging you? You can have it."

"It was yours?" The guilt descends on me like a weighted blanket. I don't want her giving me something valuable that should stay in the family. "Shouldn't you save it for your daughter?"

"I'm not giving anything this nice to my slut daughter." She sighs deeply. "Well, she's not a slut. I'd like her a lot better if she were."

I take the jumpsuit from her and hold it between two fingers so I don't wrinkle it again.

"Try it on first." She busies herself with the doll. "You can't have it if it doesn't fit over your fat ass."

That makes me laugh, because we both know that my ass is not only nonexistent but genuinely almost inverted, the kind of flatness that curves inward and defies all notions of human gravity. I shrug out of my work polo and khakis and slide into the jumpsuit, which feels cool against my bare skin. I manage to zip it up myself and then I look at myself in the eight-foot-tall ornate golden mirror that's leaning against the wall, a mirror that used to belong to the circus, one that Miri stole with her ex-husband, Hector.

I don't look half bad. The jumpsuit fits all the parts of me that normally don't look so hot in other clothes. And it's not too femme, which is nice, because I never know how to hold my body in things that have a lot of ruffles and bows. If anything, the outfit feels a bit like I've got on upscale pajamas. I twist back and forth in front of the mirror as I admire myself, enjoying how the sunshine glimmers all that golden thread.

"What do you think?" I ask. "I managed to slide my fat ass in, but just barely."

"Looks good." She holds up Velma. "And I can make dolly one to match."

I slide my hands up and down my belly. The fabric is so expensive that my skin feels nearly visible beneath the smooth expanse of it. It's the nicest thing I've ever put on my body. "I feel bad," I say. "I can't let you just give this to me for free."

"Nothing is ever free. I'm going to charge you something awful to fix this mess." She pats the doll's face. It stares up at her in wooden adoration. "And I'm still mad at you for bailing on the audition. Just because you might fuck Margot doesn't mean she'll be willing to give you a leg up professionally after the scissoring is over."

"Oh Christ, Miri."

She waves me off. "Come back in a month. Maybe six weeks."

I pay her for the makeup, plus a little extra for taking on the doll. Cash only. She doesn't show me out; she's already focused on reattaching the dummy's elbow. Just yells at me to get out when I try to thank her again. On my way through the living room, I take a closer look at the framed photos tacked up on the walls. The photos start off black and white, and as time passes, they slowly shift to color. Plenty of circus images: Miri on the back of an elephant, Miri doing a handstand under the big top with her legs in a wide V, Miri holding a chimpanzee that is wearing a fireman's hat and clutching what looks like a real axe. Some with Hector, also decked out in his clown gear. There are candid pictures as well, slices of a life lived well. Her daughter, small and dark haired, pulling a wooden pony behind her in the dirt. Miri and Hector on their wedding day, her dress a frothy white cake. Friends and family and lovers. One shot of Miri with her hair chopped in a pixie cut, laughing with her mouth flung wide-open, enough that I can count all her dark silver fillings. I'm not surprised to see that she's wearing the jumpsuit. We look alike, I think, and it's not anything having to do with our faces. It's the clown shining out.

The weather is classic Florida, spring blue skies and sticky humidity. I have the windows in my Firebird rolled down, the hot breath of an afternoon breeze caressing my bare arms. The jumpsuit feels good on me, almost like I'm not wearing clothes, and I turn the music up way too loud as I speed down the back roads faster than I should, the palm scrub giving over into wide fields dotted with cattle, those fields becoming vacant lots of punky dry grass strewn with a dandruff of garbage and abandoned cars, the lots expanding into thick stands of pine and oak trees, more scrub, and then a sudden break of brackish water. Stagnant mess in a wide ditch, full of fecund life: snakes and slickscaled fish and long-necked egrets.

What's funny to a bird, I wonder, as several crows lift from a slender pine, lighting in perfect symmetry along a nearby electric wire. It dips beneath their combined weight, looking like a blackened grin with rotted black birds for teeth. They're chattering to themselves about the car speeding past, flying faster than any bird they've ever seen. In that moment, I'm the essence of something much bigger, joyful and wholly alive, and when I laugh—as loud as I want—there's the clown inside, overflowing with glee. I'm my own audience, first and foremost. Shouldn't all things funny start out with a joke that's just for me?

The library is downtown. It's early enough that I have time to park next to the lake and take a quick stroll, maybe grab a drink. Enjoy a bit of beauty before I head inside and potentially ruin whatever's been brewing with a woman I like by simply being myself. It's the golden hour, the time in Florida I love best, when everything slows down and the damp air is tinged with a sweet, holy light.

I almost never come downtown proper. Usually, it's all nightlife and the sour smell of piss, drunk people buying late-night hot dogs from carts in the middle of the street. It's easy to forget how lovely the lake and the greenery can be. At a nearby convenience store, I grab a bag of chips coated with radioactive orange powder and a tall boy that has the heft of a newborn infant. The cashier takes one look at me and immediately inserts the beer directly into its own slender brown bag; he's right, I'm going to drink it exactly where I shouldn't. The sun has sunk behind a tall wall of office buildings. I follow the curve of the lake while I eat my chips and drink my beer and try not to stain Miri's jumpsuit.

A street performer with a plastic bucket for donations is stationed next to the amphitheater. He is miming . . . poorly. Sometimes he forgets that he's not supposed to speak and he whispers the word for whatever he's doing with his body: pulling a rope, finding himself trapped inside a box, peeling a carrot with an especially dull knife and accidentally nicking himself with the blade. Because I understand how hard it is to mime effectively, something I worked at for literal years and still don't do all that well, I decide to sub into the secondary role as a few people leave without even clapping.

Dropping a handful of loose change into his bucket, I tell him the plan. "I'll be the dummy. Ready?"

He nods. This close, I can see that he's even younger than I thought underneath all that white paint. If I had more time, I'd talk him through the makeup process, but for now, it's good enough that I'm there as his prop.

Moving into position, I "sit" in front of him on an imaginary chair. This requires serious leg muscles—ones I've worked on through countless hours of squatting as I build balloon animals, ready myself for somersaults, and perform all the slapstick routines I've honed that purposefully put me face to face with my audience. That's another thing about clowning: it fucks up your back like nothing else. Kids can tell when you're fake. They've got a built-in bullshit detector that works on anyone over the age of eighteen, and they're not going to laugh if they see that you're not willing to get down on their level.

From behind, the mime takes my hands and positions them both above my head, like a ballerina posed in arabesque. Then, as soon as he lets go, I drop both arms like they weigh a thousand pounds. Immediate titters from the audience; this new set is working. He feigns frustration and then poses me again. The arms fall, this time one smacking him in the side of the head. He lifts me up and poses one of my legs, which I allow to crumple under me. He spins me to the right, and I pivot back to the left. Our movements are synchronized in complete opposition with each other. This is another simple clowning trick: the allure of magnetic bodies. Magnets attract, sure, but they also repel. It's the fight for connection that's so funny, I think, as the audience grows in number, and the laughs grow as well. We always want the things that we can't have.

Finally, he pushes my leg forward with one of his own knees, and I immediately kick it back again, taking him out. He crashes onto the sidewalk. I stand there and wait until he taps my calf with the toe of his sneaker, then I crumple beside him. We lay there, two dismantled puppets, and then, as one, we sit upright and bow to our assembled audience.

It's a good group, and we get plenty of cheers. People come forward to drop money into the bucket, some of it bills instead of change. I smile indulgently at the mime, so young and obviously well pleased with his performance, and when I look out into the crowd again, there's Margot standing across the street, watching me with an unreadable expression on her face. She's in a shiny black satin tuxedo, holding her top hat under one arm.

I just killed with that bit, and I know it. My smile skims into something slicker, sexier. She smiles back at me, mirroring my grin. I'm savoring my moment of good art, but I'm also reveling in the way that my performance made me feel. Powerful. Hot.

There's a beautiful blonde exiting the car on Margot's right.

Portia. I wave at Margot, but she acts as though she doesn't see me. I watch her offer her ex-wife her arm, leading the two of them down the street, headed toward the library.

"That was great!" The guy who'd been doing the bad miming is high on a good performance, happily shaking the assortment of money in his white plastic bin. It's a look I love; the slap-happy joy when the gig goes just right. "Let me split this with you."

"You keep it," I say. "I got to get going."

"Listen, we could put an act together! Let me get your number!"

I wave him off and hurry down the street, wiping what I'm sure are the remnants of cheese-flavored dust from the corners of my lips. There is something to be said for duo work—more gigs, more interesting material because you can bounce ideas off each other—but it also means spending a hell of a lot of time with someone one-on-one, and I don't know that guy from a hole in the wall.

The entrance to the library is two blocks away. Margot and her ex have already disappeared somewhere inside, swallowed up by the place. It's the library of my childhood. Storytime with nice librarians who read me all the classics, stuff like "Three Billy Goats Gruff" and "Little Red Riding Hood." When I got older, my friends and I smoked weed in the downstairs bathrooms. But there's something intimidating about the building itself. It's gray and forbidding, and there's just something so cold about all that uncolored concrete. It doesn't match the warmth of its interior. That's how lots of people are, I guess. Hiding that vulnerability with a tough outer shell.

There's a man at the door with a clipboard so I yank my phone out of my bag to show him my ticket. I quickly realize I could have probably gotten in without even buying one because the guy is distracted and waves me through without scanning the QR code. My audition could have happened after all; my stomach leaks acid until I feel it bubbling up my throat.

The gala is on the second floor, I'm told by a woman with a butch haircut, shaved up one side, who hands me a fluted glass of icy cold champagne. She winks at me and it's sweet. I wink back at her in return, and then I'm following a crowd of people up the stairs and into a large, heavily festooned room filled with a bevy of high-top tables and even more waitstaff in all black, serving snacks on tiny silver trays.

I'm not used to attending events; my heart is with the waitstaff and the performers. I slink backward into the room, away from the crowd up front, uncomfortable without the greasepaint there to obscure my face. There's music playing from the speakers overhead, jazzy stuff that's meant to sound like *something*, but not *too much* like something, more of an approximation of music. I stare at the ceiling, where they've draped sheets of indigo linen, dotted through with holes, so that the lights that pierce the fabric resemble clusters of stars.

Guests mingle. I listen in on their private conversations, much like I do at my own gigs. That's how you learn what makes people laugh, by listening to what they have to say and then riffing off of it. For instance, a couple at the high-top table next to me are arguing over the selection of meatballs.

"It's grape jelly," she says, taking one between her perfectly white teeth. "It's how my grandma always made them."

"There's no way these are Crock-Pot meatballs." He's wearing a gray suit with a baby-pink tie, the kind of outfit every guy who works in a law office or in finance wears downtown. "No gala event would serve something as tasteless as precooked meat made with jelly."

"I'm telling you, they are."

"How could you possibly know that?"

"Because I have taste buds, Jamie."

"Doubtful. You couldn't tell a cabernet from a Beaujolais." He takes the leftover meatball from her plate and eats it, closing his eyes as he samples the flavor. "There's no jelly in here. It's got soy sauce. Sesame, for sure. And there's some kind of umami flavor."

"Please. For the love of God. Stop saying things taste like umami."

Another server fortuitously wanders past my table, so I take the opportunity to grab a meatball of my own, rooting around for it with a yellow toothpick.

"Excuse me." I pitch my voice high, so that it carries. "Can you tell me what's in these meatballs?"

The server, a guy in his early twenties, looks bored already. "Grape jelly and barbecue sauce."

The triumphant cry from the woman behind me is enough to sustain me through the next twenty minutes, which is good because the gala opens with a very long and boring introduction by the president of the library board. I tune out, focused on the bubbles at the bottom of my champagne flute, which is quickly emptying. I look around for a server so I can grab another, but it seems they've all disappeared.

As the man drones on and on about fiscal responsibility, I decide it's penance for Margot's act. In order to enjoy it, we have to deserve it. She's an unbelievable artist, and it kills me that half the people in the room won't understand that they're going to experience pure creative excellence. The things she doesn't show, how she hides her hand—that's where the magic sits.

And then the lights dim, and up comes the spotlight.

The show begins.

MARGOT THE MAGNIFICENT

Appearance

The Magician extends her gloved hand. It might seem like she's extending it to her assistant, that begowned siren waiting just offstage, hidden in the wings, but the hand is beckoning the audience. *Come*, it says, finger crooked; *I want to show you something.* That's how the magic begins. Not with an invitation, but with the assertion of control. For the duration of the Magician's act, all expectations will be defied. Her law has become Word, and you must listen. The Magician will have your complete trust or she will have none of you. The crooked finger, the extended hand. *Come*, she says. And you obey.

That is her first trick: the Appearance. It is the opposite of Vanishing, that final desertion that leaves the audience gaping, searching out shapes in the dark. Unlike its counterpart, the Appearance is a blossoming. It is a crack in the doorway, an illumination meant to stun the viewer into complacency. Here is the coin, the card, the sudden bright bird, an explosion of feathers. It is a manifestation. Where once there was nothing, now there is *something*. Materialization, immediate, as if the Magician were God.

And you feel like she's God when she stares at you from the lonely aisle of library stacks. Scarlet cravat bloodying her throat. That same finger curled upward, drawing you away from the light. Luring you toward her next act.

Levitation

Because the Magician can conjure material objects at whim, it's no surprise that she can move them seemingly at will. The next part requires some help, so our radiant assistant steps forward. White blonde hair, gown of silver sequins. Beside her, the Magician is a dark specter, muted next to all that brilliance. Perhaps that is the point, to hide in plain sight. The assistant hands out items from a bag: tufted velvet cushion, ruby-studded apple, a floppy-eared rabbit. The Magician compels them all. Miraculously, they float.

Levitation is a natural second act because you want to believe that the Magician can lift you up too. And sometimes she does. There, in the audience, is an elderly woman with a chihuahua shaking like mad in her handbag. The Magician crooks her finger, and at first the woman demurs, but even the audience can tell that it's a false protest; the reality is that she's thrilled to have been chosen. Everyone wants the Magician's stare to land on the moon of their upturned face. Settled into a small wooden chair, handbag tucked neatly into her lap, the Magician commands the woman to *rise!* And yes, she leaves the ground. Not with a bang, but rather with a slow and steady momentum that feels as natural as the gravity she's defied. The woman's mouth becomes a black *Oh* of shock; the Magician lifts the bag too, until the chihuahua is barking several feet above the hovering chair. When finally restored to earth, the woman stands there for a moment, clutching her dog, wobbling on her heels. Once you realize that the rules aren't rigid, but infinitely bendable, it's easy to feel both exhilarated and terrified.

Away from the lights, in a secluded corner of the stacks, your stomach flips all on its own. The zipper at the back of your silk does not need to be compelled; you want it down, and the sound it makes is like fabric ripping. The Magician slides her hands underneath your hips. You're her assistant in this matter as you both work at flight, perched on the shelf, books pressing into your spine. The books fall, one by one, thudding dully on the thin library carpet.

Mentalism

The Magician knows what you're thinking. She calls out favorite numbers, birthdays, the names of long-dead pets. She presses a gloved finger to her temple, closes her eyes to concentrate. The audience leans forward, suddenly frightened. If the Magician knows the answers to these simple questions, couldn't she also know the dark, private corners of your heart? That man by the bar, sipping from a full glass of red wine: Will she reveal that he's come to the gala with a woman who's not his wife? Does she know who has cheated on their taxes? Which person has abused, hurt, maimed? Who might someday kill?

But the Magician reveals none of that. Instead, she walks the crowd right to the very edge of danger. Here's how many dollar bills are stuffed in a man's scuffed leather wallet, obviously destined for the strip club; here's the number of cigarettes in a woman's purse—rueful chuckle, she'd told her girlfriend she'd quit—and here's how long a couple has been dating: *four years, seven months, six days*, chimes the Magician, but the real answer is hidden behind those numbers: he will never propose.

. . .

The only question that the Magician refuses to answer: How does she know?

She knows because she's the Magician; she's the Magician because she knows. That's what you think as she intuitively slides both hands below the curve of your ass, headed directly to the spot that makes your legs fall open. She knows the exact place to put her tongue, the divot behind your ear that wants attention. The Magician knows that if she sweeps her thumb just along the edges of your nipples, without actually touching, you will likely come. She reads your mind without having to ask.

Penetration

To penetrate solid matter means that you must enter it correctly. Any type of object can be breached: silver hoops clang before suddenly marrying, a slim dart with a green feathered tail pierces the heart of a wooden board. The Magician can force a fountain pen through the eye of a silver dollar. She holds it up to the light for inspection. Heads swivel, trying to catch the seam where the trick could be revealed. Certainly nothing solid can open like that and accept the pain of total violation, you think. Yet it happens easily.

The assistant glides offstage and returns with a long rolling cart; it's time to be sawed in half. She opens the lid of what might soon become her coffin, then wheels it slowly in a circle so the audience can peer at its lined interior. The Magician helps the assistant climb inside, then allows her a moment to arrange her glimmering dress. Does the Magician take the ball of her thumb and caress the assistant's cheek? Maybe it's simply a trick of the light. Down goes the lid. Three metal blades enter, guillotines in search of an aristocratic head. They swiftly penetrate the wood and possibly the soft flesh and dense bone directly beneath.

. . .

When the Magician slides her fingers inside you, you're all wonder. Because there is magic in the Penetration of a once solid object, but the real thrill comes from the display of the Penetration itself. The Magician bids you look down at the place where you've been joined, to see the reckoning of your merger. When she starts to thrust, you bite down on your own lip until you taste the hidden swell of blood.

Restoration

Once the Magician has presented the hewn woman to her captive audience, it is time to heal the gap. And it's undoubtedly swift and easy work to remove the trio of blades. Unbuckle the lock, open the lid. Our audience waits with bated breath. Will she be whole again? The Magician extends her hand. Out steps the assistant, good as new.

Restoration occurs throughout the act. Someone's dollar is taken, ripped into pieces, burned with a match, crumbled into ash, and then produced whole and crisp from the Magician's palm. It is the Jesus miracle: the dead thing brought back to vibrant life.

It's possible someone in the audience will remember this type of Restoration trick performed for them as a child. A primitive version of it, maybe; that time when someone "magically" removed a thumb. How it waggled about, still living though decapitated, held in the grasp of the other, unmaimed hand. Perhaps they remember the person behaving as though removal of the thumb was unbearably painful. Perhaps not. But they remember the Transformation most of all: the return to normalcy as the body resumed its clean and unbroken position. Thumb once more sitting easy in its socket.

. . .

After orgasm, the Magician slips free of you, and there is the wet, slack sound of your body returning to its original shape. There is an ache lodged inside you. The Magician herself is unrumpled, aside from her mouth, which must be as wet and swollen as your own. Here is your silk garment, crumpled on the floor between your feet. Now is the time to return to it, to seal yourself up inside its swaddling, good as new.

Transformation

As the audience recovers, the Magician chooses to overload their senses once again. This is done through the use of Transformation. A pale bird becomes a wild rabbit. Blue balloons pop and reveal they were orange all along. Mirrored table turns to clear glass with a clutch of roses stashed inside. Her hands, initially full of marbles, reveal a fine mist of feathers when she throws the contents of her palms at the crowd. Suddenly, the assistant's dress, once a shimmering silver, explodes into a slick of bloodred satin. She appears engulfed in flames.

And though you allow the Magician to help you dress, the clothes no longer feel right. You are aware that though everything should have been returned to its original state, your insides have somehow shifted into a completely new shape. Your heart, for instance, is no longer your own. It has become a bird in your chest, one that flaps and quivers just as violently as the white dove you saw the Magician set free onstage. You want to be taken back into the warm breast pocket of the Magician. You are ready to give yourself over.

Transposition

The assistant pulls forth a cabinet from a darkened corner of the stage. Its door stands open. The Magician shows off the interior to the audience with a wave of her hand—empty, all empty—before beckoning her assistant to climb inside. The Magician closes the door and spins the cabinet thrice.

Then she does something unusual: she leaves the stage.

Against the back wall sits a secondary platform that holds the cabinet's twin. As she stalks through the crowd, the audience is quick to notice how slight the Magician is up close. They smell the musk of her perfume; catch the way her lipstick has dragged down into one corner of her mouth, bloodying it there as if she's been struck. The Magician waves to the crowd and then climbs inside the second cabinet and closes the door.

Moments later, both women emerge. But the assistant is now waving at the crowd from the back of the room. And from the main stage emerges the Magician. The Transposition is complete.

. . .

It's unfair that she stays so unrumpled, a perfect God, while you're left quivering beneath your antique silk. You want to change places with the Magician, you think, so you grab her by the satin lapels. And though she leans into the kiss, and you can feel her relax beneath your hands, it will be only for a moment. It's an illusion, that softening; you understand by the sudden rigidity of her spine. She will not change places with you, not for the world, because the Magician never reveals her hand.

Vanishing

And here is where the Magician leaves us. Under the direct glare of the spotlight, she turns on her heel, the satin of her cape flaring outward and swishing around her legs. She climbs back inside the cabinet. But this time, when the door flies open, no one is there.

Possibly there never was.

KNOCK-KNOCK JOKE
(PART I)

I'm belting out a fairly solid rendition of "Home on the Range." Many people don't know that the 1910 version has what amounts to six entire verses, not including the original chorus.

And yes, Bunko knows them all by heart.

Tiny rhinestone cowboy hat dipped low over my brow, I swagger as I croon, hitching up my blue-and-orange-striped pants (though I don't need to because the shiny gold suspenders haul them up quite nicely all on their own). People get a real kick out of the way my padded behind bounces up and down as I walk. There's a life-size cutout of a horse set on the corner stage. The thing's enormous; it's the epitome of a true bucking bronco, complete with rearing front legs and a windswept mane. Bunko's terrified of it. Every time I reach the end of a verse, I make eye contact with the fake horse, and my voice cracks. I shiver and shake in my oversize clown shoes. I hide my painted face behind the safety of my gloved hands.

You'd think the audience would tire of the whole phobia bit, but I could sing the song through twelve more times if I wanted. Every time I guide myself too close to the horse, Bunko screams in terror, and everyone laughs like their guts are about to bust.

The kids closest to the front are nearly trampling one another in their glee. They love to point out the thing that makes me afraid. "Horse," they scream, pointing toward it with their sticky little fingers. "Watch out for the *horse*, Bunko!" Sometimes the parents will do it too. They forget it's all pretend. On the stage, it's life or death for Bunko. People can't help themselves. They love it when someone else is scared.

But it's been fifteen minutes already, and I've gone over time. The woman in charge taps her watch, circles her finger in the air—the universal sign to wrap it the hell up.

Alas, all good things must come to an end.

By the time I've reached the last verse, my voice is shot. Arms spread wide, I shout the final line of the song, then "accidentally" slap my hand onto the horse's cardboard saddle. Bunko turns, sees what he's done, and shrieks in dismay. My eyes roll back in my head. I fall in a dead swoon, crumpled onto the stage in a heap.

The crowd goes wild.

I hide my grin as I lie motionless; I'm supposed to be knocked out cold. Nothing hits harder than knocking a child's funny bone. Their comedy dial is turned all the way up to eleven, so jokes aren't just amusing, they're *hysterical*. It's never a chuckle; it's a full-on belly laugh. When you're *really* funny, kids will let you know. They're your biggest fans. They're rooting for you.

Which is good news for me, because Central Florida Kidfest has booked me for the entire afternoon. It's a spring carnival funded by the city that hosts a plethora of "family-friendly entertainment." It's good work, even if it doesn't pay well, because it's high visibility and it makes up (a little) for the fact that I blew off the audition for the much better gig that performs statewide. I can get other work off this, no problem.

I might even get another audition invite. I'm not the only clown here; there are performers spread out across the wide prairie of the open park, and I've already seen one guy I know. Marshall Jackson, stage name Gloomy Greg, is posted up near a guy selling empanadas from a cart. His artistry and craft are next level. Gloomy Greg's set is exactly what it sounds like: he's always morose and serious, a clown for whom nothing ever goes right. Marshall's been on the local event circuit for over ten years and has never been stingy when it comes to sharing gigs. It's always nice to talk shop with someone else who's got just as much skin in the game. He has set me up for multiple gigs and has talked me up with his own agent, who is better than mine and doesn't "forget" to call me back.

"Fifteen-minute break." A woman holding a clipboard thrusts a bottle of water at me. "Then you're over at face painting."

"Thanks."

"Don't be late. You'll be penalized."

She says the first part of "penalized" like how a person might pronounce "penal colony."

"Yes, sir!" I say, chopping out a hasty salute. "Right away, sir!"

"It's ma'am." She looks me over. "God, I hate clowns."

I decide she might make good material. Some kind of military clown. Structured body language, medals and regalia, possibly an exaggerated march. People who think they're in control are always the funniest.

I pull my phone from my pants pocket and check my messages. I, too, am apparently the funny kind of control freak, because I think that by looking at my texts, one from Margot might magically appear. There's nothing, of course.

Music floats toward me from the opposite side of the park, near the fountain, so I head in that direction. Darcy doesn't normally agree to gigs outside of RHINOPLASTIZE, but her old drumming instructor talked her into this one. They bring out different kits and set up stations for hands-on activities as a way to make art seem more accessible for kids. Darcy is a sucker for that kind of stuff, and so am I.

The first time I realized I wanted to be a clown was at a school carnival when a woman named Linda Lovely in a bright green wig taught me how to make a dog out of balloons. She spent fifteen minutes helping me get it exactly right, smiling face full of slick greasepaint as she guided my fumbling fingers through the motions. Her trust made me feel capable and worthy. All kids need that reassurance; without it, our passions wither and die.

In the past, when my mother has asked me why I do it, I've tried my best to come up with an answer that might make sense to her. There's something about clowning that makes it nearly undefinable for those who live outside its chokehold. People ask: Why do you want to do it? How do you expect to make a living? What exactly are you looking to get out of this experience?

My answers to these questions change on a daily basis. I know that I want to make people laugh. I know that a lot of why I chose this passion project for myself is because I miss my brother so horribly, and I think that I'm trying to re-create myself in his image. Even if he didn't quite get the clowning stuff, I know he would get a real kick out of how much my mother hates it. I want to perform in a way that feels meaningful, and right now, listening to those kids screaming with joy, I feel like I'm headed in the right direction. But I'm not trying to monetize my craft; it reeks of capitalism, and that takes all the laughter out of it. Mostly, I just want to feel good in my own body. Clowning allows for that. Not always, but sometimes.

I pass a tent with puppets for sale, painted wooden ones shaped like zoo animals with dangling, hinged parts. A slew of middle-aged women have gathered around the table, sharing white Styrofoam cups of steaming coffee. One of them surreptitiously pulls a silver flask from the hip of her peasant skirt and pours a healthy amount into her cup. She sees me watching and pockets the flask again before putting a finger to her lips. I mime locking my own and then toss the imaginary key over my shoulder. More power to them, I think. Every day should be a party.

It's hot enough to override my deodorant; the smell wafting from my pits is a mix of hot polyester and body funk. Mosquitoes halo my head. Sweat leaks down my rib cage and wets the elastic waistband of my pants. Rides are set up helter-skelter: kiddie stuff composed of chair swings, a merry-go-round, a smaller version of the whip, and even a miniature roller coaster that's painted to resemble a fire-breathing dragon. There are worse ways to spend an afternoon, I think to myself, slipping through the center of the park. Food tents have been erected, and grease permeates the air, saturating the breeze with the savory smell of onions and peppers and the spicy heat of grilled sausages. People clutch plates of sugar-dusted funnel cakes and kebabs of smoky meat, passing red-and-white-striped bags of kettle corn. The scent is so overpowering that if I opened my mouth, I feel like I could taste it in the air. I do exactly that, walking with my jaws opened wide, like a baleen whale seeking out clouds of krill.

Darcy is lounging outside the music tent, hoovering up a fully loaded hot dog. Relish and mustard squirt from the side and slide down her palm. A glob of it plops onto the ground between her spread legs, narrowly missing the top of her left boot.

"Bite?" she offers, as she holds out the soggy end and shakes it in my direction.

"Absolutely not."

"Your loss." She stuffs the rest in her mouth, and her cheeks bulge. I worry that she might choke to death. Even though I've read the poster in the break room what feels like a million times, I still don't know the Heimlich maneuver.

"Hey, Bill." I wave at an older guy with a thinning, gray ponytail who's showing a boy how to use the tall conga drums. He slaps out a quick pattern: *bang-bang-bang!* Repeats it, then lets the kid try.

He walks over to us and leaves the kid to mess around alone on the drums. "Bunko. How's it hanging?"

"Low and a little to the left."

Bill rolls his eyes. "God. Get some new material."

"Oh, you want something new?" I sketch a quick two-step and spin around, arms outstretched, fingers wiggling. "Knock-knock."

"Who's there?"

"Tank."

"Tank who?"

"Oh Bill," I say, fluttering my nonexistent eyelashes, gloved hands pressed girlishly beneath my chin. "You're welcome."

Bill sighs deeply. The kid, however, is grinning ear to ear. He's going to run off after this drum lesson and tell that joke to everyone he knows. Knock-knock jokes spread like infectious diseases. You can catch them by hearing them from three feet away.

That's it, I think, watching the boy's face. That's what it means to clown, in one gleeful expression.

"I'm going to take a walk," Darcy announces, and I follow her back into the crowd.

While we wander, I check the messages on my phone again. Still none from Margot, but I can also see that she hasn't read the last two I sent her. Those were sent after we fucked in the library, which was four days ago. In the first message, I told her I'd had a nice time. In the second message, I apologized for describing our sexual interlude as "a nice time" and then asked when I could see her again. No response to that, obviously. I wonder if she's finally turned off her read receipts, and then I wonder if she turned them off specifically because she doesn't want me to know that she's seen them. The thought makes an interesting mixture of excitement and embarrassment mingle in my belly, like I've introduced a wedge of lemon to a warm glass of milk.

If my plan had been to somehow get Margot to help me network, then it's probably true that we shouldn't have fucked before talking about it first. Classic Cherry, I think. Mentorship issues aside, the library sex was incredible.

A performers-only pavilion has been erected behind a long, colorful row of gaming tents. They've set out folding tables that hold trays of turkey and ham sandwiches and bowls of plain, unsalted chips that everyone has already dug their filthy hands inside. Darcy and I head in together, narrowly avoiding a mother who's waving me down for a picture. She's clutching the hand of her pigtailed daughter; a girl of about four years old who does not look thrilled to see me. I can tell a screamer when I see one, and I know for a fact that if I even look at this kid the wrong way, she will shout bloody murder.

We duck into the pavilion and into sudden, blessed coolness. I'm sweating under my wig. I grab a stack of napkins from the folding table that holds the plates of sandwiches and blot at my neck and forehead, trying not to smear my makeup.

Darcy hasn't said three words to me since we left the drumming tent. We're standing together, yet I feel like she's actively avoiding me. She's looking at the free food like it's about to offer up some real words of wisdom.

"How much are you getting paid for this?"

She laughs. "You think I'm getting *paid*?"

"I guess not." I'm getting two hundred bucks for the event, which isn't much, but I'm banking on pulling a few other private gigs from networking at the festival. Already a couple different moms have taken down my information; I'm hoping to snag at least three more before the afternoon is through. Time is quickly slipping through my gloved fingers. Right now, I am twenty-eight, but soon I'll be thirty-one, and then I'll be forty-eight, and after that fifty-six, and on and on, and maybe things will always be this way, until finally, I'll be seventy-nine and die alone in bed and never have made it onto a comedy tour or even a carnival circuit. Any one of these gigs I snag could be the golden ticket. I can't afford to let opportunities pass me by.

"I'm just doing it for Bill," Darcy says. "He's retiring this year."

"How do you retire from drumming?" I ask. "Can't he just keep doing it forever, or at least until his arms stop working or he gets arthritis?"

"No, you dumbass. He's going to sell the shop."

"Wait, what?" That shop has been around forever. Before Bill ran it, it had belonged to his father, and before that, his grandfather had opened the place. It's been a fixture of Central Florida since before either Darcy or I were born, one of the few original family-owned businesses that somehow managed to flourish while everything else was steadily pushed out by corporations with more money and not a single lick of originality.

"It sucks." Darcy grabs a turkey sandwich from a nearby table and takes a big bite. A fly loosens itself from the deli slice and floats toward her face, bloated on sun-warmed mayonnaise. She bats it away with a lazy hand. "Jesus, this shit is stale. I'm about to lose a tooth on this hard-ass bread." She spits the mouthful into a black garbage can and chucks the plate with most of the sandwich in after it.

I imagine that Bill's business, a big corner shop near downtown, will probably be taken over by a big-box chain that will demolish the original structure and replace it with something that looks like every other new build on the block. It's a sobering thought, and I can tell by the sour look on Darcy's face that she's already considered it. Orlando is like any other place that's being slowly but steadily gentrified; we're swallowed by the sinkhole before we're even awake enough to know that the house is halfway underground.

I can't believe she hasn't told me about this before now. My feelings are actually hurt.

"What if you bought it from him?" I say, talking over the lump in my throat. "I bet Bill would cut you a deal. He loves you."

She looks at me like I've grown a second clown head next to my first one. "Am I going to buy it with my Aquarium Select III part-time salary?"

"Maybe your mom could loan you some money."

"Grow up, Cherry. It's not happening."

I have a strong urge to hug her, but that's not something we do. My arms stay pinned to my sides. Sometimes there's just nothing a person can say to make a situation better. It's just going to suck, and that's it. Haven't we moved through Florida this way all of our lives? Mourning something only as long as it takes to mourn the next loss. We each take a bottle from the water table. I pour mine carefully into my mouth as Darcy chugs half of hers in one go.

"One bottle each." It's the lady with the clipboard from earlier. "One bottle *per person*." She has a pinched mouth that makes her look like she bit down on an aspirin.

"Sure thing," Darcy says before snatching up three more bottles. We leave the pavilion as the woman stands there sputtering. I laugh, delighted, and make a mental note to add that aspirin face to my military clown act.

"I've got to get back to work."

"I'll meet up with you later." I thumb in the direction of the crowded parking lot. "Over there?"

She grunts and stalks off through the crowd. I figure it's as much of a response as I'm going to get.

I've got dinner with my mom tonight, likely a supper of so-so vegetarian casserole and a bowl of salad fresh from the prepackaged section of Publix, plus a side of meet-and-greet with the lucky woman my mom is now sleeping with. I'll need to get my ass home beforehand so I can scrub all the evidence of clowning from my face.

It's not my fault that my mother hates clowning, but I guess it's not her fault that she wound up with a kid who's obsessed with it either. It's simply one of those mysteries of the universe.

I try to imagine having a child like myself and can't picture it without wincing. I was a colicky, sick baby and from there grew into a bratty kid, one who was picky and snotty (literally and figuratively) and cried a lot. My mom had no qualms about voicing what a pain in the ass I was over the years. It's not her fault that the kid she loved more died. Even as a young child, he was funny and charming and easy. There were pranks, sure, but he also cleaned his room and always remembered Mother's Day. My mom and I are both gay, which should have made things easier, but my mother has always preferred the company of men. She's one of those dykes who says that women are hard because they have too many "feelings." Dwight, lunkhead that he was, never voiced his emotions aloud. I screamed mine from the rooftops. I'd have picked Dwight over me too. I'm sure my brother is laughing about that, wherever he is. Still the favorite after all these years.

At the face painting tent, I apply a variety of colors to an assortment of dimpled faces. Kid skin is super elastic and poreless, and that makes the job a lot easier than swabbing it on my own skin, which has lost some of its youthful tightness and now drags beneath my tools like I'm trying to stretch leather. One boy becomes a tiger, complete with whiskers; a girl who loves ponies shifts into a purple unicorn, shiny golden horn affixed to her forehead with rubber cement. I morph kids into colorful squawking parrots, silvery robots, neon-hued kitty cats with blushing red cheeks, black-and-white pandas, and even a flamingo with feathery pink accessories, especially fitting for a steamy Florida afternoon.

Toward the end of my shift, a woman escorts her daughter to the metal chair and sets her down in front of me. "She'll be a fairy princess." She squeezes the girl's shoulder through the thin fabric of her T-shirt. "Go crazy with the glitter. Seriously. It'll drive her father nuts when he picks her up for visitation." She digs her phone out of her purse. "Hope it gets all over the interior of his new Mustang."

"Do you want to buy the matching wings?" I ask. "It's an extra ten dollars."

"Cici, sit still for the nice clown, okay?"

Her phone rings and she holds up a finger before I can take her payment, ducking out of the tent and leaving the two of us alone with each other. I look at the girl sitting in front of me, short legs dangling, knees pink with the memory of old scrapes. Dark circles raccoon her eyes and her mouth is set in a thin, unsmiling line. It's a festival for kids, which means it should be fun, but this little girl is obviously miserable.

I'm about to begin when she utters a startled cry. Something has landed on her arm.

"Just a ladybug." I set my fingers against the girl's bicep and let the ladybug walk from her bare pink skin onto my white glove. I hold the ladybug up for her inspection. It sits on the tip of my pointer finger, crawling in slow circles. "Did you know that if one lands on you, it's good luck?"

Cici shakes her head. The ghost of a smile winks out from behind her pursed lips.

"Well, it's your lucky day. Make a wish." We both blow on the ladybug like she's an especially tricky birthday candle. It finally has enough of us and takes off again, fluttering out into the hot glare of the afternoon.

"Now." I turn to face her again, getting my pots of paint and brushes sorted. "What do you *really* want?"

Straining around in her chair, she glances back at her mother, who's still on the phone, looking pissed. Probably talking to the dad, I think, noticing the way she keeps jabbing her finger in the air, as if she might actually stab the breeze.

"Tyrannosaurus rex," Cici whispers. "A really mean one."

I nod, impressed by her choice. "You got it."

I'm halfway through her paint job when the shouting starts. "Stay put, kiddo," I say, and leave her sitting half-done beneath the safety of the tent. Her mother is still on her phone, but she looks worried, staring at the people by the entrance gates.

"Something's happening," she says into her phone. "I have to call you back."

It's hard to tell exactly what's going on from so far away, but there's a lot of yelling, and that's never a good sign when there are kids around. I try to hurry, but it's hard in my clowning outfit, which is made for laughs and not for speed. Frustrated and hot, I kick off my oversize shoes and carry them, speedwalking across the field wearing only my socks and praying I don't step on any loose glass shards.

People are blocking the entrance with their bodies, performers and parents and a handful of service workers from the food tents, arms linked. Men in black tactical gear have gathered outside the gate to the festival. Their hats are pulled low over the foreheads, and bandannas obscure their faces.

I know who they are.

I've seen them at Pride events, their numbers growing steadily in Central Florida year after year. They huddle outside abortion clinics with the evangelical church groups, squawking angrily at anything that moves. One of the men is holding up a white poster board with GROOMERS written on it in bold black ink. The word is surrounded by a vivid red circle with a slash through the middle.

"Keep those pedos away from our kids," he yells. "Send those freaks home!"

Drag Story Hour has started at the back corner of the park. It's hosted by one of the local queens; they have a weekly showcase at the neighborhood gay bar. There aren't a lot of gay bars still standing in Orlando, and the community remembers the violence that ended one of them forever. This particular queen volunteered to read to the kids before the big music act at the end of the festival. Drag Story Hour is always well attended, and the event today is possibly the biggest crowd yet. More than fifty kids are stationed on that corner of the field.

The shouting escalates. Men holding signs are pushing through the blockade of people at the gate. I spot Darcy's hair; she's at the very front, toe to toe with a guy who's at least two feet taller than her. I press into the mass of bodies, but I can't get through the crush. Some of my greasepaint rubs off on the shoulder of a woman next to me. I remember I'm still dressed as Bunko; this is a children's event, for God's sake. The men with their tactical gear look like they could be carrying assault rifles, though it's tough to tell what's under all the padding.

The guy with the GROOMERS sign starts a loud chant that includes the words "pedophile" and "kill." Everything is loud. My chest hurts from the pressure of someone's elbow colliding with my ribs.

"There's kids here, man!" Marshall is still in his clown costume, wig knocked askew. It falls off his head when a man reaches over the chain-link fence and pushes him, hard. He stumbles backward into a line of interlocked arms and nearly vanishes beneath the mass of tangled legs before someone yanks him up again by the neck of his spotted shirt.

A woman in the front, a mother I recognize from earlier in the afternoon—I'd painted her child's face with rainbow zebra stripes; they'd both been delighted—screams hoarsely as one of the tactical-geared men grabs her arm; she wrestles with him as he tries to yank her out of the way. Everyone pushes relentlessly forward. Marshall cries out. There's thudding, flesh on flesh. He goes down. When he claws his way up again, his clown paint is smeared and blood is gushing down his chin. The police, who've been down the street "watching traffic" throughout this altercation, finally arrive on the scene once Cici's mother leaps the fence and screams for them to get off their asses and do something.

Things gradually cool off. The police escort the tactical-geared men and their signage to a long stretch of weeded grass directly across the four-lane highway. Some parents and performers stay by the entrance gate to keep watch. The crowd has managed to block most of the unpleasantness from the children's view. Drag Story Hour continues for the kids gathered in the sunlit patch of grass next to a towering group of oaks, trees that have been on this land for more than two hundred years. They'll listen to the story and enjoy being kids. Afterward, they'll move to the bandshell and dance joyfully to the music, moving their bodies wildly, because they are young and full of life and feeling that freedom. And after that's done, they'll head home with their families, none the wiser about what happened one hundred feet away from their play. But there is always the next time, I think, or the time after that. All it takes is time for things to finally wind up spoiled or broken.

It's like whiplash. That's the only way to describe it. Over and over again, violence, and then we're expected to immediately return to normalcy. But I'm not sure we know what "normalcy" is anymore. Is it normal to be a queer person living in a place with a government that actively tries to harm you? Is it normal to know that you might attend a gay club and be gunned down in the middle of the night? But if you don't return to "normal," what kind of life are you living? If there's no joy, then what's the point?

And though it makes me hate people, it also makes me cling to the small bits of humor that I can glean from any situation. Because if I can't find something to laugh at, how the hell am I going to make it through anything?

People have wandered off, drama over. Marshall sits beside the chain-link fence, head slung between his bent knees. There's dead grass caught in his dark, curly hair. His clown wig, a bald cap with lank blue hair dangling from either side, is filthy and matted from being stomped under people's feet. He clutches it in his hands and doesn't look at me. Just keeps breathing heavy, face trained at the ground between his spread legs. He spits a mix of snot and blood.

"I think you're supposed to tilt your head back," I say, not actually sure if that will help. I'm remembering someone with a nosebleed on TV.

He looks up at me, and I see hurt in his eyes.

Marshall shakes his head. "I'm done."

"You don't mean that."

"Yes, I sure as hell do!" He's dabbing the blood and spit from his chin with his fingertips. Finally, he whips off his oversize shirt and uses it to mop his face, smearing all the greasepaint. It all mixes together in a confused swirl of color. It's hard to tell what's blood and what's clown.

"But you're great!" He needs to stop rubbing off his makeup. Clowns aren't supposed to transition in public; it's one of our rules, a code of ethics that requires us to maintain the illusion of our personas. We disrobe only in private. Much like superheroes in comic books and movies, our identities must remain secret.

Marshall squeezes the balled-up shirt until his knuckles bulge. "Nobody cares how hard I've tried."

"I care."

He throws down the shirt and swipes some dirt from his bare chest. "My sister lives up in Jersey. Her husband had a heart attack last fall and can't work too many hours anymore. She asked me to move up there to help out. I'm going to do it."

"Come on." I laugh. He must be joking.

"I'm going, Cherry."

A family of four walks past, headed toward the parking lot. They're smiling and laughing. The little girl has got a wad of cotton candy in her mouth, and her mother is trying to clear the blue stickiness from her cheeks and chin with a wet wipe.

"Don't give up. You're going to make it." I don't say what I'm thinking, which is really more like, *If you quit and you're a better clown than me, how will I ever make it? What was any of this for?* My gloves are fully gray with dirt. The knees of my pants are in tatters. I'll have to leave the festival early and take a pay cut, and already the money was barely worth my time.

Marshall laughs, and that's when I know that he's really done, because all the light has gone out of it. "I'm forty-two years old. I can't do this anymore." He gets up and dusts off the seat of his wide blue-and-red-striped pants. Dirt flies in the middling afternoon breeze. "And man, come on. I'm not even *from* here. I can't keep pretending I want to stay in hell when this place has got me beat down to a pulp." He holds up his fingers, fingernails still stained with his own blood. "Florida can keep it. I'm out."

I want to tell him that all he needs is a little more patience, that he should give it another try, but the swell of words sits lodged in the back of my throat. The truth is simple and sharp: not everyone makes it. Art is hard, sure, but so is home. Florida's not always nice. And sometimes the mean can be too corrosive, acid eating out the bottom of your heart until the whole thing drops free of your body, leaving you cold and empty inside.

Who am I to tell anyone else what's best? I can't even get my own mother to engage with my work. And Marshall has had years more rejections than me; who's to say I won't be saying the exact same thing in another ten years?

"Here." He empties his pockets and hands everything to me. Most of it is stuff I don't need, but there's his wilting rose too, which is the staple of his act. Gloomy Greg longs for romance; it's his whole shtick. But every time he tries to hand this wilting flower to a beautiful woman, it collapses in on itself. It sits in my lap like that now, broken and miserable. I remember the first time I saw him incorporate it into the act. The gleam had been in his eyes then, that light that good art can conjure.

"Fuck y'all!" He gives the tactical-geared men across the street both middle fingers, and then he stalks off into the crowd of happy, oblivious people.

After he leaves, I stand there processing the fact that I've just permanently lost a friend and that the world at large has lost something very special. Then I stuff the rose in my own pocket and get up to find Darcy.

The vibe bums me out as I walk through the tents. It's like nothing happened. The cheery music piped through the overhead speakers is shrill, grating. All the laughter feels forced. To my wounded ears, it sounds more like screaming.

Darcy's back at the music tent, giving drum lessons to a bespectacled girl with braids. "Hit it," Darcy says, using her own drumstick to wallop the snare that's in front of them. "Smack it hard."

The girl looks up at Darcy, blinking owlishly behind her glasses, and taps the drum gently. One staccato rap.

"Oh, come on. I know you can hit harder than that!" Darcy kneels down, jeans digging divots in the dirt. "Think about a time you were really mad. Okay? Maybe your mom wasn't being fair, or a kid was being a jerk to you at school. Maybe someone told you no to something you really, really wanted. *Feel* that angry feeling, okay? Channel it. And then I want you to take all that anger, send it shooting down your arm, and whack it right into that drum."

The girl looks back down at the drum, eyes narrowed to slits. Her arm swings high over her head, and then she brings the drumstick down, hard. The wild smack produces a terrific bang, sound bouncing off the plastic walls of the tent. She hits the snare again and again, gritting her teeth through the whacking motions.

Darcy cheers her on. "That's it! Just like that!"

That small flash of promise when she connected to the drum, that gleam brightening her eyes—it's a new world full of incredible possibility. I can't interrupt it with my personal hurt and my worries of grand-scale failure.

None of it is funny.

The times when I have to take off the clown feel too hard to bear sometimes. I want to sit inside my greasepaint and hold out the flower, to make anything bright for even a moment. I can't stand how hard the world is, how much like the blade of a knife home can feel when wielded by people without empathy or care.

Instead of waiting, I slink off quietly. I pass people without seeing them, the smells of the fried food turning my stomach. Near the car lot, I see the mom from earlier who'd been drinking from the flask. She's with a few of the other mothers, and they're talking loud enough for me to hear them.

"I wish they'd let those men in," she says. "Might have done some good. Family day used to be respectable."

I drive home and walk inside my apartment, marveling at the mustiness of the place; the thick scent of mildew never leaves the floors or walls or the furniture, even with all the windows open and three different air fresheners plugged in. Florida is smothering me. The thing I love doesn't love me back. In the bathroom, I strip off my clown gear and leave it piled in a dead clump on the floor. I scrub at myself in the shower like I might peel off my own skin. I don't want there to be anything left of the clown when I see my mother, don't want her to find a trace of greasepaint along my hairline, or a slick of white pressed in the divot beside my nose. I don't think I could stand it if she even looked at me wrong tonight; I worry that I'd have a reaction like Marshall and leave my art behind forever.

Here's a joke: I have a queer parent and know I can't talk to her about what I experienced today. A real laugh riot.

By the time I emerge from the steam, my skin glows red from too much exfoliation, and my body feels like a heated-through sack of meat. For comfort, I slip on an old T-shirt and a wrinkled pair of jeans that just barely hangs on to my hips. I've lost weight again; I haven't been eating because I'm so focused on clowning, trying to make something happen with my art, transcendence always just out of reach. And if I'm being honest, it's not just about the work anymore. There's also the woman who's been on my mind: the one who won't respond to my messages, the one who fucked me in a library and then left me alone.

If she could make real magic, I think, then maybe she could successfully vanish herself from my brain.

Fifteen minutes later, I'm standing on my mother's front porch. It's the house from my childhood, which has stayed picture-perfect after all these years: pale blue paint, the same terra-cotta pots set neatly in their standing copper wire baskets, flower petals still glistening from their afternoon spritz with the garden hose. My mother loves petunias and bathes them daily, without fail, almost robotic in her routine. I've never been able to keep a plant alive; I can't help but think it's all Nancy's fault. If I didn't associate flowers with my mother, maybe I'd do a better job of raising them.

"Knock-knock," I say, starting the joke for no one but myself, and then I rap my fist hard against the door.

A tall blonde woman answers, wearing a baby-pink Juicy Couture tracksuit and rhinestone-studded flip-flops. Portia, woman of a thousand sparkling evening gowns. She smiles at me with a mouth full of perfectly white teeth.

The better to bite me with, I think.

"You must be Cheryl," she says. "You're late."

GUESS WHO'S COMING TO DINNER (PART I)

B efore we go any further, I need to reiterate that not all clowns are interchangeable.

For instance, I wouldn't call myself a circus clown, though my makeup and clothes are essentially modeled after their traditional, capering style. Consider the folks from Barnum & Bailey, those jewel-toned pioneers of the craft, prominently featured in all the circus marketing and ad work. You can't think of the circus without thinking of the clown; they're inextricably linked. But much like Diet Coke isn't regular Coke, these circus clowns and their artistic choices differ from mine in a few distinctive ways.

First of all, circus clowns don't tell jokes. At least, not in the traditional sense. The theater of their work is the circus tent itself, the veritable big top. Not only is it too large a venue to allow for voicework, the tent means that the clown must gambol and cavort beside a bevy of other attractions and not take the focus too far away from the ringmaster. They're supporting actors, not the main event. Lions, tigers, and bears, oh my! Circus clowns slip through the gaps of these entertainments, drawing your eye from one amazement to the next. They serve as guides.

That leads me to another difference between us: they work as a unit. When I say "circus clown," what does your brain immediately conjure? It's not a single face, it's a full-on horde: multicolored bodies spilling from a minuscule car or tumbling from a "burning building," like in the movie *Dumbo*. Individually, they don't do much other than cartwheel and tumble, but together they mime out fantastic scenarios that allow us to consider the humor that comes from surviving dangerous situations. Isn't that what the circus is all about? Defying death and living to tell the tale?

Clown work has been around since the very first chucklehead decided to paint a joke on a cave wall. There's what feels like a million types of clowns: Whiteface and the Auguste, the Tragic and the Harlequin. Tramp and Jester and Character (consider Bunko and his debilitating horse phobia, all wrapped up in the role of cowboy hopeful). It's been said that the original clowns weren't simply providing entertainment, they also served spiritual roles, doing double duty as priests or shamans. It makes sense when you think about it. Who better to understand the human condition than a person whose whole job is to uplift and delight the spirit?

Laughter is the best medicine. And even if it's not, it sure goes down a hell of a lot easier than Robitussin. Which makes what I'm about to say next a particularly bitter pill to swallow: I can't clown my way out of this situation. I'm having dinner with my mother and her new girlfriend, and the new girlfriend is the ex-wife of the magician who recently fucked me in a library and now refuses to call me back. In theory, this should be hilarious. But no one who would find this funny is present, and that means I've got to keep all my little jokes to myself.

Sometimes clowning can be lonely.

"Cheryl, could you make yourself useful and set the table?"

"It's Cherry," I respond automatically. This exchange will happen for the rest of our lives. My mother will call me by my given name, and I will correct her; she will ignore my correction, and we'll move on. That's our bit together, forever: Nancy Hendricks, the straight man to my fool.

Portia sits on the leather sofa, leafing through a copy of *Reader's Digest* that's been living on my mother's coffee table for the better part of the last decade. She's holding a big glass of white wine studded with ice cubes. She sips it with her pinkie out, as if she's quaffing tea with the Queen and not drinking from a liter bottle that I know my mother must have bought on sale at Publix. One of her rhinestoned flip-flops dangles as she alternately sips from the sweaty glass and flips the pages of the ancient magazine. I keep watching, waiting for the sandal to drop from her pedicured foot, but every few seconds she clenches her toes and the flip-flop slips back into place.

This doesn't seem like a good topic of conversation, that dangling flip-flop, but my other choices are:

So, you're sleeping with my mother?

Or

So, I guess I slept with your ex-wife?

"I like your shoes," I say. "Very shiny."

Portia smiles politely and takes another sip, condensation from the sweaty glass plopping onto the leather sofa. "Thanks." She wiggles her toes. "I got them at TJ Maxx. Seven bucks. Can you believe?"

I cannot and tell her so.

She beams at me. "So wild."

She's different than I'd imagined. Kind of ditzy.

My mother pokes her head out of the kitchen. "Table setting. Now, please."

It's as though I'm twelve again and not nearing thirty. Our dynamic has never been what one might call congenial, but there's no point in arguing unless I want to make an already awkward dinner even more uncomfortable. Portia stays seated comfortably in the living room, as out of place as a Vegas showgirl at a Cracker Barrel restaurant. I wave her off, acting like she's offered to help, when in reality she's completely absorbed in a magazine so ancient that the person on the cover has been dead for the last ten years.

"Really, it's no trouble at all," I say. "I've got it."

As I pull out the guest plates from the cabinet (Target purchase from twelve years ago, set marked down from $49.99 to $12.99; my mother has told this same story at least fifty times), I decide that even if dinner won't be funny, it should at the very least be civil. There's no reason Portia should dislike me. Margot wouldn't have mentioned anything about our time together; who tells their ex-wife about a one-night stand they had with a woman half their age? But still, there's a bad feeling bubbling in my gut that I can't deny, something that makes me wonder if her dumb-blonde shtick is all just an act.

"Can I help you, Nance?" asks Portia from the other room. Voice high and darling, like Snow White calling to a group of forest animals who all love her unconditionally. "Need me to fix you a drink?"

"No thanks, sweetheart. You just sit and enjoy your wine."

Nance and Sweetheart! Almost as toxic as Sid and Nancy, I think, collecting the braided place mats and assorted silverware. Cabernet-colored cloth napkins and their accompanying hammered silver rings. Cut-glass candlestick holders that contain white tapers, never lit. The dining room has been set by me since I was old enough to be trusted with the knives. Three cushioned chairs at an antique mahogany table with an embroidered runner. One setting for my mother, one for me, and one for Dwight, positioned at the head of the table. The dining room windows overlook the backyard, its lawn manicured to the point of military precision. Privacy hedges ruthlessly trimmed so that they no longer resemble plants, more like a child's set of building blocks. There's not a birdbath or hummingbird feeder in sight. Just harshly clipped greenery, lifeless, free of lizards and squirrels. No self-respecting animal would dare choose to hang out there.

Out go the mats and the plates, then the napkins stuffed in their silver rings, spoon and fork and knife, water glasses to the left, fresh wineglasses to the right. Bread plates and the butter dish that belonged to my great-grandmother, shaped like a roosting hen. Dwight hated that dumb bird. He called it "The Cocksucker," which drove our mother crazy, not because of the swearing, but because she claimed it was "misgendering the chicken." That bit always made me laugh even though she didn't mean it as a joke. I can't think of a single meal that I've had in my mother's lonely house where I haven't mourned the loss of my brother's bulky, oversize presence. I can feel the hole of him in every room, sucking up all the air.

What must it have been like to be Dwight? I wonder all the time. He never had to try hard; people loved him, regardless. But there's another part of me, a long-buried bitter part, that reeks of jealousy and anger, that wonders if people thought he was so goddamn funny and charming simply because he was a boy. Boys get to pull pranks and make "jokes" that are really just insults, and everyone laughs because that's just how boys are, that's how they get to be.

My mother enters the dining room, glass casserole dish clutched between her oven-mittened hands. The mitts are shaped like alligators; one is female (pink bow tie and lipstick on her snout), and the other is male (mustache above the row of sharp pointed teeth, formal black bow tie). They were a Christmas gift from her previous partner, Patricia. I wonder for a moment if Portia knows about her, but then figure it doesn't matter much since that relationship has been over for years. The moratorium on jealousy of an ex probably runs out at the ten-year mark.

"You didn't set out the trivet," my mother says, sighing deeply. "The glass is too hot; it will ruin the wood."

I pick the trivet up from its spot on the sideboard. It's shaped like a star, and I hold it up to my chest like I'm declaring myself the sheriff of these parts. "I wasn't finished setting the table," I say in my best John Wayne voice.

"Well, can you? I'm not getting any younger."

I could argue that I'm not getting any younger either, that none of us are, but instead I'm transfixed by the sunbeam that has landed on my mother's head. She's dyed her hair. It's not anything bold; in fact, I'd say that she's stayed pretty true to her natural hue of dull cinnamon brown. Well, no, I guess it's a little different from her original color. This is more of a toffee, I think, or possibly hazelnut; my brain has fixated on baking terms in order to process the change. The strands of wiry gray that have been threaded there since I was in high school have somehow magically disappeared.

"Cheryl, please! My hands are burning!"

I throw the trivet down on the middle of the table, and she places the steaming casserole dish at a slight diagonal, same as always. Even with blisters probably forming on her fingers, my mother has to have everything perfectly in its place.

She whips off her oven mitts and pairs them together, the cartoon gators locking jaws as if they're about to perform the death roll. "What's wrong with you? Are you on something?"

There are a million jokes that I could make based on this comment alone, but I'm still stuck on toffee and hazelnut. "Did you *dye* your *hair*?"

She pats the short, shellacked shell of it self-consciously. "Yes. Portia took me to her stylist. It's an umber tone."

"*What*?"

She looks put out. I'm shocked to see the start of tears forming in her eyes. "Why do you always have to make me feel so self-conscious? I'm allowed to change too, you know. I'm not just a parent; I'm a human being. With *feelings*."

Now I know that a pod person has officially replaced my mother, because I cannot for the life of me remember a time when she wore lipstick, much less knew a single thing about hair tones. "I thought you told me that only women with low self-esteem dyed their hair after fifty?"

In true Nancy Hendricks fashion, she sniffs at this question. "I changed my mind."

"Really? After twenty years?"

She waves me away, as if I'm an annoying gnat she'd like to swat. The tears are gone. "Get the breadbasket. It's time to eat."

This is the most interesting my staid, routine-driven mother has been in years. I'm trapped in a web of jokes too intricate to untangle without losing my mind. My brother would have been delighted by all of it; he'd have placed dye inside her shampoo bottle, kelly green for Saint Patrick's Day, or something harsher, like bleach, just for the thrill of it. And even though she would have hated the prank, she'd forgive him because she loved him, but also because when Dwight thought something was funny, you couldn't help but laugh. Even if the joke was at your expense.

God, what I'd give to have that talent! But I know that it's more than that; I'm remembering him the way that I want to, not necessarily the way he was. Maybe he didn't feel funny all the time either. Maybe he got tired of having to make jokes. Dwight never gets to change now. That's part of being dead: you're the same person forever.

Portia and my mother are murmuring in the kitchen—quiet, cuddly tones, a sound like two lovers sharing a secret—and the seriousness of it sobers me up quick.

I parcel out five rolls from the breadbox (one roll for each person, plus two extras, because "you can never tell how many people will want a second piece of bread, but it won't be everyone"—my mother claims it's a statistical improbability). They walk back into the dining room together, laughing at some private joke. My mother looks younger when she laughs. She doesn't do it often, but when it's there, I see my brother stretched out in the grooves of her cheeks.

It's one of the greatest losses of my life that I can't manage to make her crack a grin.

Try harder, dummy.

Dwight in my head again. He's always showing up when I need him there the least.

Then stop thinking about me. Get your own life.

We gather around the table while the last of the afternoon's dying light bleeds across our arms and faces. Tonight, the sunset is all butter and caramel and mango sorbet, painting the walls like we're inside the witch's candy house from "Hansel and Gretel."

Still smiling, my mother sets down the wooden salad bowl, which is three parts romaine, two parts iceberg, shredded carrots, cucumber quarters, cherry tomato halves, and an unholy amount of cracked black pepper—ratios engrained in my memory since it's the only salad my mother makes. My mother sits in her usual chair with her back to the bay window, facing me. Portia pulls out Dwight's chair—although no one has ever sat in it but him, my mother claims.

How long have they been together? What else has changed in my absence?

We fill our plates. The silence isn't exactly comfortable, but at least we've got something to occupy our mouths so we don't have to acknowledge the fact that there's nothing to say. I have a hard time with awkward silences, par for the course when it comes to being a clown. If I were anywhere else but my mother's house, I would have cracked five jokes by now, most of them inappropriate. Clowning means I'm generally never at a loss for words, even if they're the wrong ones. It's not exactly her fault, but my mother sucks all the good humor right out of me.

I poke at the casserole with the tip of my fork. I can't tell from looking at it, but it's possible that whatever's in it isn't fully cooked. My mother isn't the greatest chef. There have been several instances when I've fallen ill after eating her food. The consistency of what's on my plate is akin to firm Jell-O. I scrape it to the side and focus on my salad.

"So, Cheryl. Your mom tells me you're into marine biology," Portia says.

She's got that same vacant look in her eyes from earlier. It's like the lights are on but no one's home. My mother's sawing away at her gelatinous casserole with a steak knife. The casserole wriggles like a jellyfish as she works at it, as if desperate to escape back to the sea.

"Actually, no," I reply, because there's no point in beating around the bush. We are what we are, and no amount of embellishment from my mother will change that. If she wants me to talk about my day job instead of my actual passion, I can work with that. "I work part-time at an aquarium store," I say.

Thousand-yard stare. "Which one?"

"Aquarium Select III."

"I don't know much about fish." She hums thoughtfully, pink lips closing around her fork. "And what is it you do there, exactly?"

I could say that I'm passing the time between fucking other people's mothers. I could say that it's a front for my real passion, which is inverts—a term I can thank John for, my dead brother's high school friend who bought his kid a dying hermit crab. I could offer up everything I know about clowning or tell a long and complicated story about how I need to be the one making all the art in my family since Dwight's no longer around to be the funniest guy in the room. But I say none of that, because for some inexplicable reason I am trying to be kind to my mother, who is wadding her napkin between her fingers in nervous anxiety.

"Just restocking," I say. "Service desk. Cashier. You know, basic grunt work."

"Oh." Portia laughs, tinkling silver bells. "I thought maybe you swam with dolphins or something. Like Shamu. You know, at Sea-World?" Portia sets her glass down, and my mother hurriedly refills it. It's a hefty pour, nearly to the brim—one you'd tip happily for at a restaurant.

Silence descends again and everyone continues eating. I poke at the casserole, which has firmed up a little as it's gotten to room temperature, but I'm still not totally sure what it might contain. "What recipe is this, Mom?"

"Thai curry with tofu." She forks a large bite of it into her mouth and chews, putting up a finger when I try to ask a follow-up question. "I got it from Martha."

Martha Stewart is a longtime favorite of my mother's. She's adamant that Martha Stewart is gay. I've told her repeatedly that this is not the case, that Martha has never come out as anything but a white lady, but there is no convincing my mother otherwise. She latched on to her from an early age and has decided that she must model Martha's entire lifestyle. I'm not sure why this is the case, since my mother has never been especially good at hosting parties, or decorating, and her cooking is like something from a botched science experiment gone horribly awry. It's one of the most unintentionally funny things about her. But I decide to focus on the part that matters in the moment. Because it could mean life or death for her only surviving child.

"It doesn't have peanuts, right?" I stab it again with the tine of my fork, leaning forward to sniff. "It smells like peanuts."

"Of course it's got peanuts in it." She keeps eating. Portia smiles sunnily. My mother pats her hand. "It's a Thai curry."

"Mom, I'm allergic to peanuts." She looks confused, so I hold up my fork. "One bite of this shit could kill me."

She frowns. "Don't say 'shit.'"

The fact that she's focused on my swearing and not on the fact that my throat could have closed up into a pinhole in under fifteen seconds flat has me flummoxed. "Why, out of all the meals in the entire world, would you serve the *one* thing I'm allergic to?"

My mother takes a sip from her water (served in a clear pint glass, crushed ice, squeeze of lemon; this is the drink she pairs with every meal), then has another large bite of the casserole that could have killed her me.

"Portia likes Thai food," she says, shrugging. "It's her favorite."

"Mom."

"And you don't have any allergies."

That is news to me, a person who has spent her whole life dealing with a very real peanut allergy. "*What* are you *talking* about?"

"You didn't have any allergies as a child." She rolls her eyes at me, good-natured ribbing. "Unless you decided to develop some as an adult, just for fun?"

My mother reaches across the table and takes Portia's hand. The two of them smile, stare dreamily into each other's eyes. It's like I'm not even in the room. I begin to wonder if they are planning my murder. It's possible that my mother could have taken out a life insurance policy on me at some point. There's got to be at least an easy two hundred thousand she could get out of my peanut-fueled death.

"Seriously, Mom?"

She's not paying attention.

"Mom!"

"Didn't I make you peanut butter and jelly sandwiches? For school?"

The question makes me laugh, and it's a honking, donkey bray of a sound, more akin to Bunko's hilarity than to Cherry's sense of humor.

Nancy Hendricks raised her children to be "self-sufficient," which, according to her, meant that we had to do everything on our own from the time we were able to tie our own shoes. She learned that from her own mother, a dour woman who worked long days at a school cafeteria and had very little time for laziness from her only child. I did my own laundry, I cleaned the bathroom, I took out the trash, I got myself home from school, and I made my own food. "You never packed any lunches. Maybe for Dwight, but never for me."

"Oh, not this again. You're always so sure that I loved your brother more, but that's not true. I never played favorites with my kids." My mother pushes the bowl of salad toward me. "Just eat this if you're so worried about your 'allergy.'" She says the word like it's in quotation marks, as if I'm making up some wild lie about peanuts just for attention. I'm almost thirty and she thinks I'm trying out some tricks that a middle school kid might attempt, as if I were meeting my new stepmom for the first time and throwing a tantrum over it.

"Do you want to go to the farmers market this weekend?" Portia asks, turning to face my mother. "We could try that new pickle place out. Kiki said they have horseradish!"

"Kiki really loves her horseradish."

I have no clue who Kiki is, so I decide I will help myself to more of the salad because I'm hungry and I don't have money to buy groceries right now. I wonder what Margot is up to, aside from ignoring my texts, and wish that I was back in that library getting fucked by her instead of here with my mother and her ex-wife, a beautiful dummy of a woman who is slathering so much butter on a piece of bread that it resembles cream cheese. A large glob of pepper gets caught in my throat and I begin to choke, spraying a piece of shredded carrot across the table. My mother attempts to get up—to do what, I have no idea, possibly smack me on the back like an infant whose Cheerios have gone down the wrong pipe—but I wave her off and head to the bathroom.

As I stumble down the hall, eyes watering, I pass what used to be my childhood bedroom but is now a crafts space (my mother occasionally makes tacky Christmas ornaments from wine corks or gets into a quilting project that is abandoned almost as soon as it's begun; as previously stated, she is no Martha Stewart, gay or otherwise) and then pass Dwight's on my way to the shared hall bath. His room hasn't changed much. Some might think this type of behavior reads as abnormal, but there's actually a perfectly reasonable explanation for it. Back when my brother spent his savings making those expensive ads, he'd return home to try to cut down on costs. The room is now an odd mixture of teenage Dwight and adult Dwight; posters from bands that no self-respecting adult would ever admit to listening to, signs from his real estate business. His clothes are all mixed up in the closet, depicting two very different timeframes of a man's short life. Beat-up board shorts and sensible work slacks. He'll never have an old man's saggy windbreaker to hang up beside them.

I close the bathroom door behind me and splash water on my face, cough petering off, then realize that the faucet is different. I've figured it out by touch alone; the previous iteration had separate handles for hot and cold, but this one is just a single lever. Every time I enter my mother's house I'm struck by the keenest sense of vertigo. The place stays essentially the same—same blue-gray terrazzo floors, same brown leather furniture, same configuration of pastel-hued desert prints full of cacti on the walls—yet every year or so she'll abruptly change some small thing, which leaves me feeling like I'm inside one of those *Highlights* magazine's "Can you spot the differences?" pictures.

It feels like everything is changing too fast, even when the change is happening too slow. I miss my brother, I want him here, I'm starting to forget what he looked like or how his hair smelled when we hugged the night that our elderly cat died. The past is now yet also already far away, long distance in the rearview, so foggy I can't make out any distinct shapes. I've got motion sickness from it and close my eyes to try to settle my stomach.

When I return to the dining room, I see that my mother has cleared everything from the table except for my food and my half-drunk glass of wine; the rest of the dishes have been swept away like they were never there at all. I wonder if I'm expected to sit down and eat the casserole that I'm allergic to; perhaps my mother has set a timer in the kitchen for me like she used to when I was a kid, prepared to send me to bed early if I didn't finish my food before it went off. It's funny how Dwight never had to finish a meal if he didn't feel like it. I can't remember a single time my mother ever set the timer for him.

Speaking of my brother, I can hear him talking in the other room.

Zombielike, I follow the sound of his voice. My mother has pulled up one of his old commercials on the enormous television in the living room. She and Portia sit side by side on the leather sofa, holding hands, as my dead brother smiles widely at the camera, giving his spiel about haunted houses and poltergeists and the booming real estate market. Skin still plump, cheeks rosy with health, hair thick and cowlicked at the crown. He's so young, I think. Just a baby.

"Turn it off," I say. My voice is thick from all the coughing. It sounds like I've abraded my vocal cords with a meat tenderizer. "Turn it *off.*"

My mother halfway turns, but she's still staring at the TV. Her thumb rubs concentric circles into the skin of Portia's palm. "She hasn't seen these yet, and your brother is just so funny." She turns again to Portia. "He came up with all of this himself. Haunted real estate! Isn't it a riot?"

"*Turn it off!*" I yell.

Now I've got her attention. She looks confused, then concerned. "There's no need to shout."

There are a thousand reasons a person could get upset. Every single day in this country it feels like there are exponentially more reasons to scream bloody murder, but this particular reason—my dead brother's voice, his hands, his face, presented as if he were a carnival attraction and not a ghost himself—is reason enough for me to yell. "Turn it off!"

"Calm down," she says, getting up to pat my back, like I'm a riled-up toddler on the verge of a tantrum. "It's almost over."

She's not taking me seriously. No one ever takes me seriously; I'm a clown, I'm good only for a laugh. Dwight's still talking, using that goofy "adult" voice that he'd perfected for his ad work, one that's a mix of Timothy Dalton and Duffman from *The Simpsons*. He'll never have a real adult voice of his own. I run over to the TV to try to turn it off myself, but it's a new model and there are no buttons to operate it on the box itself, only the ones on the remote, which my mother is holding.

"Give it to me!" I say, attempting to yank it from her.

"Cheryl, stop!"

I head into the dining room and retrieve my plate, then park myself back in front of the television, facing the two of them.

"Please," my mother says, throwing up her hands. "This is so childish."

"If you won't make it stop, then I'll make it stop." I pick up my fork and use it to scarf down the cold, gelatinous casserole that's still sitting on my plate.

After ten seconds, my throat begins to close up. My vision restricts to pinholes, and my limbs feel fuzzy before losing feeling altogether. As the plate drops from my hands, it seems to fall a long, long distance. My mother screams. Then I'm lying beside the spilled plate, the sharp leg of the coffee table digging into my shoulder. I want to tell her there's an EpiPen in my bag, but that's maybe the funniest part of this whole mess because I can't get the words out. I'm about to die in the middle of my mother's living room while the TV plays the last moments of my dead brother's haunted realty comedy routine. I point at it the best I can, fingertips grazing the underside of the leather before my arm goes completely limp. Portia, apparently not as dumb as I'd previously thought, grabs my bag and rifles through it, unearthing the EpiPen. She stabs me, hard, in the thigh.

My voice comes back in a rush. "Fuck." I wheeze. "Jesus."

"Cheryl," my mother says, sobbing. "Don't swear."

A great prank, I think. Dwight would have loved it.

AQUARIUM SELECT V

Extremely metal," Darcy says, poking at the rainbow-hued bruise covering the top of my left thigh. "You should tell women you got it in a bar fight."

I roll the leg of my khaki work pants down again, trying to smooth out the wrinkles with my hands. "Am I supposed to say someone kicked me? That's not very metal."

"True." She chews on this for a moment, rubs her finger under her eye to dislodge a nugget of eyeliner-darkened sleep crust. "She should have stabbed you in the heart. You know, like they did in *Pulp Fiction*."

"That character OD'd on heroin."

"What was yours from again?" Darcy asks.

"Peanut allergy."

Darcy sighs and punts a box with her booted foot, sending it sliding across the polished concrete floor. "That's not very metal at all, actually."

"You're right. If I'd died, it would've been a lot cooler."

It's Aquarium Select III's semiannual sale, meaning 75 percent off all bulk coral and half off assorted aquarium supplies and select fresh-water fish. For seventy-two hours, shoppers descend like a plague of locusts, scooping up "Megawatt Deals." Mister Manager coined this term himself and is obnoxiously proud of it. We're required to use the word "megawatt" every time we interact with a customer, no excep-tions. Mister Manager reaches peak asshole during these sales events. Even Wendall isn't immune from these blasts; whenever he forgets to say "megawatt," he's docked one fifteen-minute break. And yes, that shit is illegal, and we all know it. But this won't stop Wendall from taking at least five of these breaks per shift, dock or no dock, so Mister Manager can get away with it.

Darcy and I each grab a box to move to the opposite side of the storeroom, both of us competing to see who can move the slowest. Mine is suspiciously light. I look inside and find that it's actually empty. I decide that it doesn't matter. All I'm trying to do is make it through the next three hours without screaming at someone, or jumping off the roof, or both. This job is a joke, I am a joke, my career is a joke. Might as well lean into it.

"So, was it weird?" Darcy says.

"Was what weird?" I place the empty box on my head and hold out my arms, walking forward with it balanced there like a tightrope walker. It immediately tumbles to the floor. I put it back and try again.

"Meeting the woman that your mom is boning."

"Jesus Christ, Darcy." The box topples off my head again, and I scoot it along with my foot. "My mom is obviously a bottom. She'd be the one getting boned."

When we reach the back of the stockroom, we toss our boxes and lean against the wall, sliding down until our asses hit the floor. There's a 75 percent chance that Mister Manager will find us slacking and fire one of us (but not both of us because he doesn't have enough trained staff for that). We both know that the other will threaten to quit, so no one will get fired. Everyone's mood has taken a turn for the worse. Darcy and I haven't been this testy with each other since "The Great Rumble of 2018" (my coinage), in which we fought for two weeks straight over a piece of chewed bubblegum that *someone* left on a chair, effectively ruining a pair of clowning pants. That someone was absolutely Darcy, but she'll never admit it.

Aquarium Select III really is the place where creativity comes to die, I realize, wondering when I'll finally quit. Bunko needs a lot more of me than I've been able to give. I think that I should expand the act, generate new ideas. For instance, is there a way I could somehow incorporate a real horse into my gigs—say, a very small pony? It could chase me around the stage, and afterward I could give all the kids pony rides. Now that's a good idea, I think, and I wonder how many other good ideas I've missed out on because I've been so focused on a job I hate. Not to mention on a woman who wants nothing to do with me.

"How come whenever I have sex, my brain stops working?" I ask. "It's like it just turns itself off."

"She's a magician, right? Not your fault. She's got that magic pussy."

"She's got a solid disappearing act, that's for sure."

Darcy winces. "Maybe getting laid really is bad for you."

She gets up and stretches, forearms brushing the sides of her mohawk, which today features black and green stripes, like a seasick zebra. I fight the urge to kick the back of her knee, worried she might decide to kick me back. I haven't told her yet who my mother is dating. I'm not sure how she'd react to the news. Knowing Darcy, she'd want me to talk to my mother about it, as if the twisted intimacies of our dating lives would result in an easy conversation. I find this exasperating because that's how close Darcy is with her own mother. In their relationship, secrets are unheard-of because they both genuinely respect each other. I can't remember the last time my mother was curious about my personal life, outside the time that she pointedly asked if I was paying my taxes. Darcy's closeness with Brenda makes it hard for me to trust her sometimes. Even though I know it's not right, something in me turns away from her when I see how easy she's had it.

"Assistance needed on the floor." Mister Manager's voice crackles over the intercom. "Report to the register, *stat*."

"We're busy," Darcy drawls into her walkie-talkie.

"Megawatt busy," I add, clicking in with a last-second save, but it's too late. Mister Manager doesn't respond to either of us, which means he's on his way to the back to ream us out in person.

I pick up two empty boxes and pretend as though I am struggling beneath their weight. As I round the corner of the overstock shelves, Mister Manager bursts through the stockroom door. He's breathing hard and looking bullish, khaki pants riding low enough on his hips that I can see the elastic of his white underwear peeking over the top.

"What are you doing back here?" He's looking over my shoulder for Darcy, who has wisely parked herself behind a stack of twenty-gallon tanks.

Grunting, I heft the empty boxes up again and nearly toss them over my shoulder. I'm really flexing my acting chops today, I think. "Restock. Got to get these goods out on the shelves, Chief."

"I'm not your chief; I'm your boss." He's still mad, but there's too much going on in the store to spend much time yelling at me. In his mind, every second we're back in the stockroom is another important sale lost. "Get back out on the floor. Help Wendall."

I think that Wendall, who couldn't find his own ass using both hands, needs more help than anyone can give. But I bite my tongue. I wonder if it's possible to get an ulcer from capitulating to patriarchal bullshit.

"I'll get right on it," I say, and follow him back out into the shop.

It's like someone shouted "Fire sale!" in the middle of a Walmart Supercenter. The store is packed with bodies, people squabbling over bulk bins of fabulously colored coral and snatching 50 percent off aquarium gear from one another's hands. New trainees have been stationed in front of anything that's alive. We can't be sure that someone wouldn't just reach into the cages and grab at the animals, like they're raiding bulk candy bins instead of elbow-deep in a fish tank. A young trainee with a rash of acne on his cheeks has his back to the ferret display, trying desperately to ward off a roving pack of pre-teen boys.

"Hey! They bite!" He slaps at the grasping hands of a kid wearing a beanie and a hooded sweatshirt. The idiocy of it fills me with nostalgia. In Florida, in the summertime! Oh youth, I think, and briefly reminisce over the times I wore sweaters that dragged down over my hands and nearly died of heatstroke all because my friends thought it looked cool.

"Um, excuse me? Where's filtration?" A frazzled-looking mother with a fussy baby on her hip stands in front of me, toddler drooling something down its chin that looks like mashed banana.

"Aisle six," I say. "Can't miss it." She gives me a grateful look before hoisting up her infant and heading in the opposite direction of the aisle that I'd indicated.

Mister Manager is pricing out gravel for three different women who are all talking over him. "Ladies," he says, and they speak even louder, forcing him to put up his hands as he backs into the line of fish tanks behind him. The water sloshes, fish bobbing gently in the wake. I wish Mister Manager the best of luck and wonder if he is finally as sick of this as the rest of us.

"Cherry!"

I turn and find the hot older lady with the bearded dragon standing behind me. "LeeAnn," I say, genuinely happy to see her. In this mass of idiot customers, she's an oasis in lime-green and electric-purple Lycra. "How've you been?"

"I'm good, real good, honey. And Bradley's doing great!" She unzips her fanny pack and roots around in it, unearthing the bearded dragon. I have to admit he looks a lot healthier than the last time I saw him. Though that wouldn't be too hard to accomplish since the lizard was on death's door.

"Nice color," I say. "Gained some weight too."

"All thanks to that new light you recommended."

I know that can't possibly be true, but I'm glad she's doing well.

"Happy to help," I say, and for once I feel glad for the work that I've done, because it's brought someone joy. And then I'm embarrassed that I'm taking credit for helping this woman when, in reality, I've done nothing but listen to her talk and look down her low-cut aerobics top.

She leans in, clutching me to her in a surprisingly tight embrace. There's that fragrance again, freshly washed linen and hints of cotton candy. It feels like the very best day at the carnival, and I lean into her just as hard, happy to take comfort where I can get it.

Something's squirming between us. I'm confused and even more turned on, wondering if LeeAnn's decided to feel me up in the middle of the store.

"Whoops!" She wrenches back and there's her bearded dragon, already halfway down the top of my navy-blue work polo.

Bradley escapes into the crevasse between my breasts before I can grab the end of his tail. I try reaching down the neck of my polo as Lee-Ann untucks my shirt and reaches up from beneath, accidentally scratching me with the tips of her long fingernails. I'm extremely ticklish on my stomach, so I'm cracking up, squirming as I try to dislodge the lizard that has crawled inside my bra cup as she works to unhook it from the back—she's really good at that, I think, simultaneously horny and disgusted with myself—and then she accidentally honks my breast like it's an old-timey bicycle horn, tweaking my nipple as she finally grabs hold of the reptile.

She pulls it out from under my shirt, holding the traumatized lizard up for my inspection. "Got him!"

I'm not sure who's more embarrassed, me or the bearded dragon. My shirt is still rucked up around my chest, and I'm blushing hot enough that my entire body is covered in a rash of red hives. Over the rush of blood in my ears, I hear someone clapping. I turn around and there's Margot standing at the end of the aisle beside a display of coral cutters and assorted epoxy.

"Reappearing lizard," she says. "Very good trick."

She doesn't belong here, that much is glaringly obvious. All that black in this fluorescent and neon aquatic setting makes her resemble some kind of oil spill. An environmental hazard, I think. Still beautiful, though, like a rainbow effect appearing on top of the slick.

"What are you doing here?" I ask, and my voice sounds oddly high-pitched and breathy, like I'm a middle school girl desperately trying to impress a boy. I clear my throat, try again. "What are you doing here?" Too low that time, like an Elvis impersonator. I clear my throat again and nearly choke on my own spit.

LeeAnn shoves Bradley the Bearded Dragon back inside her fanny pack and offers up a quick thanks. I see him wriggling in there, like he's waving goodbye, thanking me for the good time, but he thinks we'd be better off as friends. She leaves with her lizard, and then it's just me and Margot and the dozens of feral customers fighting one another over discounted aquatic gear. I'm having a hard time reconciling the Margot standing in front of me with the Margot who fucked me in the library stacks and then avoided my calls. She doesn't necessarily look happy to see me, but she doesn't look upset either. Despite being a fellow performer, I can never get a solid read on Margot.

I wonder who she is, really, beneath the cloak of the magician. It helps me to think of her this way. Makes her seem more human.

"What are you doing here?" This time the question comes out in a normal tone of voice, and I'm thankful. The relief is short-lived, however, because I realize that it's entirely possible that she knows that my mother and her ex-wife are a couple, and that she has perhaps showed up at my job simply to warn me not to discuss our "relationship." Another stumbling block in the road to getting my mentorship on track.

"I won't say anything," I tell her. "I promise."

Margot stares at me for a moment. "I don't know what you're talking about, and I won't pretend that I do." She walks briskly forward, then reaches beneath my shirt and deftly rehooks my bra. I am suddenly redressed, and I'm aroused all over again.

"Then what do you want?" I ask, my brain finally settling on the right question.

A man bumps into me clutching a twenty-gallon tank full of bags of shiny blue gravel and green plastic plants. Margot grabs my arm, moves me out of harm's way and into the side of the aisle where traffic is less aggressive. Even when she lets go, I can still feel the press of her fingers on my skin.

Mister Manager is shouting in my earpiece.

"Assistance," he booms. "Need megawatt assistance at the register, pronto!"

"Just a minute," I say, then remember I'm supposed to use the sales event lingo. "I mean, I need a megawatt moment. I'm with a customer."

Margot raises an eyebrow at that, and I'm struck by the significance. It's not just Portia's trick, I think; the two confiscated each other's trademark moves. I wonder if that happens with every couple—a shared dialogue made up of inside jokes. Portia might be one of the only people on earth to understand the inner workings of Margot's magic act. The thought gives me a painful feeling in my gut, and I recognize in this the stirrings of jealousy.

"Does your assistant know all your secrets?" I ask, and then correct myself. "About your act, I mean."

She considers this for a moment. Bites her lip, thinking. "Not all of them," she offers. "But yes, a few. That's the nature of my work. It requires an apprentice."

Someone's hand is on my elbow, yanking me.

"Jesus," I say, turning around again. "Careful, I need that arm."

It's Mister Manager, and he looks pissed. "Well, *I* need you on the register. This is not a request."

This close to him, I can count all the oversize pores dotting his cheeks and nose. Seeing them reminds me of a woman I once dated who had trypophobia, which is a fear of holes. It's a very real phobia, even though it sounds like the intro to an incredible gay joke. I imagine what that woman would have thought of Mister Manager's face and all those blackheads—Wanda, I remember, her name was Wanda, and she had an obsession with cranberry juice; drank a half gallon a day so she wouldn't get a UTI—and while I'm thinking about this, Mister Manager takes the opportunity to grab my elbow again.

"Quit it," I say, shaking myself loose. "What's your problem?"

"You are my problem. Always."

"You can't touch your employees, Mister Manager."

"Right." He backs up, rakes a shaky hand through his hair. Its usual gelled-back boy-band look has been undone by the humidity and the weight of all these shitty customers taking up the store's oxygen. "It's just . . . There aren't enough people here today." When I look confused, he hurries along. "I mean, there are too many customers here and not enough workers. Nobody is on the registers. People are screaming at me."

"Because you were getting screamed at you decided to scream at one of your own employees?" Margot has turned her laser-like focus on Mister Manager, who squirms beneath it.

"I shouldn't have."

"So, apologize."

"I'm sorry," he says. "Really sorry."

"And you should let her have the afternoon off," Margot says. "Unless you want her to file a complaint?"

"A complaint?" The sweat that has been threatening to drip from the corner of his brow suddenly slips down the neck of his shirt. "Please don't do that."

"So, she'll have the rest of the afternoon off? With pay?"

He's nodding vigorously. I feel bad for him; I know he's a pain in the ass, but he doesn't make a ton of money either. I can't imagine trying to manage someone like me or, God forbid, Darcy. I'd quit after a week.

"I'll come in tomorrow," I offer. "Take a morning shift, if you want."

"Great," he says. "Terrific. Wonderful."

He backs away, still muttering his thanks. It never occurred to me that I could file a complaint. I sock this away as useful information.

Darcy clicks in on the walkie-talkie. "Cherry, are you on register?" I ignore her question and turn my attention back to Margot.

"Let me take you out to lunch," she says. "My treat."

"Why?" I ask again, because she still hasn't told me why she's here. Why does she want to talk to me at all when just last week she'd decided I no longer exist? Why am I suddenly so fascinating that she needs to show up at my job and defend me in front of my boss?

Margot smiles and takes my hand. "I have a business proposition for you."

I don't usually hold hands with my business partners, but it's fine, I'll take it. "Okay. But I get to pick the restaurant."

WHEN YOU'RE QUEER, YOU'RE FAMILY

Rituals establish where we sit inside the order of things.

Human beings love habit; we are creatures of it, littering our days with to-do lists and scores of checked boxes. Routines give our complicated lives a semblance of meaning, regardless of whether our customs are something simple or incredibly complex. For instance, someone's daily pot of coffee at 7:00 a.m. might be just as significant as another person's eight-step skin-care routine before heading off to bed. We return emails and texts, walk our pets at the designated hour, tune in for Prestige TV on specific nights, enjoy Taco Tuesdays and Wine-Down Wednesdays and happy hours. And not only do these rituals create value in our lives, but they also give us a sense of satisfaction. What better way to build serotonin than to manufacture situations in which we can strike a chore off our list, essentially mark the mission as complete? It's witchcraft for soothing our anxiety-riddled minds.

Finish the ritual and you're safe.

People like to find patterns in things and figure them out, trace the map of someone's psyche so that they feel they have a deeper under-standing of the human mind. Consider Bunko: a clown and a fool, yes, but also a performer on display. When the crowd views my persona, they are laughing, sure, but they're also trying to figure out what makes it so funny. Even the kids in the audience become armchair psycholo-gists; they all want to be the first to figure out what's *really* going on with the clown.

It's perfectly natural. Clowning is a living, breathing, somersaulting metaphor. And I need the people to want to look at me, to examine me, to scrutinize my jokes and fears and foibles. It's entertainment, but it has to do with a lot more than that. My art has to consume them, but it's crucial that they think they've come to their realizations all on their own. My phobia of horses, my self-deprecating jokes, my earnest pleas for "help" when I know they'll just abandon me for the next shiny ob-ject. I have to make them care.

If you really think about it, everything is a ritual.

There's the ritual of applying the makeup and donning my costume: sliding the greasepaint over the ridges of my face, building character from scraps. The act itself requires hours upon hours of intensive con-sideration and planning. And after the gig is over and I've removed my clown's face, I lay those clothes out on the floor in the shape of my body and let them breathe. It doesn't matter where I am in that mo-ment, or if they need washing, or if they're a rental; the clothes have to lay out, exactly that way, immediately after the work is done. I'm hon-oring the work that happened, respecting the time and energy that went into my art. Bunko is still there inside the clothes, waiting to be put back on again, to move through the world like a giggling colossus. When I honor the costume, I'm honoring the art.

Rituals are practice. When we continue to perform them, we're stav-ing off death.

Everyone has them. Even Margot.

Aside from her magician's rituals, which are deeply specific, she has a slew of very human ones. There's the fact that she wears her watch face down on her wrist, second hand ticking like a heartbeat against her pulse point. She applies her lipstick without using a mirror. Her fingernails are unpainted, but she's rubbed her pinkie so many times against her jeans that the nail has been buffed to a high gloss. And there's also the fact that she refuses to make any left-hand turns in her car. We've been driving for almost fifteen minutes and are still nowhere near the restaurant, which is located only half a mile away from my job.

"Turn left here," I say, certain that she won't. "It's in the same plaza as Ross Dress for Less."

"I hate that light. Everyone speeds. It's like they think they're playing bumper cars and that the accidents they cause won't be lethal." She drives past it, then takes another right the next block down. Deep sigh. Her breath smells like something I wouldn't normally associate with a mouth. Floral, some kind of lavender? "Besides, it's faster this way."

It's not going to be faster and we both know it, but I'm learning something new about her—and that matters to me a great deal. And hey, I'm getting a free meal out of it, aren't I? I don't bother asking if it's a date, because she'll just whisper the words "business opportunity" at me again like she's invoking the spirit of Steve Jobs.

After another series of right-hand turns and more minutes of muttering about "reckless" drivers—which for some reason I find endearing, as if she's a grouchy grandfather—we finally reach the restaurant.

She shuts off the car and we sit there, listening to the engine tick. "Please tell me you're joking."

"I never joke about Olive Garden," I say, unbuckling my seat belt. "When you're here, you're family. And my mother couldn't tell a joke to save her life."

As we walk to the restaurant together, I tell myself to cool it with the mom jokes. The last thing I need is a discussion with Margot about how her ex-wife is shacking up with my mother. I hold the door open for her but she takes it from me, shaking her head, ushering me inside first.

"What a gentleman," I say, hand to my brow, as if I might faint from gratitude. "And they say that chivalry is dead."

It's lunchtime but there's no one waiting inside except the hostess. She barely looks up when we enter, too busy scrolling on her phone, watching a video of what looks like donkeys playing together in a meadow. I take the fact that the place is empty as a good sign that we'll get faster service. But Margot looks around and seems concerned.

"If no one is here at lunchtime, what does that say about the quality of the food?"

The way she says "quality"—strong emphasis on the front half off the word, like she's trying to spit it out of her mouth—makes me laugh. Again, I shelve it in my brain for future reference; store it on the shelf marked "intimacy."

We're finally seated at a booth after Margot soundly rejects a two-person high-top table ("not clean enough," she declares, swiping a finger across its lacquered surface like she's in an ad for Lemon Pledge). We're handed our menus by the same bored hostess, who manages to muster up a facsimile of a smile before heading back to her frolicking donkeys.

We sit in silence and drink from plastic glasses of what is almost certainly tap water. I'm sure Margot wonders why I would bring someone like her—a person who probably learned how to make marinara from scratch from her great-grandmother—to an Italian chain restaurant. But I'm glad to be in my comfort zone. Perhaps that's a ritual of my own: allowing myself a small joke at her expense so that I can gain a little ground.

When our server arrives, I decide on three separate appetizers as well as the most expensive entrée, topping off my order with an entire bottle of wine. Margot stares daggers at me, but I'm unperturbed. In fact, the whole situation is getting funnier by the minute. The more upset she gets, the more I want to poke at her, see how she reacts. She offered to treat me to a meal, right? Well, she's about to treat me like chain restaurant royalty.

"I'll have the salad," she says, handing over her menu. "And whatever wine is . . . most palatable."

Our server looks like a guy who took this job to pay off the interest on his student loan debt. Lips pinched, I can tell he's having a hard time not rolling his eyes. "Ma'am, this is an Olive Garden. We have red and white, and sometimes there's a rosé that comes straight from a box."

"She'll have some of my cabernet, just bring an extra glass," I say, thanking him for his time. "Jesus, Margot, you're going to give that kid an aneurysm."

"No one is professional anymore." She sips from her water and grimaces at the taste. I don't blame her. Unfiltered Florida tap water has enough minerals in it to fulfill a daily vitamin's allotment.

"Where has true service gone?" she says.

This makes me laugh. "God, you're so pretentious."

She cracks a smile. "I know. I'm terrible."

When the server arrives with the bottle of wine and two glasses, Margot wisely says nothing as he works for several agonizing minutes to open it. By the time he finally manages to remove the cork, the guy is sweating through the armpits of his shirt and looks ready to throw the bottle and us through the nearest window. He pours some for me to taste, which I do, grinning up at him. "Tastes like wine."

"Well, I would hope so," he says, and hurries away again.

We drink our wine, me with considerably more enthusiasm than Margot, who is staring down into the contents of her glass like she's about to be poisoned.

"So, let's get down to it," I say, because I'm feeling a lot more mellow. "Also, I think this is the first business lunch I've ever taken in my life."

"That's very sad," she says, and I can tell that she means it, which delights me.

"You think I should care more about *business*?"

"It's how art is made accessible. And that's what you want. You said so yourself, at our last meal together. You said you wanted your art to be taken seriously, yes?"

I agree that yes, I said that, and yes, I meant it. "But what the hell does art have to do with business?"

She smiles at me again, but this one is big, full of shark's teeth. "Everything."

For the next ten minutes, Margot explains exactly what she knows about it. How from a young age, she was heavily involved in her family's glassblowing company. At the tender age of fourteen, she was already assisting her father with the financial logistics of the business, networking with distributors, posted up at parties with a glass of sparkling apple cider in her champagne flute, charming potential investors.

"It taught me that marketing is crucial when it comes to art," she says, picking at her salad. So far she's eaten only the radicchio and the croutons. "Even though I was young, I took it seriously, because how could I not? Creativity requires an audience. In order to make the art you want to make, you must first learn how to finance it."

"That just sounds like capitalism," I say, because of course it does. "Like learning to *finance* something? Come on. What does it have to do with making something beautiful or interesting?"

"Please, be serious." She holds up her hand, counts off on her fingers. "Without money, without stability, without support—you feel the lack. Instead of making art, you're spending half your time considering how best to sustain yourself. It's why great artists of the past were supported by wealthy patrons. That way they could focus solely on the work they were making, no cloud of debt hanging over their heads, obscuring the work."

I want to ask what she could possibly know about debt since she grew up in such a wealthy family, but our server has finally arrived bearing a truckload of plates. He's got the stand for the tray wedged under one armpit, struggling to get it set up without dropping all the food on the floor. When he eventually does manage to kick out the legs with his foot and heft the tray on top of it, I want to applaud. Instead, I tell him, "Yes, I would love grated cheese on everything that's arrived." He proceeds to dusts the entire table with Parmesan, a real Central Florida snowstorm.

"Anything else?" He holds up the cheese grater like he might zest some into my wine.

"We're good," I say, and he hurries off again.

"And what is . . . this?" Margot asks, using her glass to gesture at a mound of deep-fried rectangles. The wine sloshes, threatening to dump onto the table. She pours some more in her glass while I pick up one of the rectangles and dip it in the accompanying tub of marinara. I bite into it, the cheese inside stretching like a delicious rubber band.

"Fried mozzarella." I nudge the basket her way. "Try one." When she glances at it like it might bite her hand, I roll my eyes and shove it closer. "Don't be such a baby. That's my job."

"Well, when you put it that way." She picks one up with the tips of her fingers, forgoing the sauce, and bites into the corner. A thin string of mozzarella droops and she works to gobble it up before it hits the table, hissing at the heat on her tongue.

"Good?"

She chews for a moment, then dabs at her lips with a napkin. "It was not . . . awful."

"Wow! High praise coming from you."

Mommy issues. I can't escape them.

We polish off the bottle of wine, and when the server comes back, I impulsively order another. When Margot complains, I remind her that she offered to pay for everything. "Besides," I say, dipping my finger into the dish of Alfredo sauce, "you still haven't told me about the business opportunity."

"I was waiting until after the wine. I thought it might ease the conversation."

I hold up my glass, which is empty again, and fill it from the fresh bottle that the server has wisely dropped off without fanfare. "Well, I'm as loose as I'm going to get."

Margot sets down the remainder of her fried mozzarella. She stares at me, hard, and I'm reminded of how easy it is to get lost in those giant, dark eyes of hers. They're magnetic. I wonder if she's using mesmerism on me; it's possible she hypnotized me at our very first dinner together, and she's been using it on me ever since. How would I even know the difference?

"I think we should put an act together," she says. "The two of us."

That isn't the business plan I expected. And it's more than I could have hoped for in terms of mentorship. It's boots-on-the-ground employment. I'd learn everything from her, firsthand. Up close. "What, like a combination of magic and clowning?"

"Not exactly." She pauses for a moment, considering. "But yes, in a sense. I've been approached by some higher-ups. There's a significant amount of money involved, but I must be frank with you. It would require contractual work."

I know what that means. The only people who require contractual work, other than agencies, are theme parks. My excitement immediately dissipates; capitalism and art aren't friendly bedfellows. "You're not suggesting what I think you're suggesting, right?"

"We'd be able to format the show to our liking," she says, continuing smoothly. "Whatever we wanted. And we could build something brand new. That's what you said you wanted, correct? To make art? This is your opportunity. I'm handing it to you."

I shovel an enormous forkful of chicken Parmesan into my mouth so that I don't have to answer right away. She's giving me a gift, of course—access to her and her oversize network. But she's also asking me to give my rights and my identity over to a corporation that can twist it into whatever it wants. Because even with the very best contract, the parks have the money and the legal power to stab a hole through it. What's yours isn't *yours* anymore when you sign with those people. I say as much to Margot when I've finished chewing my meat.

"They'd take my work, slap their own name on it."

She shrugs. "So what, they keep it. By the time your contract is up, you'll have enough money in your bank account that you can come up with something even better."

She's got me there, I guess. Because haven't I been thinking about what it would be like to finally quit my day job, the one that drains me of all my time and creative energy, depleted as a wrung-out rag? What would it mean to finally keep my own hours, to spend my days devoted to the craft of clowning? To be able to afford whatever I needed without having to scrounge for change between the cushions of my couch?

Margot puts her palm over her mouth to conceal a burp. "I need to find the restroom. That fried . . . *thing* did not agree with me."

After she leaves, I imagine what an act between the two of us might look like. Would she want me to take Portia's place as her assistant? Bunko is a main act all on his own. I'm not sure how that would mesh with the main character arc of Margot the Magnificent, a presence so large she dwarfs everything in the room. I swirl a long, slippery loop of pasta around my fork, circling it in the marinara, and consider us onstage together. Light and dark. Effervescent and intense. Despite my reservations, I find myself energized at the prospect of making something new. It would be difficult, sure, but creatively it might be exactly what I need to rejuvenate what's recently become a pretty stale act.

And let's be honest, it's not like I haven't known what was coming.

Some hardened part of my heart has always known the sad facts of my career: watching the clown community in Orlando waste away, everyone too burned-out from the occasional birthday parties and gigs that make you feel like you're either invisible or a monster. The offer of money, *real* money, would allow me to make things that matter. I could create something that lasts longer than the time it takes for a child to get bored and leave the room. Money could make my clowning dreams a reality.

It could be something spectacular.

When Margot returns, she's cupping a wad of paper towels in her hands. She sets the collection gently on the table to the right side of her plate, then picks up her wineglass and pretends it's not there.

"Excuse me," I say, eyeballing what has certainly returned with her from the restroom. "Should I be concerned?"

For the first time in our short acquaintance, she's the one who looks embarrassed. "I'd rather not talk about it," she says. "You might find it . . . distasteful."

The idea that this woman who has more than one kind of olive oil in her kitchen thinks that *I* might find something distasteful has intrigued me. "I'm sorry, but I have to know."

Margot sighs with the deep, welling exasperation of a person who has endured far too much. "Fine," she says, and motions me forward, as if she's about to tell me a secret. We're both leaning over the table, faces positioned directly above the wadded bunch of brown paper towels. She peels them back as if she's unwrapping a sleeping baby.

"Margot!" I jolt upright. "Is that thing *alive*?"

"Of course not." She folds the desiccated lizard corpse back inside its shroud of paper towels. "Did it look alive?"

No, I admit, it did not look alive. In fact, it looked long dead, skin shriveled over its slender skeleton like it had been shrink-wrapped—

168

something that happens to lizards when they've gotten inside a house in Florida and forgotten how to find their way out again, starving to death under a refrigerator or beneath a cabinet. I have no idea why she's collected this thing and brought it back to the table, but I assume she must have a very good reason.

"Why?" I ask. "Is it for your act?" I envision some kind of Lazarus situation, Margot raising the desiccated lizard from the dead.

"No, it's because of my grandmother," she says. "She was Roman Catholic and always said we all have souls, even the smallest creatures. So now whenever I find something dead, I have to bury it. Roadkill, dead bees, even flies on windowsills. And God, especially lizards. They're everywhere here."

"That's true."

"So, I just do it. I bury them. It makes me feel better. There's something in me that won't let it go, won't let me rest until it's done." She finishes the last of her wine in one long swallow and tucks the wad of paper towels into her black designer handbag. "I know it's unhinged. But it's part of who I am."

"Oh." I'm struck, once again, by everything I don't know about this woman. Floored by the simple fact that there are a million strange things I could learn about her, if given the time. If she decided to let me in. I think about what it might be like to make art with her, and imagine making just this sort of raw, feral discovery. I'm not opposed to it, I realize. Making something new with this woman. It sounds like a lot of fun.

"Okay," I say. "I'll do it."

"You'll do what?" she asks, putting up an imperious hand and flagging down our waiter, who's been studiously ignoring us ever since he dropped off the second bottle of wine. He hustles over with the check.

"The business opportunity."

Her gaze sharpens. "Are you serious?"

I shrug. "I'm never serious. But I'm willing to try it out. See how it goes."

"Wonderful." She smiles again, teeth stained dark from the red wine. "Terrific."

After she pays the bill—"so inexpensive for so much food," she says, with wonder in her voice—we walk out the front door of the restaurant and head to the parking lot, the black pavement sticky and broiling in the late-afternoon sun. I pull the fork I've stolen from my back pocket and kneel down in the patch of weeds that sprout from a nearby median.

"This looks good," I say, digging a small hole with it, forking free the silty dirt. "We can bury him here."

Margot pulls the wad of paper towels from her purse and places it inside the hole. As I work to cover it again with the leftover dirt, she whispers a prayer in what sounds like Latin under her breath. Once I'm done filling in the tiny grave, I dust my hands off on my pants. She pulls a bottle of hand sanitizer from her purse and squirts some in both of our palms, the two of us quietly massaging the liquid into our skin as the sun bakes the tops of our heads.

Afterward, she opens the passenger door, reaching down to pull the lever that reclines the seat. Then we climb inside together. She fucks me like that, silent in the hot car aside from our labored breathing. When I come, it's so good that I bite down, hard, on the leather seat. My teeth marks remain indefinitely, a permanent reminder that I was there.

BUDDY UP

"Can you make it look like the Big Bad Wolf?"

I stare down at the strands of colorful balloons threaded through my gloved fingers and consider what might make the teeth, what could serve as torso or tail. Bright blue or sunlight yellow. Cartoonish, maybe. Doesn't sound exactly big or bad. But it could be wolf shaped.

"Can you make it look real?" he asks, tugging on my belled sleeve. "Really *real*?"

"Sure I can," I say. At least I can try, and that's what matters when it comes to kids. They only want to see that you're willing to put in the effort.

The little boy on the bed is watching my hands. He's hoping to understand how a tiny, deflated balloon can turn into something large and important. There's magic in watching things transform, which children, I think, find especially important. So much of what happens in their early life is about growth and change. They're all just learning what it means to be alive.

Two quick puffs, twist at the tip, pop, and secure. What was once a shriveled piece of rubber now holds depth and dimension. I've breathed life into it, built body parts from scraps and hot air.

The boy is transfixed. He leans closer, pokes at the inflated parts; then he slides his finger along the tube of balloon, rubber squeaking under his skin. He's thin, small for his age. Dark circles under his eyes show that he hasn't slept right in a very long time.

It's not often that I volunteer at the hospital, but today I made the time, even though I don't get paid for these kinds of gigs. I started volunteering five years ago to keep myself busy after Dwight's death and also to get more practice. My performance anxiety was through the roof, and I needed an audience—any audience—to reaffirm that I was good at what I did, that my work made a difference. But I quickly realized that it's more meaningful than that. These kids need me. Alongside their medical care, the small sparks of happiness I provide are like bursts of psychic energy, helping their bodies fight whatever is harming them. It's exactly why I got into clowning in the first place: to bring joy to people who need it the most.

Don't get me wrong, there are plenty of patients who don't want anything to do with me. Some because they're scared of clowns (TV and movies haven't done me any favors; everyone's scared of the monster that wears a clown costume), but it's also true that a lot of these children don't feel very good, which means laughter can sometimes hurt. They're sick and they miss their families. They just want to go home.

I'm careful when I'm here, approaching only the kids who seem bored or are actively eager, ones whose hands shoot up when I ask who'd like to see a magic trick or have their face painted.

A performance in the hospital isn't the same as a birthday gig, but these volunteer hours have taught me how many smiles I can get from the tiniest amount of effort. Today, as I make the wolf, I "accidentally" tie a balloon around my finger instead of correctly knotting it off. I act as though the balloon has surprised me, staring at it with shock as I try to wrench it free, only for it to suddenly attach itself to the fingers of my other hand.

The boy, whose name is Dominic, laughs, thin and raspy.

He likes robots and pepperoni pizza and has a black-and-white spotted dog back home named Scooter. Three weeks ago he turned eight. Also, he has an aggressive form of childhood leukemia that has so far been treatment resistant. He's got an IV attached to his skinny arm, the tube of it taped to his wrist. I'm careful as I sit in the chair beside the hospital bed, not wanting to pull anything I shouldn't.

His eyes widen as I yank the green balloon from my right hand, mysteriously find it knotted onto my left hand, and then somehow pull it free, only to see that it's attached to the right hand again. He laughs again, hard, revealing a missing front tooth. The new one is already sprouting up where the old one used to be, a large adult bone surfacing beside the Tic Tac of the baby beside it. I am struck by this contrast; wonder about his chances, hope that he'll live to see the other grow in.

"Can you show me?" He lisps the question.

I guide his smaller hands through the motions with my own as we pull the rubbery balloons, twist the ends tight, knot them together to form joints and legs. Finally, we mold the head.

"There he is!" My voice is high and giggly, Bunko at his brightest. "Your very own Big Bad Wolf!"

Dominic holds the wolf by its ears, staring awestruck into its cartoonish face. "You did it," he says. "You made a wolf!"

"*You* made a wolf." I search for the horn hidden inside my belled sleeve and give it a beep. I press the wolf's snout to Dominic's nose.

He cracks up, so I honk the horn two more times, bopping his head with the balloon animal before handing it back.

I paint a matching wolf on the apple of his cheek after that; nothing too big, his skin is sensitive, and the hospital staff will just scrub it off after I leave. I show him my work in a hand mirror after I'm done, and he nods approvingly. After I put away my paints and stow the rest of my balloons, a little girl in the corner wakes up from her nap. She's groggy and scared; her steady low-toned wail becomes my cue to head out.

Dominic waves goodbye, his face one big smile, the balloon wolf clutched to his chest. I wave back and hurry out the door, pulling my cell phone from the depths of my pants pocket. It's been buzzing on and off for the last hour, which is never a good sign. Nobody ever calls for anything good anymore—it's all spam and death. Once I'm outside in the visitor lot, I post up against the side of my car, heat from the metal sinking through the thin fabric of my oversize pants.

There's an avalanche of notifications on my phone. One from Darcy, bizarrely asking to meet up for coffee. I can't remember the last time she sent me a text that didn't include the word "bitch." I also can't re-member the last time she texted me just to shoot the shit. She's busy doing something, apparently, but I have no idea what. I tell her I can meet in thirty minutes. There are a few messages from Margot, check-ing in about our business discussion from the other day. She wants to come up with a strategy and talk "logistics," which is the least sexy word on the planet. The rest of the notifications are all from my bank. I've overdrafted for the third time this year. The bank is adding a twenty-five-dollar fee to each subsequent purchase that goes through, which apparently applies to purchases made several days ago. The screen shows that I have a negative balance of $187.96.

On the phone with the customer service representative—finally a real person after almost fifteen minutes of shouting key phrases to a robot, shrieking "representative" until I nearly gave myself hearing loss—I explain my predicament (that I am bad with money and need another chance), hoping that the woman can help me out.

"Please," I say, wondering how I'll pay my rent, which is due in five days. "Come on."

"There's nothing I can do." Her voice is nearly as monotonous and mechanical as the automated customer service line.

As we argue, I watch a line of crows form on the thick black power line above my head. Four of them gathered there, then five. Six. A murder, that's what a gang of crows is called; I remember reading about it as a child in a book about Florida migratory patterns. I wonder if I could bribe these crows with some stale chips, get them to attack the bank on my behalf.

An ambulance screams its way into the hospital parking lot. I wait until they turn the siren off before responding.

"Sorry about that," I say. "It's loud here."

"Are you all right?" Her tone has changed; there's suddenly some kind of *feeling* present in her voice, as if she actually cares about our conversation. "That *was* very loud."

"I'm at the hospital." Two EMTs unload an elderly woman in a sky-blue dressing gown from the back of the ambulance. She lies motionless on the stretcher, an oxygen mask attached to her face. "There's a lot going on right now," I add. "It's kind of crazy here."

"Oh God. I'm so sorry." She pauses. "Family member?"

"Yeah," I say, because I'm not really listening to her anymore. I'm too busy worrying about what I'm going to do when my paycheck finally hits and there's not enough in it to cover my overdraft fees along with my rent. Perhaps Mister Manager will let me move into the stockroom of Aquarium Select III if it means I'm willing to work the register more often.

"Listen," she says. "Since you're in a jam, I can help you out, but you've got to add funds to your account by this afternoon to cover the remaining negative balance. I'll waive every overdraft fee after the initial one—my boss checks those—but the rest I can push until tomorrow."

"Really?" I ask, feeling cautiously optimistic. For once, someone at the bank is acting like an actual human being! "Where does that leave my balance?"

"You owe seventy-six dollars and twenty-eight cents. Can you get that covered by today? If not, all the overdraft fees will reappear on your account, plus some new ones."

"Thank you, I'll handle it," I say, not sure where the hell I'll come up with that kind of money without giving plasma or selling feet pics online. "I appreciate it. You have no idea how much your help means to me."

"No problem, Cheryl. Is there anything else I can help you with today?"

I tell her no and hang up the phone, filled with an odd mixture of optimism and dread. Blood pounds in my ears as I breathe slowly, in and out, trying to settle my crazed heartbeat. Then I realize the pounding isn't coming from me. There's a man across the parking lot, repeatedly smacking his hands on the trunk of a black Honda Accord. When he realizes he's got my attention, he stops hitting the car, cups his hands around his mouth and starts shouting.

"Get out of here, you disgusting piece of shit!"

One of the EMTs has come back out of the hospital, pulling the empty stretcher behind him. He sees the man shouting, looks at me with a mixture of pity and disgust, then closes the doors to the ambulance and hurries back inside.

Thanks for the help, buddy, really nice of you, I think; then turn back to face the raging man, who's gone back to banging on the trunk of his car.

"Go on!" The man is tall, muscles bulging from the rolled sleeves of his T-shirt. He's hitting the trunk hard enough to damage the body of the car. "Leave!"

I dig through the oversize pockets of my yellow-and-purple-striped pants, searching for my keys. Like the rest of my clowning outfit, the pockets are outrageously humongous, making it hard to find things quickly. He's still ranting, face puffy and red from exertion. I can tell exactly who's being scary in this parking lot, and it's not the frightened clown just trying to get into her car after a morning spent entertaining sick kids. No, it's the large baby of a man who's the nightmare here. But his fear has turned him violent, so I'm the one who's terrified.

The fact is, this guy doesn't know I'm a woman. It's the clown. When he looks at it, all he sees is a monster. It's one thing to have to move through the world as a gay woman—especially in Florida, where the government is always trying to gut you—but it's quite another to add a layer over it that people also hate. Cherry: woman, lesbian, clown. Some days I feel loaded up with other people's loathing. I wonder if there's a single thing about me that people could just plain love.

My keys are at the very bottom of my pocket; I finally find them and hurriedly unlock the door. And though I know I shouldn't, that I could get into trouble if someone reports me to the hospital administration, I roll down my window as I peel out of the lot and tell that awful man to go to hell.

I throw up both middle fingers for good measure, but I still don't feel any better as I drive away. Instead of remembering Dominic's joy when we created that balloon animal, I will remember today as the day when a man shouted at me, and I feared the vicious force of his fists on my flesh. Not to mention the scary reality that I still need to rustle up $76.28 in the next few hours or I could lose my apartment.

Hunched down in my seat, I make several quick and superfluous turns, because I'm also suddenly afraid that the man may have followed me. I chance a look in my rearview and nearly jump out of my seat as I spot a black sedan pull into the lane behind me. But it's not the man's car, it's a different model, and the person behind the wheel isn't a day under seventy. She probably couldn't beat me in a fight.

God, Cherry. You're such a pussy.

Perfect, I think. The ghost of Dwight is sprawled out in the passenger seat of my car, talking to me like he's not five years dead.

Technically, it's my *passenger seat. You've never had enough money to buy your own car, had to snake mine after I kicked it.*

That's true, I guess, but it's not my fault he died. What was I supposed to do, leave the car sitting in the garage, moldering under some dusty tarp?

You could have sold it. Funded your "passion," or whatever kind of freaky clown shit you call art.

This is stupid, I realize. This isn't even my brother I'm arguing with; it's the version of him that lives in my head.

Bingo. That means you're arguing with yourself, you psychopath.

"I'm not a psychopath!" Now I'm laughing because I've said it out loud, proving his point; there is something very wrong with me.

Okay, so not a psychopath. Just crazy.

I'm not crazy, I think. But it definitely means something's wrong. I've conjured him up before, times when I'm stressed out, pushed myself too far and too hard. It's almost like I need Dwight around to take the edge off, to remind me that none of it is actually all that serious. Back when my brother was alive, he bullied me terribly, but he was also the person who talked me through all the bullshit. "Stop feeling sorry for yourself," he'd say, and then I'd just get over it, because it wasn't worth my time. He made every problem seem insignificant. Even the fights I had with our mother he could defuse with hardly any effort. Without him around to pop the balloon of my anxiety, my fears seem to grow larger than I can handle on my own.

Keep telling yourself that.

"It's true," I say, turning on the radio to drown him out. "It's too much."

You can't lie to me. He taps a thick finger against his equally thick skull. *Think, genius. If I'm really you, then you can handle it fine. You were the one doing it all along.*

"But I don't want to do it alone."

My dead brother shrugs. Turns up the music to a near-deafening volume. *Chill out, would you? And call Mom back. You're kind of being a bitch.*

"Takes one to know one."

Then his finger is drilling into my ear—*Wet Willie*—and my brain zaps him gone again. I swallow down the giggle lodged in my throat, because laughing alone about your dead brother really is verging on crazy. I pull over and put six dollars' worth (all I have left in my wallet) of gas in my tank at the nearest station and then call Darcy to tell her I'm running late. She doesn't yell at me for it, even though that's a huge pet peeve of hers. Weird. Then she asks me to meet her at a coffee shop that neither of us likes very much. Another indicator that something's wrong: we invite each other to this particular spot only when we have shitty news. Darcy claims that if we meet at places we don't like when we're talking about hard shit, then we'll never taint a place we actually like with a nasty association. It's pretty smart when you think about it—who wants their favorite restaurant or bar attached to a trauma response?—but after the day I've had, I'm really not in the mood for PTSD, chicken strips or no chicken strips.

The entrance to the coffee shop is awkwardly situated between two busy roads, and the lot is full of potholes. There's one spot left, and I quickly discover why no one parked there: when I pull into it, the front end of my car scrapes loudly over an enormous tree root growing through the asphalt. The accompanying noise is a loud metallic *kerthunk* that probably means I've punched a hole in something important.

I put up the window screen and change out of my clown gear in the front seat, sweaty skin sticking to the leather as I slide my damp body back into my street clothes. My real shoes are somewhere in the back seat; it takes some massive bodily contortions to finally reach them. I keep makeup wipes in the glove box for this exact kind of quick change. There are enough left in the package to get most of the greasepaint off, but not all of it. A ghostly residue remains, leaving behind a complexion that makes me look like a tourist who needs to work harder at rubbing in their sunscreen. I get out of the car feeling more like a clown than ever, hot and frazzled and frizzy-haired.

Darcy is already inside, posted up next to the front window with her computer open on the table in front of her, a rickety glass-topped thing that needs something wedged under one of its legs. The place is full of furniture like this, castoffs that someone picked up on the side of the road, stuff that no one in their right mind would bring home. Darcy's bike is leaned against the wall, handlebar resting beneath a truly horrific painting by a local artist that's on sale for the outrageous price of seventy-five dollars. The painting features what looks like a parrot's head atop a naked human body. "POLLY WANT A CRACKER" is typed out in a thought bubble next to the parrot's beak. The font is Comic Sans.

"I can't believe you rode here," I say, dropping my bag. "It's like a thousand degrees outside."

Darcy shrugs and pats the seat of her bike. She refuses to buy a car. "Have you seen the way people drive in this town? Like they've got spare lives in a video game."

This reminds me of Margot and her refusal to take any right turns. The thought makes me smile.

"I already ordered," Darcy says, staring at her computer screen. "You should put in something now; it'll probably take a year."

There's no one in line, but that doesn't matter; the baristas at this particular coffee shop operate according to their own internal clock, which means they make your drink whenever they feel like it. I approach the stained Formica counter and order the cheapest item on the menu: a large drip coffee with a splash of whole milk. The person working is someone I know through a friend of a friend of a friend: a sullen guy named John D., shadow of a mustache growing over his top lip and the beginnings of a wispy mullet sprouting from the back of his head. He's wearing what I'm sure he considers an ironic Florida Lottery T-shirt that features a pink flamingo. He sighs repeatedly when I pay for my coffee with change scrounged from the bottom of my bag, a sum total that leaves only three cents remaining for tip.

"I'll get a dollar from my friend," I tell him, but he's already gone back to ignoring me.

There's a whiff of garbage in the air, as if the can in the kitchen hasn't been emptied in a while. It's supposed to give off a disaffected vibe—young guy rolling his eyes, dirty mugs, bad service—but when it comes to Orlando, I think it would be a whole hell of a lot cooler for people to actually act like they cared instead of pretending they don't give a shit about what happens.

"They have the worst drinks," Darcy says when I sit down with my coffee. "And even worse food."

"Then why are we here?" I ask. We don't fight very often, but when we do, they're knock-down drag-outs; the kind of arguments that leave us both so angry afterward that we don't speak to each other for days at a time, sometimes even weeks. The past couple of months have been unusual because our mutual frustration with each other hasn't leveled off at all; it's just kept building. I know that's probably not healthy. I don't open up all that easily, which means that when I finally do, it's a deluge of shit, with Darcy becoming a catchall for feelings probably better hashed out with a therapist (that is if I were the kind of person who could afford something as fancy as "health care"). It's not her job to hold everything for me, I know that; but because I lost Dwight and because my relationship with my mom is long soured, she's taken on a lot of roles that she's frankly not equipped to handle. The same could be said for her; she doesn't make friends all that easily and can sometimes alienate people with her bluntness. It takes Darcy longer than me to get over things, possibly because she's a Taurus, but she'd never admit that because she's convinced astrology is for people who can't think for themselves.

She pulls a pair of horn-rimmed glasses from her backpack and puts them on before steepling her fingers. "I've made a business decision."

"Why do you look like you're about to help me refinance a used car?" I've never seen Darcy wear glasses before. She looks uncomfortable in them, pushing them repeatedly up her short nose with the tip of one black Sharpied fingernail. "Are those your mom's readers?"

"Pay attention."

I realize that this is technically my second "business conversation" of the week after a lifetime of never engaging in a single one. I zip my lips about Margot's proposition, fully aware that Darcy would ream me out if she knew I was considering it. I can already hear her berating me in my head: Why would I consider entering an arts agreement with a woman who can't manage to return a text? There are so many opportunities with achievable outcomes, why lean into the one that probably won't work out?

Because it's exciting, I think. Because even though it's scary, it makes me feel alive.

"Don't be mad," she says, and now I'm sitting up and paying attention. If Darcy is worried that I'm going to be upset, it means she's about to tell me something truly awful.

"Before you tell me, can I borrow a dollar for a tip?" I ask. I've got only a few more hours to get the money to the bank before the overdraft fees are reinstated and I have to declare bankruptcy. This is the reality of being poor. Like every moment is embarrassing because you're never able to make it on your own without help; palm extended, eyes averted in shame. "Also, can I borrow a hundred bucks?" I say, just to get it over with.

I've never asked Darcy for money before, aside from the occasional buck for coffee or beer; this is something new for us. She looks a lot more like her mother with those glasses on. And even though her hair is still in its usual mohawk, it's looking a little limp today; less shellacked. I reach out to try to touch it, wanting to see if it's as soft as it looks.

She slaps my hand away, scowling. "Don't touch my fucking hair."

"Sorry."

She pulls a crumpled five-dollar bill from her pocket and slides it across the table. I pick it up and wave it at John D.

"Jesus, a five-dollar tip for a drip coffee?" She grimaces at the mug, which doesn't exactly look clean. "What are we, billionaires?"

"Sorry," I repeat, but she interrupts me with a wave of her hand.

"I quit the band," she says. "Told them that after our next show, I'm officially done."

This is not the bad news that I'd anticipated, because this news is actually *great*. I've been trying to get her to drop that deadweight for years. "What did they say?"

"I wrote them an email." She stares at her computer. Her voice is small. "They haven't gotten back to me yet."

This is a move very unlike Darcy, who is usually the kind of direct that can be mistaken for grade A assholery. Once she made a man cry because she told him he had the kind of face that hurt your eyes when you looked at it for too long. "Picasso face," she'd said, like it was a compliment.

"What, you're going to start a solo project?"

That's something she's talked about before, at least briefly, but she shakes her head at that. "No more gigs." She takes a deep breath, then hurries on, the words bleeding together in a wild rush. "I'm going to buy the drum shop from Bill."

This isn't bad news either; it's even better than Darcy quitting the band. It's like all her dreams are happening at once. I'm beginning to think she called me out to this coffee shop just to fuck with me. It's almost too perfect to be real. I know I've been checked out due to my own drama; we have been distant from each other lately, but I feel like I should have known something about *some* of it. When I brought up the same idea last week at the festival, she acted like it was the dumbest thing she'd ever heard. "So, is your mom going to help you out with the money?"

She squirms in her seat, the legs of her chair scraping and squeaking against the worn linoleum floor. "I mean, yes. Some of it."

I finally take a sip of my coffee, and it tastes like it's been stewing in the pot for at least a week. I use my napkin to swipe the bitterness off my tongue. "Can you please tell me? I can't take the suspense."

"I just don't want you to be upset."

I'm trying to follow the thread of this conversation, but it's continually unraveling in unexpected ways that leave me looping back to my own problems. "Why would I be upset?" I put my used napkin on top of my mug, watch the syrup of coffee seep into it. "Unless you're about to tell me that you're going into business with the reincarnation of Hitler, I think we're going to be fine."

Instead of responding, she turns the computer around to face me. She's got a PDF pulled up on her screen; a business contract, from the looks of it. There's a lot of weird legalese that I can't understand, but there's her name, right at the top: Darcy Dinh, along with her cosigner, Wendall Duncan.

I'm *flabbergasted*. This isn't a word I've ever thought to use in conjunction with myself, but there's no other that accurately describes my feelings. I am goddamn flabbergasted.

"Are you *high*?"

"You know I don't do drugs."

But that's not the point. The point is that she's partnering on her dream project with the laziest man in America, a person who is essentially a slug disguised in the form of a human being. A man who routinely sits back and lets women do his work. And from the way that she's squirming around in her seat, I can tell that it's actually something worse than just partnering together. It's more than just the money. My mind goes full galaxy brain as I recall their recent interactions. How she laughs at his awful jokes, reads his terrible poetry, brings him up in casual conversation even though she knows I hate him. How she let him have access to her food. "Are you *sleeping with him*?"

"Shut up," she hisses, but her neck and cheeks have gone blotchy with embarrassment, so I know that it's true.

Aside from the fact that I'm grossed out beyond belief, I struggle with the logistics. "How the hell can Wendall afford any of this? He works fewer hours than us!"

"He doesn't have to work for money; his parents are loaded. He just does it to be around all the aquatic stuff." She lowers her voice, and I have to lean in to hear the rest. "You know, for his slam poetry."

My brain is so rattled by this information that I can feel it clanging around in my skull, like someone's shaking a tin can full of loose change. "Slam poetry!"

"It's not that weird," she says, though she obviously doesn't believe that because she still refuses to look me in the eyes. She takes another sip of her tea, then gets up from her seat to deposit the full mug back on the front counter. "This shit is vile," she tells John D., who doesn't disagree with her. He dumps the liquid into the sink behind him and goes back to reading his paperback, which looks like some kind of self-help book about raising sled dogs.

The computer is still facing me, so I look more closely at the contract. I can't understand most of it, but I do see that Darcy will be co-owners with Wendall, a man she once described as "the human equivalent of a can of expired Spam." She's putting in only ten grand—money that I'm assuming she got from her mother—which means Wendall is putting up the rest. He'll own the majority, as the one financing almost everything.

Darcy sits back down at the table and takes the computer from me, sliding it inside her backpack. "Listen. This is a good thing."

"You're telling me this asshole, a certified piece of shit who has routinely made both our lives harder, is going to help you out strictly from the goodness of his heart?"

"We're going to start an art collective together," Darcy says.

I hoot with laughter. "Will he perform his slam poems?"

"Stop it."

"You're quitting Aquarium Select III," I say, because I already know that the writing is on the wall. "You're taking that bozo and you're leaving."

"That was always the goal. We both agreed that we wanted to find a way out."

"Yeah, I get that," I say, and my voice is as bitter as my coffee. I remove the napkin and try another sip, grimacing at the burnt taste. "But how are you going to make any money? Opening an art collective is all grants and nonprofit shit, right? How will you live?"

"We'll figure it out."

We. The plural kills me.

"Sure you will." It's easy enough to transform my hurt into anger, just like slipping into Bunko, only much, much worse. I am a persona, a caricature. I'm the meanest thing alive. "You've got your mommy and Wendall to help you out, right? Money for nothing. You don't have to worry about a thing."

"Fuck you, Cherry." She yanks on her backpack, tightening the straps until the skin of her shoulders pinches white beneath them. "Just because your mom doesn't care about you doesn't mean you can take it out on me."

It turns out both of us are capable of being the meanest thing alive. "More like fart collective."

"That's the stupidest thing you've ever said."

"You're the stupidest person I've ever met," I reply. "And that's really saying something."

"If you can't be happy that I'm finally achieving my dream, then maybe we're not friends after all."

"Have fun listening to shitty poems about black holes!" I say. "Hope he recites them to you while you fuck."

She flips me off, with both middle fingers. So many birds flying around Central Florida today, I think; it's like a Hitchcock film. She yanks her bike out from behind the table, smacking into the wonky leg and sending my coffee flying. The mug breaks into a thousand shards. Dark liquid inks the wall and sprays on the ugly painting behind me.

"Y'all gotta clean that up," John D. says, and both of us tell him to fuck off.

Then Darcy's gone and I'm left alone in the terrible coffee shop with shitty coffee all over my lap and a miserable feeling in my gut that isn't just from the fight with Darcy. Because she's not the only one who has to get money from somewhere.

Maybe Bunko could magic some up for me, drawing cash from my billowing sleeves, inflating dollars like balloons.

SEND IN THE CLOWNS

I t's no big surprise that pain fuels humor.

Suffering is relatable; everyone has it tough. Watching someone else joke about their personal trauma makes our own hardships feel bearable. Jokes give us relief, like aloe smoothed over a truly wicked sunburn. And for the person making the joke, there's the control factor to consider: if we make fun of our misery first, someone else can't come along and make it hurt even worse. Our joke, our rules.

Granted, it's a little more complicated than that.

First of all, we have to find the root of the ache. No matter how original an act might seem, all jokes inevitably stem from a painful source, the flotsam of our lives lifted from the world around us and collaged together to make something new. By the time I was nine, I'd already viewed dozens of Bozo-like characters on TV. I watched, rapt, as they slipped on banana peels, rode tiny bicycles with their knees nearly pressed to their chins, and threw themselves down on whoopee cushions like army men detonating a bomb. I coveted the laughs these clowns received. I cataloged their routines in my reptilian brain, scheming and plotting.

But if we're discussing roots, I need to go back further. It all started with a well-worn *Garfield* comic book.

Dwight had already read through it, grown bored, and handed it over in lieu of buying me a birthday gift. And though I was very into Garfield at the time—what kid doesn't love a creature that's basically id personified, pure ravenous hunger and the unrelenting pursuit of pleasure—I found my real interest captured not by that fat orange cat but by Binky the Clown, a side character who took up only two or three pages in the entire collection.

Binky doesn't do anything all that new or interesting as far as clowning goes. In fact, as Garfield's antagonist, he's so outrageously annoying that most readers can't wait for him to leave. As a clown, he was hard and sometimes mean, but whenever he was in frame, he was in control of the joke, wielding cream pies and seltzer canisters with absolute authority. In a household where my brother could do no wrong and my mother barely tolerated me, Binky was exactly the kind of clown I wanted to be. After reading that comic book from cover to cover, I threw on some of my mother's lime-colored sweats, plopped a ratty yellow Halloween wig on my head, and hid behind a door with a bucket of water. And when my brother got home from school, I dumped the contents of that bucket on his head and yelled "Hey, kids!" just like Binky from the comic strip. It didn't matter that my mother screamed at me because I got the floor all wet. Because guess what? My brother laughed. And that first laugh, his huge guffaw, the open yodel of his delight, has lived on inside me ever since.

We copycat first, you see. We make the thing we wish to become. In creating Bunko, my clown persona who is afraid of horses yet wishes more than anything to romp across the wide plains of the Wild West, I also, of course, brought along Binky and his confidence, his colorful facade and sneakiness, his outright rudeness.

And didn't I bring along Dwight too? If I'm being honest, can't I admit that he was the real Binky all along: an overwhelming presence, a guy with a too-loud voice, occasionally frightening in his pursuit of getting what he wanted, handy with gags and pratfalls? Charming as hell, sure, but also completely full of shit?

I miss him like I'd miss myself. I'll always wonder what kind of clown I'd be now if he were around to see it.

He's gone for good, that wonder of my childhood. The pain of it lives inside every joke I make. And the very worst part? That son of a bitch is always going to get the last laugh.

GUESS WHO'S COMING TO
DINNER (PART II)

"I hate this goddamn planter," I say, and because I'm in a bad mood, I kick it.

I'm on my mother's front porch, and the planter in question has interlocking hearts with a hole on top for a gaggle of sunflowers. It used to be bright red, but because the planter has lived outside in the Florida sun, the color has faded to a flesh-toned putty. And in my mind, it never looked like hearts; it always resembled a pair of misshapen boobs.

Darcy would hate this planter too, I think. It's embarrassing to consider her take on things, to wonder what she might make of the fact that I'm nearly thirty years old and I'm about to beg my estranged mother for money. Not even good money either. A hundred bucks, the kind of cash you can get from selling clothes at a consignment shop. It would make Darcy laugh, at the very least. The reminder of our fight hurts almost as much as thinking about my dead brother. Another ache, another deposit for the joke piggy bank that lives in my brain.

"Piece of shit." I kick the planter again, and this time it tips over onto the welcome mat.

This doesn't alleviate my aggravation; it just kicks my rage into high gear. I stomp on the broken planter, the pot breaking into pieces beneath my feet. After I'm finally done, wet bits of plant gristle stick to my ankles and cling to the soles of my shoes. Potting soil and chipped terra-cotta litter the usually immaculate front porch. It smells like a mixture of sweat and damp, wild earth. This is probably the exact opposite of what I should be doing since I'm about to ask for cash, but I'm too riled up to care. I reach down and scoop up some of the dirt, slipping two wet fingerfuls of it under my eyes, as if simulating the black paint that football players wear out on the field. For battle, I guess, wondering if my mother will take one look at me and slam the door in my face. When I shake the remaining dirt from my fingers, residue splatters against the window shutters. I do it again and again, raining mud onto everything clean: the door, the white stucco, the freshly painted porch railing. It's oddly therapeutic. Makes me wish there were more mud to fling.

I'm a mess. And for once, I don't find that very funny.

"Cheryl?" And suddenly there's Portia, hefting an enormous mug of coffee. She's using both hands to hold it. "You've got dirt on your face."

"Yep." I can't get over the size of that mug. Like a soup tureen.

"You didn't ring the doorbell. Or knock."

That mug could hold the nation's collective outpouring of coffee, I think. "Yeah, I forgot," I say.

"You forgot how to knock?"

I can't tell if she's being serious. She's less dumb blonde today and more confused housewife. Her hair's twisted up on the top of her head. It's the kind of hairstyle that only certain women are capable of performing; because that's what that kind of hair is, a performance. Easy breezy, as if she just twirled it up without a thought, then secured it with a single bobby pin. *I don't have a care in the world*, that hair says, because it's attached to a head and a brain that never has to think about money. *Cash!* That's what her hair screams, shiny and lustrous and slick with good product and bouncy from conditioning. A few strands have slipped free, draped artfully beside her perfectly rosy cheek. I've never been able to do hair like that, never a day in my life, but that doesn't matter. I just slap on a zany wig, hitch up my persona, and call it a day. That's what I wanted, right? To be the clown?

I'll lose my apartment because I had to buy a gala ticket to see a woman who doesn't really care about me. I'll have to sell Dwight's car because money is a thing with feathers that always wants to perch far away from me. The problem is easy enough to diagnose: it's me, Cherry. But I can't even pity myself because I know in my heart that I'd do it all again.

"I like your hair," I tell Portia, and then I burst into tears.

She ushers me inside. It's impossible to know if she feels bad for me or if she's embarrassed the neighbors might see. But I don't care, I'll take whatever mothering I can get. We head through the front hall with my childhood photos tacked up on the wall, past the china cabinet that holds my great-grandmother's tea set and brass-dipped baby shoes that once fit Dwight's soft baby feet, then into the living room with the same leather furniture, the same glass coffee table, the same worn rug with the fringe that my mother has to compulsively fix every time a thread pulls out of place.

"Sit down," Portia says, and I obey. "Wait here," she instructs, and I nod. I can't stop crying. Snot runs down my chin. I yank up the neck of my shirt and use the inside to clean my messy face.

When she comes back, she's got a box of tissues in one hand (white wicker tissue holder with a mermaid stitched on the side, wearing a bra made of actual seashells, $12.95, purchased on a fifth-grade class trip to St. Augustine. It was a gift to my mother for Christmas, one of the few that she genuinely liked). Her other hand holds a half-full bottle of peppermint schnapps.

"This is all we have. You know, liquor-wise." She eyes the bottle with genuine regret. "Your mother doesn't really drink. But I guess you already know that."

I have to imagine that this particular vintage is at least ten years old; I remember it sitting on a table at a Christmas party when I was just out of high school. "Want to chug from the bottle?" I say.

Portia shrugs. "Might as well." Another tendril of white blonde hair slips from her bun, drapes along her cheek like a slick line of silk. Rich bitch hair, I think, but not without affection.

We take turns, long pulls straight from the neck. I've never consumed peppermint schnapps all on its own; usually I pair it with hot cocoa, a way to get drunk that still feels childlike and innocent. Peppermint schnapps tastes like candy, if candy could magically get you wasted. The kind of alcohol that a middle school delinquent would love.

Portia pours her next shot into her oversize coffee mug and then screws the cap back on the bottle. "I think that's enough of that," she says, and I'm inclined to agree. Already I can feel the sugar swirling in my brain, promising one of God's worst hangovers.

I feel loose and tired from drinking and also from crying. I pull tissues from the box, a never-ending silk scarf of them; three, four, five, until the box is almost empty. Comedy, I think, and use the giant wad of them to swab at my face.

She sets the bottle on the floor between her bare feet. Pedicured toenails. Baby-pink polish. The skin is soft and clean and perfectly toned. The kind of feet you could really picture pressing down hard on your throat. Listen, she might be my mother's girlfriend and I might have wiped snot from my chin using my own T-shirt, but I'm not a corpse.

"You look really pale," she says.

"Greasepaint, from clowning," I say, not sure if I should be telling this woman about my artistic endeavors since my mother hates them so much, but at this point we've shared liquor and her ex-wife's pussy, and she's seen me cry, so I guess it doesn't matter. "I had a gig earlier and I ran out of makeup wipes."

"You're a clown?"

"Yes, I clown. I clown, therefore I am. I'm down to clown." I toss the wad of used tissues in the direction of the kitchen because I can't be bothered to get up and put them in the garbage can. The ball of tissues bounces off the side of the leather recliner and lands in the middle of the rug, unfurling like a snotty snowball. "I mean, Aquarium Select III is just my day job. My real passion is clowning."

She blinks. "Oh. That's nice."

"Is it?" I ask, not sure that's the right word. Stressful, maybe. Overwhelming, sure. Akin to dancing on hot coals? Absolutely. "I mean, I don't know if I'd call it nice. Most people hate it. Seriously loathe it. A guy screamed at me today in a hospital parking lot, and I was only there to cheer up the sick kids." And, because I'm feeling sorry for myself and because I've had a prolific amount of schnapps, I lean into my bad mood and bring up some drama. "Even my own mother can't stand my clowning."

She looks unmoved. "You're an adult, aren't you? Do whatever you want; who cares if she likes it."

It's a smart idea, just one I've never been capable of accepting. Instead of listening to her, I decide to go all in on my pity party and spare no expense by immediately bringing my dead brother into it. "You don't understand. Without Dwight around, all she has to focus on is how big a disappointment I am."

Portia laughs. "Wow. You are really self-absorbed."

I was hoping for a hug. "Excuse me?"

"What makes you think that your mother would care about *anything* that you're doing? I mean, she has her own life. She's not just a mom, you know? We've been dating for months, and you literally had no idea. I'm pretty sure she wouldn't give a hoot that you're clowning around or whatever."

I'm liking Portia more and more.

"If she cared, she'd ask."

"She doesn't have to care." Her voice is gentle but firm. "You're the only one who has to care about it."

"Dwight would care."

"Sweetie . . ." She pats my hand. "Dwight's not here."

I don't want to talk about that because it will make me cry again, so I go back to the subject I love most: myself. "Clowning is the one thing in my life that makes me feel like I'm truly, authentically myself. I think about it first thing in the morning when I wake up. And it's the last thing I think about when I fall asleep at night. Acts, gigs, art." I'm unloading rapid-fire, a deluge of word vomit, all the shit I usually keep to myself because it's so mortifying to talk about how I *feel* when I could make a joke instead. "I don't just like to clown. I *am* a clown. And I hate that my mother can't understand that."

Now she pats my knee awkwardly with her pretty hand. "I mean, I get it. Who doesn't have issues with their parents?" Realizing that she barely knows me, she abruptly pulls her hand away and begins stroking her own bare knee. "Your mom is just particular. And stubborn. Sometimes it takes her longer to get her head wrapped around something."

That's an astute assessment of my mother, and I should have been able to come to that conclusion on my own. "Maybe," I say. "But that doesn't mean I have to be cool with it."

"Oh, you definitely don't. My ex-wife, she works in performance too. She's good at it, like the real deal. And her family basically disowned her for it." Portia picks up the ball of used tissues with the tips of her fingers and goes into the kitchen. I hear the clang of the garbage can as she steps on the lever with that beautiful foot. Then she washes her hands (Palmolive dish soap, original variety, three dollars; "the only kind of dish soap worth using," according to my mother) and comes back, drying them off on a red-and-white-striped hand towel. "So, she went out on her own. Made the art she wanted to make, you know? And when they finally did try to mend that bridge, it was too late."

I hadn't known that about Margot; the unexpected perks that come from chatting with an ex-wife. "So, even though they finally recognized her art was good, it didn't matter to her? She'd moved past it?"

Portia flips the towel over her shoulder. It makes her look a little like a waiter in an Italian restaurant, which I find fitting for this particular conversation. "They didn't even care that she was gay. The magic stuff was embarrassing to them, because her family is very wealthy and all invested in the corporate world." She shakes her head. "People get weird when money is involved. I don't get it, but I wasn't raised that way. I mean, both my parents are public school teachers."

"Well, my mom was fine with the gay stuff too. That's what happens when your mother is a lesbian. Can't really be homophobic."

"That's true." Portia smiles at me. It's the first real one I've ever received from her, and it reveals a row of wildly snaggled bottom teeth. I've finally managed to crack her shell.

"So . . . where is my gay mom?" I look around, as if she might pop up from behind the couch, yell at me for wearing my shoes inside and dragging dirt all over the terrazzo.

"At work." She sways back and forth so that her bathrobe shifts open and closed around her tanned legs. "She won't be home until after five."

My mother's been retired from her guidance counseling job for almost a decade. I know, how cliché—the mother who's a therapist for hundreds of teenagers can't even talk to her own daughter. She'd told me about this new part-time gig a few months ago, but it must have slipped in one ear and out the other. She's arranging bouquets, or harvesting succulents, something like that. Portia is right: as little as she knows about my life, I know next to nothing about hers. It's like we're in a competition to see who could possibly know the least about the other.

Mother? I barely know her!

"What are you doing home?" I ask, realizing that it's the middle of the afternoon and Portia is still in a bathrobe and we've been day drinking peppermint liquor. "Don't tell me you're milking your ex-wife's rich family for alimony payments."

I meant it as a joke—Florida doesn't do alimony payments, the one normal thing about this state in a sea of regular weirdness—but Portia doesn't laugh. Her eyes get hard and she stops swaying, sets down the mug again to hold her robe closed at the neck. "Absolutely not. If anything, I was financing Margot's lifestyle."

"I'm sorry," I say, and I genuinely am, because it felt like we'd made some progress. I might not have a great relationship with my mother, but I can't stand it when people don't like me—even the people I don't like—and I often find myself working hard for their approval. "Seriously, I can't keep my foot out of my mouth. It's probably a clown thing."

After a few tense moments, she softens. "It's not your fault," she says. "I'm sensitive about it."

I'm sensitive about a lot of things, so I can't really fault her for that. But I am curious about Margot—more curious than I should be, given our upcoming business plan—so I ask her why.

"Because my ex was really controlling. We always had to do what she wanted, never anything that interested me. It was always about her act. She didn't care that I had my own job, my own friends. That I wanted to travel and see new places that didn't have anything to do with networking or building her portfolio."

These are all things I can believe about Margot because I feel the same way about myself. It's part of the reason that I've struggled to maintain any kind of lasting relationship: I know that my art will come first every time. Say what you will about my mother, but she's never been a person who cared more about anything than keeping a routine. It's very possible she'll devote her entire life to making Portia happy.

And why shouldn't they be happy? Why couldn't they find that kind of good thing with each other?

"I'm a financial analyst," Portia says. "It's boring, but it pays the bills."

It's embarrassing to admit, but the news shocks me. When I first met her, she seemed so empty-headed. Don't you have to be a math genius to work in finance? "So, you just work at home? Alone?" I ask.

"Most days, yes. I prefer it." She shrugs. Another tendril of hair loosens, slips down her neck. It's almost like she's got them on a timer. "I'm really a homebody."

For years she was Margot's stage assistant, glammed up in a slew of fancy, sparkly dresses, paraded across a stage for everyone to gawk and leer at while Margot did her magic routines. I wonder what that kind of thing might do to a natural introvert.

The things we do for love, I think. The awful, terrible things we put ourselves through in order to be loved in return.

She sits back down again and turns on the TV. She hasn't asked me why I'm here, and I haven't volunteered the information. I'm not sure what we're doing, but it's making me feel better than anything else has all day. The television is tuned to a daytime talk show with a celebrity host who has more teeth than seems right for an average human mouth. We watch in silence because the TV is muted, a pile of afghans and throw pillows squashed between us. The captions are on, sliding up the screen a few beats behind the host's oversize lips.

"I like it better this way," Portia says. "Feels like I'm reading or something. I never actually get to sit down and finish a book; they always feel too long, and I get bored in the middle and start thinking about something else, like what I want to have for dinner." She laughs and puts her feet on the coffee table. "They're about to kick me out of book club."

This interests me because it feels so embarrassingly silly. I want to ask her a lot more questions. I want to know what kind of book club she's in, and if they read chick lit or contemporary fiction. What's the difference between chick lit and contemporary fiction? Aren't book clubs just an excuse to drink wine? What did she love more about Margot, her forthrightness or her dark sense of humor? But right now, I need to get to the bank, because if I don't, it's likely that I'll end up moving back into my mother's house. And I don't think our relationship—or frankly, Portia and my mother's relationship—could handle that kind of strain.

"Could I borrow a hundred dollars?" I ask. "I need it because I'm very bad with money."

"That's all you're going to tell me?"

"That's the short version of the story."

"What's the long version?"

I think about this for a moment. What's the best way to describe my financial situation without telling her about my dalliance with Margot? "The long version is that I had enough money to cover my rent a few weeks ago because I blackmailed a woman I had clown-fetish sex with during her child's birthday party, but then I spent it on a gala ticket and a bunch of clowning accessories. Now I'm broke again, and if I don't get a hundred dollars in my account by this afternoon, I'll lose my apartment and I'll either have to live inside my car or move in with you guys."

Portia listens to all this with a stoic expression. "You were at the library gala?"

Too far, I think, and immediately backpedal. "I bought the ticket but never went."

It doesn't look like she believes me, but I can see that it doesn't matter. "You really are bad with money." She sighs heavily and gets up from the couch, grabbing her purse from the front hall. She pulls a stack of twenties from her bright pink wallet and counts out five bills. (What is with these women and stacks of loose cash? How do rich people just have this shit lying around?) When I grab for them, she steps backward, keeping the money just out of reach.

How embarrassing, I think, eyeballing the wad of cash like a child in a desperate rush for the ice-cream truck.

"You have to do something for me."

"What is it?" I ask. "Whatever it is, I'll do it."

"You have to promise me something."

The countdown clock to bankruptcy is ticking steadily downward in my head. "Sure, yes, I promise."

"I'm going to ask your mother to marry me." She puts her wallet back inside her bag. "And you're her only living child. So . . . I want you to officiate the wedding."

The ask is galling. "I'm a clown, not a priest."

"Anybody can be an officiant these days. And it will mean a lot to your mom since Dwight can't be there."

Of course, I'm second choice to a dead man. And the fact that this woman with a bunch of money is offering me such a paltry sum to do something that I know my mother wouldn't want—would actually pay me *not* to do—has me second-guessing how well suited they are for each other after all. But whatever she wants me to say, I'll agree to. I figure I can pay her off at a later date, change my name, go into witness protection, flee the country.

"Okay, I'll do it," I say, and Portia hands over the cash.

Pussy, Dwight says, shaking his head at me. He's lying on the recliner, arms tucked behind his head. My anxiety must be through the roof.

Fuck you, I mouth at him once Portia's got her back turned.

I take the money to the bank, but when I hand it over to the bank teller, my heart does a terrible flop. My brother would never have taken that money; he would have done anything to avoid it. I'm not sure what kind of person that makes me.

But hey, what can he possibly know about any of it? He's dead. He doesn't have to worry about disappointing anybody ever again.

BREAKING YOUR
FUNNY BONE

Line starts there," the woman says, pointing in the direction of a nearby hallway with a ballpoint pen. The cap has been savagely chewed almost to a point sharp enough to cut flesh. This is a person who has so much rage trapped inside her body that it's manifesting in violence.

"How long will I need to wait?" I ask.

The pen goes back in her mouth. Two more hard chomps, then it emerges again, slick with spit. "You should get yourself warmed up now. Five minutes with the panel, that's all the time you get."

The line she's indicated stretches down the length of the hall. It's packed with dozens of eager young women dressed in assorted clown gear, all of them at least five years younger than me. Some are probably ten years younger, if I'm being honest. One limber person has her right leg stretched up on the concrete wall, the tip of her dance shoe almost touching the low drop ceiling. She leans into her own thigh, hugging it hard to her stomach.

The woman with the anger management problem and the spitty pen slaps a square sticker in my hand. Number 44.

"Put that on your shirt," she says. "Right side only. *Not* left. If they call your number and you're not there within thirty seconds, you lose your spot. Understood?"

I nod. Her breath is scorching, full of coffee stink. I discreetly huff into my palm, wondering if I should have used mouthwash. Jokes are never as funny when the audience is busy gagging on your bad breath.

Another vicious chomp. "I'm going to need a verbal response."

"Yes, I understand."

But she's not listening to me anymore. She's turned to a guy who had the audacity to place a refill jug for the water cooler in the wrong location.

"Water delivery goes to administration, not casting!" She chases after him. "Administration! *Not* casting!"

I'm in an office building that reeks of clove air freshener and toilet cleanser. The overhead lights, all long fluorescent tubes set in the drop ceiling, are flickering like I'm on the set of a horror movie. It does feel a little horrifying, I think; everyone's skin washed out to a zombie gray-green hue. Let's face it, nobody looks good under fluorescent lights, not even girls who're barely eighteen.

In the hallway with the rest of the hopefuls, I sit on the floor because the line hasn't moved since I arrived fifteen minutes earlier, and there aren't any chairs. The linoleum is gritty and yellowed with age. I wonder if the seat of my orange and red clown pants will be stained from plopping my ass down on the filthy tile, then shrug it off. I'm a clown. Who cares if I'm dirty? I'll just pretend it's part of the act. Tramp clown, down on his luck. Dust from the trail dotting my drawers. Makes it all feel more authentic.

Listen, it's whatever. This place—corporate, theme parks, all that bum-out jazz—isn't really what I want. But I am interested in what it might turn into, or at least how Margot made it sound. So, I'm willing to stand here and perform like a trick pony.

I haven't decided yet if I'm going to offer up Bunko to these talent scouts. There are other characters I could play instead, personas I've honed over the years: Laurence the Cowardly Lion Tamer with a fondness for kittens; Greta Goldfinch, the aspiring opera singer with a voice like someone scraped her vocal cords with a rusty fork; and Von Jovi, which is my riff on Bon Jovi, except this clown is his long-lost cousin who hates the guitar. None of them are as good as Bunko, though. If I want to impress the panel, then I'll need to pull out the big guns, and Bunko has guns, even though they're only clear plastic water pistols filled with blue raspberry Kool-Aid.

"You shouldn't sit." The girl who'd had her leg up over her head is now leaning over me. Along with her lavender-hued leotard and matching sheer dance skirt, she's got a dusting of silver glitter on the tip of her nose. Her curly wig is the color and consistency of strawberry cotton candy.

"You shouldn't sit," she says. "It's bad for your circulation."

"I'm not trying to circulate," I tell her, pulling my knees up to my chin. "I want my body to completely atrophy. Let me turn into a statue. That will *really* impress the committee."

The jokes aren't landing with this one. She stares down at me in confusion, wide blue eyes fringed with false lashes the exact same robin's-egg hue as her irises. "Cold is bad for your muscles," she says. "Your tumbling will be stiff and less fluid from sitting on that chilly linoleum." She lifts her leg up again and leans it against the wall over my head. Because of my seated position on the floor, this puts her crotch directly in front of my face. I turn to the side and cough, hoping she'll take the hint. She doesn't. Instead, she switches legs and begins stretching the other one out, nearly bumping into my head as she lunges forward.

"I don't have any tumbling in my routine," I say, pointedly staring down at my lap. "I mean, I've got like a somersault. But that's about it."

She slips her other leg back down to the floor. Her mouth, stained with a rose-colored gloss, puckers into a moue. "Everyone has tumbling in their routine."

"Not me."

"No gymnastics? Ballet?"

I shake my head.

"What about a musical act? Fire breathing? High wire?"

"Are you messing with me?" Looking up at her that way hurts my neck, so I decide I'll stand after all. It takes me longer than I'd like to get up from the floor. Both my knees crack, loudly, and when I'm finally on my feet, my back feels like it's been run over by a tiny clown car. "Be for real."

"What do you mean?" she asks.

"Why would I need any of that shit? Acrobatics?" I gesture at my ensemble, stick out one red-shoed foot. "I'm a clown. A regular gag-and-punch-line clown, just like everybody else here."

"I mean, yeah. You're kind of right? But not totally." She puts her arms overhead and stretches, side to side, then back to front. She's a full head shorter than me, but her posture is so good that it feels like we're the same height. "Everyone here is doing at least three of those things in their routines."

I'd clocked that everyone was younger than me, but I hadn't noticed that almost everyone looks like they're gearing up for *America's Got Talent*. Pliés and jetés paired alongside wild acts of contortion, arms pulled nearly out of sockets, legs walked backward like a flamingo. Grunts and lunges and thrusts, gyrations that make the building vibrate. There's a woman down at the end of the hall doing a modern take on the robot; her body moves in ways that don't seem human. People doing splits, clutching electric guitars, holding coiled lengths of ribbon for gymnastic routines. Makeup that's obviously been applied by a professional's hand.

"You can't *just* be a clown."

"I can't?"

Her cotton-candy wig is full of iridescent butterflies whose wings open and close, mimicking the behavior of insects. "*Everyone* here is a clown. You have to bring something special in order to compete. Something unique."

"Oh," I say stupidly. "Really?"

I've been banking on the fact that my basic routine is enough, that *I* am enough, just because I'm funny and I've been doing it for so long. And the fact that it's for the parks has made me think that my originality, my uniqueness, puts me at the top of the pile. I don't want *them*, so surely, they'll want *me*, right? That's how it always works in my head. But looking around at all this talent—all this young, eager (did I mention young?) talent—I realize that I've gone about this all wrong. Suddenly, I'm sweating bullets beneath the large sail of my clown shirt. I flap my purple-and-green polka-dot tie, trying to work up a breeze so I can cool off and get a handle on my spiking anxiety. I smack myself in the face with the tail end of it, white greasepaint streaking a pale line down the underside of the fabric.

"Don't freak out." She pats me on the shoulder. This tiny fairy of a girl who looks like she graduated high school last week is trying to comfort me, employing a tone that someone might use to soothe a toddler who woke up cranky from a nap. "Listen, is this your first audition?"

I nod reluctantly. Someone's number is called. Ahead of us, a young woman in rainbow-tinted tights cartwheels into the open doorway. Katy Perry's "I Kissed a Girl" blasts from the speakers; there's no way she's worked making out into her clown routine, is there? If so, I'm impressed.

"Then you've got time to come up with something new before your next one. Add some pizzazz. Something that only *you* can bring to the room."

"What next one?" I realize she means the next audition. "*Next* one?"

The butterflies in her wig don't just flap, they glow, brightening and dimming in her pink curly hair. "I mean, hey—this is my sixth audition this week."

It's Wednesday. Only halfway through the week and she's on her sixth audition. They don't want *her*, a girl who can put her entire leg over her head. She's beautiful and young and talented. So what if she's not funny? I can't even get off the floor without my knees making a noise like someone's stomping on Bubble Wrap.

This is all Margot's fault, I think, and for the first time in our short acquaintance, I experience a real rush of anger toward her. I've never felt any bad feelings toward her before. Not when she ghosted me after we fucked, not when she bailed on our first date, not all those times she talked down to me or ignored me. I didn't care that she seemed indifferent; I chalked it all up to her magician's persona. I took her work seriously, and she looked at my clowning and thought it could stand in a lineup with about a billion other women. It's not just my heart that's hurt; she's fucked with my dreams.

She'd called me two nights ago. It was strange, because Margot had never called me before, only texted and sent pictures, and hearing her voice travel through the earpiece of the phone was like slipping inside a dark room together. She'd informed me that I'd need to show up at casting today. "You have to audition" is what she'd said. That surprised me because I was under the impression our act was a done deal, that she was the one who got to select who she'd be working with in her showcase. Wasn't she in charge? That's what had drawn me to her in the first place: the fact that she knew more about everything, that she had everything completely under control. She'd been quick to reassure me, claiming that the process was "merely a formality" required for everyone involved, because of the theme parks' strict contracts. As long as I showed up and performed my routine, everything would turn out just fine.

"I'm rooting for you," she'd said, deep and breathy in my ear. It was the same voice she'd used in her car when she told me to take off my underwear. "Remember, I chose you."

I'd believed that Margot had power. Part of this was because she had power over *me*. I looked at the way I responded to her—her body of work, her body in general—and assumed she had that same enormous impact on everyone else. But that's obviously not the case. She has just enough power to get me a standing audition with a slew of other nobodies.

"Number forty-three!" The woman with the pen problem pokes her head through the open doorway. The line has continued to move while I've come to life-altering realizations. "You have five minutes!"

I'm bizarrely out of place in this audition line. I've got padding in all the wrong places and a face meant to make you scream with laughter. Every other clown here is young and dainty and looks like a Disney princess, as if some clown prince is waiting in the wings to come sweep them off their feet. Is this what Margot wanted? Some classically lovely girl with a face like a painting and legs that can stretch sideways like a yanked-apart Barbie?

Down the hall, a clown-girl with long yellow hair tied in looping bows at either side of her head opens her mouth and honey spills out. Her voice is hypnotic; she has the kind of talent that lets you enjoy the performance without ever worrying that she'll fall flat. What's so funny about being good at something, I wonder. Does it make your clowning better to excel at everything you touch? What made these perfect specimens want to be clowns? I turn to the delicate fairy beside me and ask her exactly that.

"What made you want this?"

"Want what? To audition?"

"To clown. Why'd you choose it?" I ask.

Those big blue eyes slide wide. "I don't care about clowns. I just want to act."

"Clowning isn't acting," I say. "We're joke makers and storytellers. We make the world come alive."

She shrugs and the butterflies flap fruitlessly in her cotton-candy hair. "It's the easiest way in. Hardly anyone clowns anymore. There's less competition."

Now I get it. These women are all looking for a way to sneak their real dreams inside by donning the gear. They won't be funny; how could they be? But maybe if they're good enough at hiding behind the clown mask, they can get the thing they actually want: to be seen for their talent. I can respect that, I guess. It also tells me exactly what I need to do to succeed in the audition. Just be myself.

There's no one like me. And maybe that's the part that Margot forgot, or never knew in the first place. There's only one Cherry. And unlike these other clowns, I don't wear a mask. I'm all clown, all the time.

"I'm Cherry, by the way," I say. "Sorry, I never got your name."

"Lauren," she says. "But my stage name is Stacy Sparkles."

"Good luck, Lauren."

When they finally call my number, I strut into the room like a bow-legged colossus. I strike a pose and ready my bag. Lift up my chin. Spotlight, stage left.

And then the real show begins.

CHUCKLES BITES THE DUST

Ladies and Gentlemen and Swamp Folk, creatures of all ages!

Step right up! Don't be shy!

Welcome to the biggest little showcase this side of the I-4 Eyesore! We're here to entertain you, to dazzle you, to make you forget about the internet for at least five whole minutes! What sights await you! What wonders abound! What undeserved gifts you're about to receive and plunder, you ruthless pirates of creativity!

Destiny has brought you here; it's fate! Five ravenous beasts, gathered under the flickering lights of a corporate big top with greed gleaming wetly from your eyes.

But no matter. Let's get on with the show!

. . .

Behold,

The Central Florida Clown!

See how she inflates beneath the spotlight like one of her colorful, stretched-out balloons—a true master of her craft! Though she's shrunk incredibly over the past few months (years, if we're being honest, folks), today she will grow as wide as the room allows. Watch her head swell to three times its normal size, now four times, now five; an ego unmatched by even the Grinch's fabled heart! She's never been able to contain her excesses, and we see it here, now, in the ways that she spends more than she can afford, the oversize demands she places upon her family and friends, even the grandiose ways that she views her own "art." Swollen with self-importance, the clown blooms riotously, entirely full of herself, yet sick from all the excess. She won't stay puffed up for long—take her in while you can! Soon the world will needle her small again, popped and deflated, humbled by her hubris, yet continuing this tedious routine for the foreseeable future with cyclical regularity.

Now, a separate showcase! One that requires your utmost attention!

Our clown is ready to tell your fortune:

I see, voice a hypnotic hum, *quite a few jokes in your future.*

Because above all, the clown is funny! She knows exactly what will make you laugh because she's trained her whole life to anticipate your every need! Gaze now upon her bent form, see how she bends low like a crone because you want your women small and biddable, wilted into compliance. And here, she shifts again, padded to extremes, shoes so outrageously long that they trip over themselves, puppies unused to their brand-new gangling limbs. She's bumbling and idiotic, a classic fool who's desperate for your approval. She courts your goodwill because a laugh means you like her, that she's necessary for this world, that people couldn't possibly do without her!

Jokes spill from this clown like water dribbling from her flaccid daisy boutonniere! *Like me, oh please like me,* she pleads, ad nauseum. It's the unspoken punch line to each of her jokes, manna to her love-starved soul. But the laughter quickly evaporates, doesn't it? That good feeling always fades, and then she's forced to dig up more of herself as payment rendered. Oh, this clown will never run out of bits, because every gag is taken from the endless wellspring of her own self-loathing! Here, she offers up parts of herself in lieu of manufacturing any self-esteem: lungs for the belly laugh, hands to hold the seltzer bottle, throat to sing and wail and shout, and her heart, a truly desolate thing, served up on a gilded platter. It sits surrounded by bright red noses and whoopee cushions and horns that bleat like a struck goat when squeezed.

Don't turn away from the spectacle; the pain means it's working!

Look up! Gaze with delight on a true winged wonder of the world, the yellow-bellied chicken! For the clown, the high wire is a balancing act of great desperation and cowardice. It requires endurance, a willingness to bolt if anyone ever calls her out on her bullshit. Look how she holds tightly to her brother's death, refuses to let go of the fact that her mommy never loved her enough! The weights of these grievances keep her perched on a tightrope of her own creation, refusing therapy in favor of cracking jokes. Bunko might be afraid of horses, but this clown is afraid of something much dumber. Never before has there been a clown so scared of her own success! The urge to create a thing that will outlast her, remembered long after she's in the grave, is at odds with fear. What will it cost her to bare herself in ways she never has before?

Now, come closer. Witness real transformation.

Our clown is a chameleon in a trench coat, flashing bits of her true self with each unholy flick of her wrist. Her face is painted in a wide-mouthed scream, neck chalked white, hands gloved, clothes baggy enough to contain at least five other clowns.

Maybe you all would like to climb inside and see what it's like? Try her on for size? Pull her body over yours so she can host you like a clutch of blood-drunk parasites?

Every wig she dons, every wide-flapped tie she wears, all of them hide the truth of her body. She's a plain bird hidden beneath a peacock's iridescent feathers. The clown deceives the eye, tricks you into believing that she's more than just a whittled-down nub. The confidence is a cape, draped artfully over her insecurities; the mirror catches the light, showers sparks of glitter in order to distract from the hollow center.

And finally, a true horror of Central Florida; witness a terrifying spectacle guaranteed to linger long in your nightmares!

Behold, the snake handler, trainer of exotic species, immune to death itself. But this clown doesn't just handle snakes, she has become one! Slick and reptilian, cold-blooded in her need for success and approval. She'll do anything to get it, wager any friendship or relationship on the smooth scales of her body. Our clown is a creature of cunning, poised to strike. But there's no need to fear for your safety, folks—the skin she chooses to pierce will always be her own. See her bite down hard, fangs snagged deep in her own flesh. Cannibalizing her work and time and creativity to feed off herself, regurgitating the same old shit instead of choosing to make anything new. Ouroboros clown, forever swallowing her own polka-dot tail.

Have you seen enough? Dear audience, will you pilfer from the clown to increase your own depleted creative stores? Grab at the very things that have long held her back? Snatch and snatch until what once brought hope to her bleak life becomes just another corporate Florida shell?

Here's Bunko. You can have him. He's all yours.

And now we must bid you adieu, our rapt and soulless audience, and entreat you, without question, without qualm, and with great pleasure on behalf of the clown, to please,

Go fuck yourselves.

AQUARIUM SELECT INFINITY

I curtsy for the judges, my carnation splatting a lukewarm piss of water onto the floor. No one says a word as I exit the room.

And though I hadn't anticipated the outcome, shedding Bunko feels good. It's like taking off a pair of jeans you've worn so long that you hadn't noticed how ill-fitting they'd become, how constricting. Now? I'm naked but I'm free.

In the hallway, a clown wearing silver lipstick and half a disco ball as a hat is slouched in the room's only chair, cutting every one of her fingernails with a small pair of clippers. I take a moment to appreciate the nasty looks that the rest of the room is giving her. The steady *snick-snick-snick* is shockingly loud, sound amplified by the echo chamber composed of filthy linoleum and a hollow drop ceiling. Bits of discarded nail clippings ping off the tile and ricochet across the hall.

"Nice intimidation tactic," I tell her. "Color me impressed."

She smiles up at me, and I see that her two front canines have been replaced with sparkling silver fangs. Cute, I think, and I decide to ask for her number. She's not my usual type—too close to my own age, also a performance artist—but I figure if I've given up Bunko, then it might be time to throw out everything.

"I'm Cherry." I extend my hand and she takes it, still holding on to the clippers. Her handshake is stronger than I anticipated; it feels like she's got me in a vise grip. "I'm a clown," I add. "If you couldn't tell."

"Britta. Also a clown," she says. She lets go of my hand and reaches into her lap, picking something off the front of her pleated silver miniskirt. "Want a nail clipping? You could use it for spellcasting." She pulls off her disco ball hat, revealing a gray pixie cut. "Or you could have a hair trimming, if you'd like?"

"I'm not a witch."

"Are you sure?" She looks me up and down. "You look like a witch."

"Thank you," I say. I've never been told that before, and I feel oddly flattered. I decline her offerings as courteously as possible, and because I'm feeling generous, I hand over Bunko's tiny rhinestone cowboy hat. While she's attempting to stack it on top of her disco ball, I walk away, plugging her number into my phone. I wonder if she bites her partners during sex and am suddenly dazed by the possibilities. There is no way the uptight panel of theme park people are going to give her a second glance.

Two girls stare contemptuously at me as I pass. They could be sisters, in pink and purple pigtailed wigs with matching pleated skirts and knee socks, the whole sexy schoolgirl bit. People say that clowns are scary, but these two in their fetish gear, auditioning for a gig that's intended for families at a theme park, are honestly freakier to me than anything having to do with Pennywise.

I look around but don't see my friend from earlier anywhere, the fairy princess clown named Lauren who can twist herself into a human pretzel. I imagine her somersaulting around the room that way, the butterflies in her wig blinking spastically on and off like a strobe at a rave as she rolls past the table where the judging panel patiently jots down notes. *Impressive form*, they might write, *but can she tell a joke while she does it?* Laughing to myself, I squeeze through the people crowded around the exit. "You make a better door than a window," Dwight used to say, and I crack up even harder.

I walk to my car and slap my bag on the sunbaked asphalt beside the driver's-side door. I decide to free myself of Bunko entirely: inflatable pony and braided lasso and spare cowboy hat, even the fake sheriff's badge I'd bought for less than a dollar at a party store. I place these items on the windshields of a few other cars in the lot, hoping they'll go to good homes.

"Goodbye, Bunko." I salute the air and click my heels together, feeling freer than I have in years. "And hello, Cherry."

When I climb inside my car and start the engine, my brother isn't there—but I can feel him radiating all around me, swirling through the interior, slipping through the cracks of the air-conditioning vents. There's a smell, musky and sweet; just a hint of burnt sugar. I breathe it all in, then roll down the windows and crank up the radio, just the way Dwight would have liked. Classic rock, songs about drinking and fighting and fucking and dying. Songs about living. And I'm young enough, and I'm free enough, and I'm driving in a very hot car down the wide stretch of Central Florida highway, remembering what it's like to sit inside my own body. Because *I* am the clown. Not Bunko. Not any other iteration. It's me. I've lived here all along, and I'm going to see how everyone else likes it. It turns out I like Cherry just fine.

By the time I pull into the Aquarium Select III lot, I'm feeling larger than life, like I could take on the world. I'm the baddest clown you've ever seen. I kick a stray Coke can and it spins sideways, spraying dark liquid on the side of Mister Manager's midlife-crisis Miata. And when I march through the front doors and see Darcy finishing out her last week at a job she hates, I wave at her with a giant grin plastered to my face.

"I'm coming for you next," I say, which I know sounds a lot like a threat, but she takes it from me in good spirits. Probably because I'm still dressed up like a goddamn clown.

"Fuck off," she says, but I can tell she's glad to see me.

A woman with a small child in her shopping cart claps both hands over her daughter's ears, as if that might retroactively take back the swear.

"Momma, lookit! It's a funny man!"

I wave at the kid and honk the horn hidden in my sleeve while booping the end of my red nose. She claps her chubby hands, delighted, and I march off to the back to find Mister Manager.

He's sitting in the breakroom with the same goddamn tuna sandwich laid out in front of him. He stares at it bleakly, obviously unenthusiastic about having it again for the millionth time. It's the saddest thing I've ever seen, but it gets a little funnier when he finally notices me standing in the doorway. My wig is askew so I right it, and the pressure from my bicep makes the last of the water squirt from the flower in my lapel. Mister Manager's mouth drops open. A giant glop of chewed-up tuna falls directly on his lap.

"You're supposed to swallow," I say. "Not spit."

"Cherry?" He looks confused but also a little scared. "Why the heck are you dressed as a clown?"

"Don't worry about it." I take the chair opposite him, spinning it around so that I'm straddling it. I lean my arms across the back and rest my chin on them, unconcerned with the white greasepaint that's swabbing across the slick polyester fabric. "I'm here to ask you for a raise."

His eyes grow even wider behind his wire-rimmed glasses. Mister Manager only wears them on days when he has to speak to upper management—maybe they're fake lenses. I figure I've caught him at a good time; he always comes back from those meetings feeling chastened.

"Raise?" He reaches for a napkin, which has migrated to my side of the table. "Why in the world would I give you a raise?"

I pick it up and hand it to him. "Well, I guess I misspoke."

"Oh," he says, swiping at his mustache.

"I'm here for a promotion."

He stops mid-swipe. "You're joking."

"I know I'm in clown gear, so it seems like I would be, but I assure you, I'm not."

Mister Manager's brow begins its initial descent into storm cloud squall. "What on earth makes you think you deserve a promotion?"

Though I'm playing this completely off the cuff, I feel surprisingly ready to take on this question. If I'm going to remake myself and my act—turn it into something weirder and brasher and ballsier than I've ever dreamed of before—the first thing I'll need is stability. And stability means a full-time job with actual health care. "For starters, I've been here for five years. That's longer than anybody else, including Darcy. Speaking of Darcy, I know that she put in her two weeks' notice. And so did Wendall, I'm assuming? So, that means you're down two of your most important employees. All you have left are the newbies and some assorted trainees, who as far as I can tell aren't even worth the paper they were hired on. And upper management is pissed that our sales have been down. The sales event didn't go so hot, huh?"

"Yeah," he says, then shakes his head, correcting himself. "I mean, no, that's not entirely accurate."

I lean in and Mister Manager tips his own chair back, smacking against the wall. "So, you're telling me that if I quit, you can manage to keep this store afloat?"

"Is that a threat?"

I smile hugely because I know I've got him. "It's not a threat. It's a guarantee. If you don't promote me—and I mean a *real* promotion, with benefits and a raise and normal hours—I am going to quit, right here, right now. And I know that you can't afford to lose me, Mister Manager. Because if I quit, you're going to have to admit to your higher-ups that you're out another employee. And then guess who else will be out of a job?"

While he's pondering his next move, I reach across the table and grab one of his potato chips. They're salt and vinegar, and the bite of them stings my mouth, drool puddling up in my cheeks. I'm certain if I let a lick of it spill from the corner of my lips, Mister Manager would run screaming from the room.

"You'd have to undergo training first," he says. "It wouldn't be right away. I couldn't just move you to a management position out of no-where. I have to clear it with my own boss. These things take time."

"We'll get it figured out." I stand up abruptly and dust off my gloves, chip crumbs falling like yellow snow on the cheap fake wood of the table. "Good talk, Mister Manager."

He shakes his head, but he doesn't correct me like he usually would. "I don't know why you think that's so funny, but I guess you'll have an opportunity to find out what it's like to have someone disrespect you the same way you've disrespected me." He puts out his hand. "Welcome to the team."

That's awfully big of him, I think; I put my own hand out, letting the buzzer slip down into the crease of my palm. When he shakes my hand, it zaps him and emits a high shrieking noise. He screams and falls back in his chair, nearly overturning onto the floor.

"See you next week, Comanager!"

I can hear him loudly cursing me as I make my way back up front. One of the trainee-turned-newbie employees is stocking boxes in the reptile enclosure aisle. When he sees me strutting past in my clown gear, he drops the box he's holding, which sends a whole wave of boxes cascading sideways, falling like a rack of oversize dominoes onto the scuffed linoleum.

"Better pick those up, Frank." I wag my finger at him, and he visibly pales. "I'd hate to have to reprimand you."

Darcy's sitting cross-legged on the counter beside the register, unrolling an entire container of receipt paper. She wraps the blank white strips around her legs and arms, tucking the ends in place. "Well, look at you. Clownie's come a-courtin'!"

Torn pieces of receipt paper litter the floor. "What are you supposed to be, a corporate mummy?"

Darcy snorts. "More like a corporate dummy."

I take one of the rolls and wind some of it around her neck, pretending that I am going to choke her with it. A man walks inside, sees us standing like that at the register, and immediately leaves.

"This is going to be great for business," I say.

She snatches the roll from my hands and begins winding it across her chest in an X shape. "Who cares about business? Fuck this place."

"Well, I care now." I puff up my chest and put my hands on my hips. "Guess who's going into management."

"Please say you're joking."

"I'm always joking, but not about this."

I grab the trailing end of the receipt paper from her and yank at it, tugging at her like I'm pulling a dog on a leash. "Come on, let me buy you a drink."

She resists. The receipt paper doesn't break; it's surprisingly strong. "If you're a manager, you should know it's not a great idea to let one of your employees run off when they still have an hour left of their shift."

"You're not my employee; you quit." I tug at the paper again, and she lurches forward. "Remember?"

We head out the front, abandoning the cash register. "Frank, cover the front!" I yell, and Frank drops another box. There's an ominous crunch this time. Definitely broken glass.

Darcy's still trailing behind me as I lead her back to my car. "Fine, we'll do drinks. But you're buying. You owe me," she says.

"For what?"

"For being the world's biggest bitch."

I watch as Darcy struggles to fit her mohawk inside my car. Today it's stiffer than ever and dyed a very deep black. The style is unusual for her—she's normally all greens and blues and aquarium pastels—but hey, we're both going through some life changes, and that's okay.

"It suits you," I say, reaching over to poke at it. She slaps my hand away, then shrugs down in the seat until her ass is nearly on the floor.

"What is this, a car for clowns?"

"Something like that."

We drive away from the store, and I roll down the windows. The music is still up pretty loud, so I turn it down to say what I need to say next. "Hey. I'm sorry."

"What was that?" Darcy turns to me. Spikes of spray-hardened hair are striping lines across the Firebird's cloth-covered ceiling.

"You heard me."

"I'll need you to repeat it," she says.

"I said I'm sorry. I am apologizing to you."

She wiggles around some more, and one of the spikes of her hair gets twisted in the fabric. When she yanks it out, the cloth covering pulls down too, detaching from the roof of the car. It hangs there limply, a red tent dangling over her head.

"Goddamn it, Darcy, that's going to cost a fortune to replace."

"Not my problem. Use your manager's salary."

I sigh deeply, then go ahead and turn that sigh into a high-pitched yodeling scream. Darcy screams along with me, the two of us weaving through traffic, sun blazing hot overhead as it sinks into the line of palms that sits along the entrance to the interstate. We stop at the light there, both of us still screaming. The noise disturbs an entire flock of ibis, who'd been pecking at the line of scrub near a brackish retention pond coated with scummy green algae. The birds fly up and away, headed in the direction of downtown.

Our screams taper off. I cough, and it's a hacking, wheezing sound that gets caught in my throat. I pound it out with my fist, whacking my chest until I worry that I've cracked one of my ribs. Darcy slips all the way off the seat, sitting on the floor with her back pressed to the leather, watching the world shift past in a blur of blues and greens. She hangs her hand out the window, cupping the faint breeze. Outside smells like motor oil and exhaust mixed with fertilizer, but I don't have it in me to close the window. Her fingers look small. She is small, I remember; Darcy has a big personality, but sometimes she's still just a little kid at heart. Her feelings get bruised so easily. I forget sometimes that she's not in my head with me. We're so close that there are times I expect her to read my mind. But she can't fill every role for me. She's not my therapist or my sister. She's just my friend.

"I'm sorry, too." She doesn't look at me, but that's fine. Darcy can never look anyone in the face when she's admitting she's done something wrong. "I should have told you about Wendall. I was just—"

"Embarrassed?"

She scowls. "No, I'm not fucking embarrassed. He's my boyfriend. And I like him."

"That's hard to accept, but okay."

"I'm sorry because you're my best friend, and that means I shouldn't keep secrets from you. But sometimes you can just be, like . . . really judgmental."

This bit of honesty makes me laugh, but it also makes me sad that she worried I would stop caring about her over it. I need to vocalize my feelings aloud more often. It would probably solve at least 84 percent of my problems. The remaining problems are in God's hands. "Darcy, our entire relationship has been built on sarcasm and judgment. It's how we show our love."

"I know."

"I accept your choices. I just reserve the right to give you a really hard time about them, that's all."

"This coming from a clown who fucks moms."

"It's part of my charm."

"Whatever you say," she replies, but I can tell that it's past now; the fight is over. We'll go back to being okay again; things are on the up and up. We dealt with our feelings in a mature and healthy way. The thought is revolting. Suddenly, I can't wait to get that drink. I speed up through the next yellow light, and a guy waiting on a motorcycle does a double take when he sees there's a clown driving the car next to him.

I park down the block from the bar, in the suburbs again near a row of neat ranch-style houses. "Just in time for happy hour," I say. "Our lucky day."

We walk down the street together, just a clown and her best friend, headed toward our beer. When we reach the weed-riddled front yard of the bar, Darcy stops dead in the middle of the sidewalk. Here it sits, the place where we've attended a thousand shows, drank a thousand shitty vodkas, held each other's hair back while we puked, found dates, lost dates, cried and laughed, and laughed until we cried again. The Pussy Palace is not only closed, it's completely boarded up. Splintered planks have been nailed haphazardly in front of the door, screening all the windows. There's a big sign in the front yard for a corporate real estate company that has been steadily buying up local property to create strip malls. Yet another iconic hangout in town will be bulldozed and demolished, with something indescribably boring and beige and basic built in its place.

"No," I say, dropping to the curb. "Fuck me."

"Indeed. We are fucked."

Our unofficial queer space. Vanished. We'll build another, we always do, but it'll never be quite the same. A handful of us will remember the good times, then those people will slowly forget, and eventually it will be gone for good.

Darcy and I sit on the curb until the sun dips below the horizon and stains the sky red, mourning something beautiful and deeply Central Florida that we'll never enjoy again.

KNOCK-KNOCK JOKE
(PART II)

There's immense power in absurdism.

Take, for instance, the Greek myth of Sisyphus, destined to roll that goddamn boulder up the same goddamn hill every goddamn day, only for it to roll back down to the bottom once the job was completed. I'm sure I've told you this before. Haven't I? Regardless, you've heard it somewhere. We're all retelling the same old stories for all eternity. When we look at this in relation to our own paltry human existence—heading to the same job, day after day, for the same pay and same lack of respect, the same measly benefits—and compare it to Sisyphus's plight, things don't seem all that dissimilar.

And comedy? It thrives inside this echo, beating onward, forever building on itself.

Every day we wake up, eat, breathe, shit, fuck, walk, talk, drink, and then we sleep. The next day, we get up and do it all over again. There's some variation on these points, but not many, not usually. And if we do decide to switch things up, the freshness can't possibly last.

After a while, the latest idea becomes just as restrictive as the original thing; you're trapped in a habitual current. Life turns stale. The new thing quickly becomes the old thing, and so on, etc.

But hey, that's humanity! It's silly and pointless, aside from punctuations of brightness afforded by love and friendship. There's that good feeling when you see a puppy or a duckling, for example; no matter how many times you spot them out in the wild, they're going to engender a sense of delight. Cute is gonna be cute, no matter what.

Or:

Remember the last time someone told you a real gut buster of a joke? You know the one I'm talking about; it was so funny you still laugh about it years later, even if you can't remember all the particulars. That joke is different for everyone, but it affects us all in the exact same way. Sometimes it's not even a joke, is it? It's just something that managed to grab your funny bone at the perfect moment, whacked you hard, and then *bam!* You laughed until your entire body ached. And you remember that ache for the rest of your life; you keep it stored in your head, pulling out the memory when you want to reminisce about how good it felt to laugh that hard. And after you remember it, you tuck it away again. You continue on with your day, but the memory remains, waiting for the next time you need it. And on we go like that, throughout our numbered days, until we reach the end of the line.

Knock-knock!

Who's there?

Death!

Death wh . . . [keels over, dies]

It's not even that funny of a joke, but it worked on me because it was Dwight who'd told it. The way he'd clutched his chest! How he'd swayed there, propped in the doorway to my childhood bedroom, before eventually falling over backward into the hall. And yes, I'd laughed so hard I'd peed myself. And yes, I'd gone to school the next day and told that joke to anyone who would listen: kids in my third-grade class, teachers, even the custodial worker who was not, in fact, a fan of knock-knock jokes. And even now, when I remember that original telling, I smile. It doesn't matter that my brother is dead or that the joke itself was about death. It doesn't even matter that the idiot told it wrong! Death's not supposed to kill himself, after all. It was the principle of the thing. Because in my childlike mind, mortality was a concept as silly as a knock-knock joke, and now, as an adult, I understand that there's not much of a difference.

I'm thinking about that when I pull up to Miri's house and find a cavalcade of cars in her front yard. That's unusual for plenty of reasons, but first among them is that Miri never allows more than one person into her home at a time. This has nothing to do with fears of shoplifting or robbery; she claims she's a shit host if she's forced to divide her attention between customers.

I'm old as hell and I've only got so much whiskey, she likes to say. *Two is tea service, three's a crowd.*

Another indication is that the multicolored paint has been pressure washed clear of the driveway, the asphalt faded to a dismally murky olive. The house looks colorless and depressing, not at all like Miri. I park next to a midsize U-Haul truck half-packed with boxes and hurry up to the front porch.

A woman in a beige business suit opens the door before I can even knock. It looks like she's been traveling for days; her dark hair is flung up in a frizzy bun, and her suit is wrinkled along the knees and hips, her lips are cracked and dry.

She looks pissed that I've interrupted whatever's going on inside. "What do you want?" she says.

I smile as nicely as I can. "Hi there! I'm here to see Miri."

The bags under her eyes are carrying their own bags. The woman looks beyond exhausted, but she also looks familiar.

"Well, you can't talk to Miri," she says. "It's not possible."

I have a bad feeling, but I go ahead and ask anyway. "Why not?"

"Because she had a stroke last Saturday. And two days later she died."

Now I understand. This is Miri's daughter. I can see the resemblance in her high cheekbones and in the shape of her thick, dark eyebrows. But where Miri's face is lined from years of smiling, this woman has creases in all the wrong places: a deep crevasse in the midpoint between her eyes from excessive frowning, long lines dug into either side of her jowls. This is a deeply unhappy woman. No amount of sweetness from me is going to correct that.

Oh, she's dead! I think. My friend is dead. And my eyes flood with tears.

"You're Camila," I say. "Miri's slut daughter."

She chokes on a shocked laugh. "Wow."

"I'm just repeating what she told me."

She leans against the doorway and presses her face against the frame, chuckling weakly. "Oh, Mama."

"I'm not here to bother you. I just came to get Velma."

She looks back at me again, and there are tears in her eyes. The hardness has gone out of her face, and the tightness in her jaw has dissipated.

"Who's Velma?" she says.

"My doll."

"You came here for a doll? Are you some kind of collector?"

"It's my ventriloquist's dummy," I say. "And I'm a clown."

"I believe it. Your jokes sound like hers."

"Thank you," I say, because that's an incredible compliment, even though it makes my heart ache. "I wish I were even a fraction as funny as your mother."

Camila steps backward into the house and motions me inside. "You're going to have to help me look. The place is a wreck."

Cardboard boxes fill the living room. The curio cabinets that line the walls are empty, their assorted memorabilia flung down onto the floor in a jumbled heap. Some of the figurines have been wrapped in Bubble Wrap; others have been tossed into bins marked for Goodwill. We step carefully around the piles; colorful window drapes clumped and tangled, an assortment of afghans and quilts, and then we dodge a precariously stacked collection of plates and cups.

"Where's Priscilla Presley?"

"Who?" she asks.

"The dog."

Camila sniffs. "One of my mother's friends took her in. My cat would have a fit if I brought home a pit bull."

Bottles of whiskey are gathered together on the braided rug in front of Miri's famous car-seat couch. Most are unopened, necks sealed shut with red molded wax. So many good moments were shared here, I think, sipping from those rose-dusted cups in the dwindling afternoon sun, getting day drunk with an old woman who'd lived so many lives.

"No more tea service, huh?"

Camila doesn't spare the bottles a second glance. "I'm sober and so is my husband."

She yanks a stack of outdated entertainment magazines from a pile and tosses them into a bin marked GARBAGE. "Take the booze if you want. I'm just going to throw it out."

I consider it for a moment, then decide I'd better not. "Thanks, but I'd rather remember her drinking it. She was such a cool old gal. And God, she loved an afternoon cup of whiskey."

Camila doesn't seem as endeared by the memory of her drunk mother. "Loved it a little *too* much, in my opinion."

I follow Camila into the next room, where a guy in a dusty white T-shirt and chinos is unloading a crate of clown clothes into a large plastic tub. His suit jacket is tossed over a nearby armchair. Large patches of sweat dampen his underarms.

"Can we turn down the air? Please? I'm not used to this swamp heat." He runs a rag along his brow, leaving behind a smear of gray. "I'm dying in here, Cami."

"Switch on the ceiling fan." Camila jerks a thumb at me. "This is . . . wait, what's your name?"

"I'm Cherry."

"This is Cherry. Cherry, this is my husband, Roberto."

We wave half-heartedly to each other. I can tell the guy doesn't give two shits about me; all he can think about is the heat. He's obviously not from Florida. Inside the house, it feels almost cool to me.

"The fan isn't going to do much," he says. "See, the blades are loaded down with dust."

"I'm not paying for extra air-conditioning just because you're a baby," she replies, obviously the boss in their relationship. "Only keep the fabric, okay? I don't want any of that clown shit coming home with us." She turns to look at me. "No offense."

"None taken," I say. "Lots of people hate clowns."

"Maybe you would hate them too if they were all your mother cared about."

We continue into Miri's sewing room, where there are hundreds of dolls spilled on the floor: wooden puppets and rag dolls and blonde-headed dollies and porcelain babies that eerily resemble real children. All of them are fully dressed as clowns, their faces painted white, bright reds and blues lining their eyes and lips. I pick up one that looks older than me, cracks running down its face, the mustiness of its ancient cloth body puffing into the air around me as I clutch it to my chest. Miri held this doll, I think. Miri had loved it. Cherished it like a real child.

"I didn't realize she had so many," I say, unearthing a stack of zoo animal finger puppets. "How did she manage to sleep at night?"

She shrugs. "Mom was always kind of a creep."

"She really was," I say lovingly. "The very best kind."

After ten minutes, I've sorted through all the dolls on the floor and still haven't found Velma. It's possible Miri shipped her somewhere to get her limbs professionally rebuilt, or even have her head reconstructed. It hits me that I might not ever see my doll again. And even though the ventriloquist's dummy was never a very big part of my act, I experience a swelling sense of intense loss. It's not just the doll. It was Miri. She'd put so much time into everything. So much work into *me*.

"I'm sorry," I say, voice thick. "I don't think she's here."

"Are you sure? What did she look like?"

"Kind of like Velma, from *Scooby-Doo*?" I put my hands in front of my eyes, miming goggles. "Chunky glasses and bobbed hair. Miri was making her an outfit; it's like a silk jumpsuit? It matched one that she gave me that used to be hers. Oh! There's a picture of her wearing it!" I point back toward the living room. "By the front door."

Camila's smile vanishes. "Wait here," she says. "Don't move."

I stand there awkwardly. The dolls on the floor all stare up at me accusingly. When she returns, she's holding Velma. My ventriloquist's dummy, fixed up good as new.

"Where was she?"

She thrusts the dummy at me. "Here. Take it."

It's obvious that Miri took her time repairing the doll, cleaning and completely repainting her face, rejointing and oiling the limbs so they move just as seamlessly as my own. Even the doll's hair has been re-styled; it's a deep walnut brown, glossy and slick. But it's the jumpsuit that's floored me. The one she's sewn is almost identical to the one that Miri gifted me: the same soft swirl of pastel silk, the same cap sleeves, the same pinned waist and shiny gold thread.

"Gorgeous," I say, running my fingers over the slick fabric. "Your mother did an amazing job."

"I'm sure she did."

I turn the dummy over, continuing to examine her from the crown of her head to the soles of her shoes. Those are also modeled after mine; she's wearing the same brown brogues I had on the night of the library gala.

"Seriously, you don't understand how good this looks." I turn the dummy around to face her. "It's like the spitting image of the real jumpsuit."

"Oh, I know it is." She's still standing in the doorway, arms crossed over her chest. Though she looks calm and collected, it's her bare feet that betray her. Her toes are scrunched up tight in the nap of the carpet, digging in like angry fists.

"Are you okay?" I ask, wondering what it is about this particular doll that has set her off. "What's wrong?"

"You want to know what's wrong?" She circles her finger in the air, taking in all of me and the dummy. "This. *This* is exactly what's wrong." Her voice gets hard and mean. "Did you know that jumpsuit belonged to my grandmother? *That's* the person who raised me, in case you were interested. Miri and Hector were too busy with clowning and each other to take care of their own child. While they were off gallivanting around the country, I got dumped with an old woman who could barely walk, much less take care of a kid. And when that old woman reached the end of her life, who was the one there to take care of her? Not my mother. Me." She laughs. "And yet here you are, a stranger, telling me that my mother gifted a piece of my grandmother to you. *You*, a nobody, instead of her own daughter."

I think of the million framed photos that have long crowded the walls of Miri's house. It's almost all circus folk, her time as a clown the most formative experience of her life. There are pictures of her with nearly everyone: trapeze artists, dozens of other clowns with their arms slung companionably around one another's shoulders, lion tamers, the ringmaster himself in a tall black hat, a slew of exotic animals including elephants and chimps wearing suits and roaring tigers, and tropical birds that perched on her thin arms like a bunch of brightly hued flowers. Almost none of the photos in the house, save for very few, feature Camila.

"I'm sorry. I didn't know."

"Save your sorries." Her voice breaks. "I thought she'd made that doll for me."

There's nothing I can say that will make her feel any better, so I don't bother. I know all too well what it feels like to be the forgotten child.

Camila clears her throat and swipes her hands down her wrinkled pants.

"Take anything you want. I don't give a rat's ass." She turns in the doorway to give me one last look. "You can let yourself out."

A ROMANTIC JESTER

Without warning, the Magician has become the Clown:

Margot's been calling nonstop for the past week and a half. It's the kind of funny that hangs waiting in the air like an unspoken punch line. She calls again and again, but I never pick up. The phone screen lights up my dark bedroom, painting the walls electric blue. I experience a sick thrill each time the phone rings, excited by the fact that now she needs me more than I need her.

The big cosmic joke is that apparently what I wanted all along was to be wanted.

I'm not even angry. That performance she put me through at the casting call was a godsend. It allowed me to scrape free the rot of my current act, to toss out all the stale parts that produce canned laughter.

A clown walks into the bar that she's set for herself. She wrecks her ankles tripping over it, because in this joke, the bar was on the floor.

It's time to raise the bar.

I've been busy figuring out my new act. I plan and scheme, piecing together my costume and trying out makeup. I gather my props. I plot out sets. There's meaning embedded in everything. I'm not in a rush anymore, at least not how I used to be when it came to clowning: scurrying around, bailing water from the sinking ship that was my life with a tiny paper cup.

"Could you scratch my nose? I've got paint on my hands." Darcy sticks her face into mine.

I buff Darcy's snub nose with my palm. "Better?"

"Much."

We're at the new storefront. Darcy's been here every day since she and Wendall made the down payment. I stop by whenever I can, roped into providing the kind of free labor that doesn't require a license or any actual skill. Today I'm helping paint the interior of the building before I head off for my first managerial shift at Aquarium Select III. My manager's polo is crisp, collar standing smartly at attention. My name's embroidered in white cursive script across my right breast.

"You look like an enormous douche in that," Darcy says. She dips her brush in the bucket before running it carefully along the baseboard. "*Cherry.*" She says my name how the cursive might make it sound, girly and saccharine.

"That's Mister Douche to you. I'm management now." I slap the paint roller on the wall and drag it up and down in giant V shapes, excess paint running down the stucco in long stripy drips. It's bright pink, the same color as the late, great Pussy Palace.

Darcy takes the roller from me and clears off the excess before handing it back. "Don't fuck up the floors."

We stop to lay some tarps down over the tan and maroon speckled terrazzo and then go back to painting. Wendall's gone to grab subs from a place down the street. He offered to pay for everyone's food, which I have to admit is a classy move. I've never offered to pay for someone else's meal in my life. Wendall's been more active here than he ever was at Aquarium Select III, knocking down non-load-bearing walls to create an open-concept workspace, hauling old carpets out back to the dumpster, even unclogging one of the toilets in the ancient bathroom. I guess all it took was a real project to finally get him motivated. Or maybe it's just having a girlfriend. Some guys are like that.

"You girls are doing a horrible job," Brenda says, coming in from the back lot.

Darcy's mom has been outside discussing plant options with a landscaping company. The lot used to be weeds and a bunch of trash, but Darcy wants to make it an event location. Native plants and scrub and oak trees and dangling string lights. Spaces for chairs and tables too. Maybe a projector screen against the wall. They're still working out the details. We're the kings of DIY in Central Florida. We might not have the money, but we've got the creativity and the willpower to make it happen.

"Then why don't you take over?" Darcy dips her brush back in the bucket, then flings the end of it toward her mother. Bright pink splatters across the front of Brenda's white tank top. One especially fat drop runs down her neck.

"Darcy!"

"What?" Darcy attempts wide-eyed naivete, but the effect is more cartoonish than innocent. "I thought you were going to show us how to paint a wall."

"Actually, I think this is how you do it." I run my roller down the back of Darcy's black shirt. It leaves behind a wide pink bar, a femme skunk stripe.

"Asshole!" She swipes her brush down the side of my face.

Her mom runs for the bucket and grabs the extra brush, flinging paint into Darcy's mohawk.

It's an all-out paint war. Brenda tries to wrestle the roller from me, and I stripe a swatch of pink paint down her thigh. Darcy picks up the smaller bucket and douses her mother with it. Brenda rubs her paint-coated arms all over Darcy's back.

"What's going on?"

Wendall's arrived with a sack of sandwiches.

The three of us pivot toward him as he holds out the sack of food like a shield, but it's too late. By the time we're done, there's paint on his head, his shirt, his pants, and even his shoes. The three of them are laughing together, covered in paint. They're enjoying themselves and appreciating one another. It's a sweet moment but also a painful one; I'll never see that configuration and not be reminded of my brother and the way he held our family together.

Brenda's mom helps me up off the floor, and I try hard not to stare at her bare legs in her cutoff jean shorts.

"Don't even think about it," Darcy says, clocking my gaze. "You freak."

"I am what I am."

"Yeah, a pervert."

I inspect the ruin of my new manager's shirt. One especially vivid pink handprint sits directly on top of my left boob. "Well, time to get to work," I say.

"Don't forget your sandwich."

Darcy tosses it to me. I catch it in one hand and then unwrap the top. White sub roll with roast beef and double horseradish plus extra onion. I take a huge bite, then another, stuffing all that onion and horseradish in my mouth before breathing my thanks directly in her face. "My hero," I say, and she stumbles backward, gagging.

"You monster. Get out of here."

I borrow a tarp to drape over the front seat of my car so that I don't get paint on the leather interior. The day is warm and the sky is a startling, burning blue. Every day in Florida feels like the very first time, as if the day gets freshly repainted before the sun starts its morning climb.

In the middle of all that beauty, I find two lizards fucking on my windshield. I chase them off and settle into the car, plastic crackling around my thighs. I have two missed calls from my mother.

Now what, I wonder, and call her back.

"Hello," she says. "I've been trying to reach you."

"About my car's extended warranty?"

"What?"

My mother doesn't get the joke. Must be a day that ends in y. "Never mind," I say.

Silence. It stretches on for miles. Even when we're talking, we're not really; it's a silence we've constructed together, waiting for Dwight to speak.

The front of Darcy's building still reads BOB'S DRUMS (AND MORE) on the plain black-and-white marquee over the front door. I've asked Darcy about changing it, have offered to climb up a ladder in order to switch the arrangement of the letters on the white board, but she wants to keep "Bob" up there. "He built this place," she says, "and we've still got *drums*, and we've also got *more*. So, what else could we possibly need?"

"Cheryl, are you still there?"

"Cherry," I reply, automatically correcting her. "Cherry, Mom. My name is Cherry. It's been Cherry for years now. I'm gay and my chosen name is Cherry. As another gay person, you should respect that. You don't have to understand it, but you have to respect it. Please, for the love of God, call me Cherry. I am begging you."

She sighs and there's my own sigh hidden inside hers. Our voices share the same frequency and timbre; maybe that's why we can never hear each other.

"Fine," she says. "Sure. Cherry."

She did it, I think. She listened to me.

"You know, I like you fine," she says. "You're the one who doesn't like me."

"Mom."

"Cherry."

I don't say anything for a while. It's harder than I thought it would be.

"Are you there," she says. "Hello?"

"Yes. I'm here."

"Okay." She sighs again. I hear Dwight in it too; is it possible that all three of us share the same voice and inflection? Do I never hear it because I'm too busy listening to my own echo?

"Portia told me you came by the house a few weeks ago."

"I did." How much did she tell her? Did she say that we got day drunk? Did she tell her that I borrowed money? That I cried in her living room?

"She said she talked to you about a wedding."

"Yes," I say, proceeding with caution. "She said she was going to ask you."

"Well, she did. We are." She sounds flustered, tripping over her words. "I mean, we're getting married."

"Oh."

"Yes."

Talking to my mother feels unbearable. I think of Camila, the frozen look on her face when she spoke about Miri, like the sentences themselves were dragging her down. Perhaps that's always the way between mothers and daughters. So focused on the bad alignment that we can never appreciate when our paths do cross.

"I'm glad," I say, and I mean it. "I hope she makes you happy."

"Thank you. I hope you're happy too."

And maybe it's enough that we can wish that for each other. We don't have to do any heavy lifting. We can just exist in orbit, occasionally drifting close enough to reach out and touch.

Family are the people we choose to keep. And I'm choosing to let this one go, with love.

When we hang up, I pull Dwight's video up on my phone. I watch his eternally youthful face caper and grin. He nails joke after joke. He's funny, I think. But I can be funnier.

Fuck you, says my dead brother. *You're dripping paint on my steering wheel.*

I put away my phone and drive to work.

When I pull up to Aquarium Select III, I'm already twenty minutes late for my first managerial shift. We've been refreshing the mural on the outside of the building, and it's finally finished. Ugly as it is, it's still a Central Florida landmark, one that kids will remember long into adulthood. Someday they'll show it to their own children, reminiscing about those hideous whales and misshapen seagulls and jagged tsunami-like waves crashing down over a beach strewn with radioactive mutant starfish. Mister Manager and I came up with the idea together. Get people in the parking lot to look at the updated mural, and they might even mosey inside and buy something.

It seems to be working. Mister Manager stands next to the mural, just inside a roped cordon that's been erected beside the building. There are tons of people in line, a strange mix of young families with kids and assorted groups of twenty-year-olds who are obviously there to take selfies. The babies and the hipsters are dressed oddly alike, I think. Both are wearing funky sunglasses and ironic bucket hats.

"What the heck happened to you?" Mister Manager says, looking at me with genuine horror. Paint is all over my new shirt, and there's cast-off on my khaki pants.

"Tragedy at the Pepto-Bismol factory," I say. "We lost a lot of good men."

"Single file," he announces to the mob behind him, cupping his hands around his mouth to form a megaphone, then turns back to me. "I need you to go inside and grab the cashbox."

"Why?"

"Five dollars gets you two minutes." Mister Manager taps a cardboard sign that announces the same thing he'd just said aloud. He's attached it to the yellow plastic rope that cordons off the wall from the parking lot. "Have your picture taken with the mural."

"This isn't Wynwood!" I wonder if he's officially lost it, charging people to take pictures with a deformed seashell. "People aren't going to pay actual money for this."

Mister Manager unearths a wad of cash from his bulging pocket. "They already have."

A guy wearing a T-shirt with a tuxedo printed on it cuts to the front of the line. "If we pay ten dollars, can we get five minutes?"

"Two minutes per customer. If you want more time, you have to get back in line."

Heat is steaming off the tacky black asphalt. A kid who looks much too big for the stroller he's strapped in sets up a long and sustained wail. It's the kind of crying that makes everyone else want to cry; soon half the kids in the line are shrieking like a horrible choir. The same guy with the tuxedo shirt comes back to ask if we're selling any bottled waters or kombucha.

"Absolutely not," I say. "What do you think this is, Disney World?"

"Cherry." Mister Manager points to the front of the building. "Get the cashbox."

Inside is a relief after standing in all that direct sun. The air-conditioning is running hard enough that I can hear the metal vents rattling in the ceiling. Despite the crowd out front, there's barely anyone inside. A lone customer is perusing the plastic bottles of fish food. He surreptitiously stuffs one down his pants, and when he thinks that no one notices, he grabs another, and then a third bottle. I turn away, pretending that I don't see it. If he needs the fish food that badly, then who am I to judge? Nobody gets paid enough in this life to rat out a shoplifter.

Frank, the new guy, is standing at the register and scrolling on his phone. As soon as he sees me there, he hurriedly stuffs it in his pocket, and I wonder why, until I remember that now I, too, am Mister Manager.

"Don't sweat it," I say. "I'm not that kind of manager."

He doesn't look like he believes me, but he nods anyway. "There's someone waiting in your office."

"What do they want?"

"They said they wanted Cherry."

I think I have a pretty good idea who it might be. And when I open the office door, there she is, seated in the beat-up green office chair on the other side of the desk. Margot the Magnificent. As usual, she's dressed all in black: skinny black jeans with a black turtleneck; her black hair streaked with gray streaming loose down her back. She's wearing a pair of black-framed glasses. They remind me of the ones that my ventriloquist's dummy wears, and I tell her so.

"Her name's Velma," I say. "Like in *Scooby-Doo*."

Margot kicks one foot impatiently, showing off shiny black riding boots with tall, chunky heels. "Why haven't you returned my calls?"

I could say that I've been busy, or that I wanted to give her a taste of her own medicine, but for once I decide to be honest. "I don't know. I just didn't."

"What is . . ." She gestures at my clothes. "All this. The pink."

I pull my shirt away from my chest. It peels off uncomfortably, still clammy. "I was helping someone paint."

"And you came to work still wearing it?"

"I ran out of time to clean up."

She stares at me, eyes dark and wide behind the surprisingly thick lenses of her glasses. "You're like a child."

"Is this why you came here?" I ask. "To insult me?"

She stands abruptly. Again, I'm reminded of the fact that she's a full head shorter than me, even in those heeled boots. I always forget how short she is because she talks like she's the biggest person in the room. Margot has an unholy level of self-confidence. It's an incredibly attractive quality.

I take two steps backward to create some distance between us.

"I'd like you to come over," she says. "To my home."

"I'm at work."

"This is about work." She picks up her bag, also black, and slides past me through the doorway. "Come."

Because there was never any other way this was going to go, I follow after her, an obedient acolyte. When we pass the register, I alert Frank that I'm leaving and pass him the cashbox. I tell him to hold down the fort.

"What fort?" he asks. "There's a fort?"

"Ask Mister Manager," I say. "He'll tell you where to find it."

Margot has parked her black car directly beside mine. "That is not art," she says, nodding at the line of people congregated next to the mural. "People depress me."

Even though I know she's not trying to be funny, she still makes me laugh.

There's a mother snapping pictures of a small boy who's pretending to fight off one of the demented-looking sharks. He hooks one of his hands into a small fist and acts like he's going to punch the shark directly in the nose.

"I think it's kind of nice," I say. "Art can be silly, too."

We climb into our respective cars. I change into a semi-clean shirt scrounged from the back seat and don't bother telling Mister Manager where I'm headed. This seems appropriate for my first day on the job, a real "show versus tell" when it comes to my managerial style.

As I follow Margot out of the lot, I realize that I don't know where she lives. And she drives fast, much faster than she should; speeds through yellow lights, barely slows down at intersections, and cuts everyone off in traffic. I'm tailgating her the best I can when she rockets us both onto the highway. It feels like we're in some kind of high-speed chase; I'm waiting for the blue and red strobe lights of the cop car to flash behind me. When we finally pull off the highway and into a suburban neighborhood, my breathing quiets. Surely, she'll slow down here, but no, she's still clipping along at nearly fifty miles per hour. My tires screech as we slip around corners—all right-hand turns, which has to be why she bought this house. Finally, mercifully, she turns into the driveway of a large two-story home.

I park on the street, engine ticking as I hyperventilate in the front seat. Sprinklers dug in the emerald green lawn suddenly activate. Margot's house is an exact replica of every other cookie-cutter home that you can find in any suburban neighborhood in Central Florida. I wonder how I've wound up here.

She truly is a magician, I think.

Before I get out of the car, I look at the Post-it note I've still got taped to my dash. WHAT DO YOU WANT TO BE REMEMBERED FOR? has been modified, several of the words slashed out so that it reads WHAT DO YOU WANT? An important question, and one I'm still considering. Now, I take a pen out of my bag and correct it again, rearranging the words until the new note reads DO YOU WANT TO?

Satisfied, I climb out of my car and see a familiar sign that reads DRIVE LIKE YOUR KIDS LIVE HERE.

I've been here before.

I turn clockwise, and yes, there it is, three houses down at the corner of the block: the white-and-yellow colonial where I fucked someone's mom in the family bathroom. The husband who threw a shampoo bottle at my head is out mowing his front lawn, cutting long, symmetrical stripes into the perfectly lush grass. I wonder if his wife is inside pouring him a big glass of lemonade. Maybe they'll have sex later using the makeup that she bought off me. I consider what he'd look like as a clown: paunchy and thick. Maybe some kind of fireman clown? He could throw her over his shoulder, pretend that he's saving her from a burning building. I wave at him and he waves back, one hand clutching the runaway mower, and for a moment it seems like he might recognize me too.

"Nice car," he yells.

"I know," I yell back. "You told me last time."

Then I let it go, walk up the paved path that leads to Margot's front door, and step inside the house.

It's not exactly what I'd anticipated. For one, the color scheme is all sunshine-bright reds and blues and yellows; the place screams elementary school art teacher. I head down the wide front hall with its large abstract prints and shelves full of carnival glass and find Margot in the enormous kitchen, pouring us some dark, berry-colored wine. Wearing all that black in the middle of the entirely white room gives off the effect that she's sucked all the color from the place. She's like a beautiful black hole, I think, taking one of the stemmed glasses from her outstretched hand.

"Isn't it a little early for this?" I ask, before remembering that not too long ago I drank half a bottle of peppermint schnapps with her ex-wife at three in the afternoon. I will never tell her about that; I will never reveal that my mother is marrying her ex-wife. It's my secret to keep. My own disappearing trick.

"It's never too early for wine." Margot holds her glass up to the light, inspects the jewel-like hue. "This is very good. You can tell by the legs."

"Great legs," I say, though I have no idea what she's talking about.

She holds out her glass to me. "Cheers."

"Cheers to what?"

"To our success."

We clink glasses and taste the wine. It's better after a few more sips, but wine always tastes better after I'm already on my way to drunk. "What success?" I ask, because I can't imagine what we have to celebrate.

"The casting office loved you," she says.

"They *what*?"

I follow her from the kitchen into a sunken living room that looks out onto a large backyard full of riotous green plants. Cardinals flit past; a female and a male, the two of them lighting on an expensive feeder that's been installed near a wealth of fragrant jasmine. It's so succulent, I can nearly smell it through the window glass.

Margot pats the seat beside her. "You thought they'd hate it, didn't you?"

"Yes," I say. "I told them to go fuck themselves."

Margot laughs, red lips parted to show all her back teeth. Silver fillings. My mother has the same ones. "I'm sure you did."

"And they liked that?"

She shrugs, sips more of her wine. "You weren't trying to impress them. An original, that's what they called you. They like that, you know. People come in, day after day, show them the same old thing." Margot picks up a deck of cards from the glass-topped coffee table and shuffles through them professionally before holding them out to me, face down.

"But I was vulgar. I mean, I swore a blue streak. I talked about *sex*." I pick a card from the center of the deck. Jack of hearts. "The parks don't go for that stuff."

She takes the card from me and puts it back in the deck. She shuffles the cards again. They flip and scrape against one another in a pleasant whir. Her hands are small and delicate, they fly like birds at their work. "They don't care about content. They just want someone authentic. Someone totally new." She has me choose another card. Two of spades. Then she takes it back, shuffles again.

The wine has relaxed me. Sun dapples the wall behind her head, streaks her black hair with glints of garnet. "So what? They want me?"

"They do." She displays the deck again. I reach out limply, feeling sleepy, and choose another card. Four of clubs. I slip the card back in, she shuffles for a third time, then holds the stack out to me.

"Kiss it," she says. "For luck."

I press my lips to the top. Then she sets the deck back down on the coffee table. "And I want you," she says. "That's all that matters, isn't it?"

I nod. She knocks her fist against each of my knees. "Open your legs."

And I do, peeling my thighs slowly apart. She reaches between them and pulls a card out from under me. Four of clubs. She places it on top of my right thigh and then dives back down, drags out another. Two of spades. She puts that one on my left thigh. She smiles at me and then, sliding her fingers down the seam of my crotch, produces the jack of hearts. She presses it firmly against me, rubbing through the slick paper.

"Is this your card?"

"How'd you do that?"

She doesn't answer, just slides the edge of the card down my cheek and across my neck. She holds it there with her thumb, taking my face in the bowl of her hands. She kisses me.

It's as good as ever, a drugging, deep kind of kissing that always makes me forget where I am. And I probably would have stayed in that foggy, unknown place too, except when she pulls away to kiss my neck, I see a large arrangement of framed photos next to the couch. Half a dozen pictures of her ex-wife are on display.

"Oh," I say. "Oh boy."

She sits back. Her lipstick has smeared across her chin. "Is something wrong?"

I pick up one of the framed photos. Portia on a tire swing, a flower crown in her hair. Portia wearing a floral-patterned apron and holding up a platter, displaying a Thanksgiving turkey. And a wedding portrait, the two of them wrapped in each other's arms. "Margot . . . why are these still up?"

"We were together a long time," she says. "Of course I have some mementos."

As I look around the living room, I begin to understand why the house looks the way it does. It's all Portia. Her colors, her art. Her furniture selections. This is the house they built together. It's a shrine to what came before.

"It's okay," I say. "I get it."

"Do you?" She slips a long curl of dark hair behind her ear. "I don't. Not really. I didn't want a divorce."

I'm sure she didn't. Just like I'm sure that Portia is going to marry my mother. Just like I'm sure that I'm not going to take that job at the theme park. Margot isn't over her ex-wife, and I'm still trying to figure out how to be Cherry. We'll fuck and we'll hurt each other and we'll lose each other. And then maybe we'll find each other and do it all over again. Life is like that, I think. Intimately messy, but never boring.

In that moment, in the room with all its light and Margot in the center of it like a fresh bruise, I consider what I want to do. I decide that right now, I want to take Margot to bed. And tomorrow can be whatever it might be. And the next day can be something different too.

DO YOU WANT TO?

Yes, I think. For now.

I wind my fingers through hers. I follow her to the back of the house. And we work to make each other disappear.

CLOWN OF THE YEAR

A clown's greatest asset? The element of surprise.

This applies to your audience, sure, but above all else, you must be able to surprise yourself. If the clown already anticipates the punch line, the joke will inevitably fail. Despite how carefully you apply your greasepaint or how much effort you put into your costume, the crowd can always tell when a gag has worn itself thin from repeated use. Better if you tumble into the bit blindly and without artifice, occasionally falling flat on your face. At the very least, the audience will appreciate the effort. Maybe you'll screw up, but hey, at least you're not phoning it in. It's like free-falling from the plane but with a sack of jumbled props strapped to your back instead of a parachute. Dangerous, but always good for a laugh.

I'm in the parking lot of my local 7-Eleven. It's late afternoon and I'm sipping from a Big Gulp that's mostly Bacardi mixed with too much crushed ice and not nearly enough Sprite. There's a plywood sign erected next to my car, announcing that the next show will start in less than fifteen minutes.

COME SEE CHERRY, it says. Drippy pink paint on bare wood, leftovers from Darcy's repaint. Flashy gold glitter. 3 PM SHARP!

People pull in and out of the lot, pumping gas, buying soda and milk and turkey sandwiches and scratch-off lottery tickets and overpriced antacids and fresh hot coffee. The allure of the convenience store is its *convenience*: you stop in for what you need, and then you leave. What better place to try out a new act? If I can get them to pay attention here, I can grab them anywhere. I wave to a woman in a white sundress and strappy heels; she pretends she doesn't see me and hurries inside, wedging her bag tightly under her arm.

In just a few minutes, I'll pop open the trunk of my bright red Pontiac Firebird and start the show. To be perfectly honest, the car has gotten me more looks than either my sign or my costume. People assume that I'm either part of a nearby car show or that I'm putting her up for sale. I have to admit she looks good in all that late-afternoon sunshine; the shiny red paint and gleaming chrome are sparking jealous looks from guys filling up their eco-friendly tanks.

I slurp heartily from my steadily emptying cup and let the condensation drip freely onto the asphalt between my feet. The costume isn't my usual fare. It's no Bunko with his lasso and his chaps, his rhinestones and sequins and bright blue curly wig. But I made it myself, piecing everything together like a seamstress Frankenstein, and I can say with 100 percent certainty that no one has ever seen anything quite like it before.

Josiris props open the front door to the 7-Eleven and leans against the plate glass. I met her a few weeks back when I attempted to perform this same showcase inside the store. She's an entertainer herself—an aspiring actress who's booked roles in local car dealership ads and community college commercials—so instead of booting me completely from the premises, she offered up a parking space. And now she's tapping her watch; she's going on her smoke break, already two puffs into her Marlboro red, which means that it's time to start the show. I clap my hands together twice, which startles some pigeons that are digging through a nearby dumpster. I clap again and a few heads swivel in my direction. That's something, I think. Once I feel ready, I pop open the trunk.

And behold, a puppet theater. The interior of the trunk has been outfitted to resemble a makeshift courtroom. Dolls occupy two rows of assembled chairs crafted from discarded pieces of plywood and cast-off fabric scraps. To the right, behind a large wooden lectern, sits my ventriloquist dummy. Instead of her jumpsuit, Velma wears a black robe with a white collar. Her wooden hand clutches a gavel. She's got a mean glint in her eye, and her hair is pushed back in a black headband. A boom box hidden in the spare-tire well plays the theme from *The People's Court*.

At the very top of the trunk hangs a glittered taffeta banner. It's the kind of sash you might see on a homecoming queen, but this one is announcing something much more important.

Outlined in red sequins, the sign reads THE TRIAL OF CHERRY HEN-DRICKS.

The bailiff stands up, ready to announce my charges. In this instance, the bailiff is a floppy-eared stuffed collie that I've hollowed out and turned into a puppet. Most of the jurors are puppets that I took from Miri's house after Camila threatened to toss them. The giant-headed doll with its cracked face stares moodily into the parking lot, both of its blue glass eyes pointed in different directions. Barbie sits beside her, dressed for a day of aerobics in fuzzy leg warmers and a neon-green leotard—one of Darcy's brood that she recently freed from the walls of her mother's house. I understand that Barbie's inclusion is tantamount to my stacking the jury, but it's a risk I'm willing to take.

As the bailiff lists my crimes—shoplifting (stole a Big Gulp from the 7-Eleven—I take a huge slurp from the straw after this is announced), bribery (offered Josiris half my Bacardi if she'd let me have a free Big Gulp), kidnapping (I didn't tell Darcy that I was taking her Barbie, and she's been looking for it for well over a week), and identity theft (stealing bits and costume ideas and gags and jokes)—a crowd begins to accumulate. It's not much, but it's something. There's a guy pumping gas; his wife's got the front window rolled down, and she's watching me from the front seat. A middle school kid stares at me, straddling his bike while holding a Slurpee cup and a bag of sour gummy worms, dipping one of the worms repeatedly in and out of the frozen liquid before sucking all the residue off. A sixty-something woman in a bright pink sun visor and a pair of white plastic sunglasses has parked herself on the curb next to the store's entrance. She waves at me and I smile back.

The thing about these trials is that I never know which way the jury is going to lean. That's probably because I play the defense attorney as well as the prosecutor. I've painted my face and altered my clothes to represent all three parties: my right side is the prosecutor, a no-nonsense woman with steely-gray hair and immense shoulder pads; my left side is the defense attorney, a sharpshooter with a thick Southern drawl and wire-framed glasses; and the center is me, Cherry, hair skunked down the middle in its usual grease-slicked black, a stripe of Aquarium Select III polo and khaki pants running the length of me. Depending on whose turn it is to speak, I pivot to display that persona to the audience.

I've gotten better at ventriloquism. Sound spills and slips across the lot on a current, words popping from Velma's mouth with barely any help from me. Sometimes I forget that I'm the one voicing her. Velma's the toughest judge on the circuit.

JUDGE: You've stolen from every act you've ever seen. Is that correct?

CHERRY: No, Your Honor. Not *every* act.

JUDGE: So, you're saying that you've taken some of them?

CHERRY: I mean, it's hard to explain why theft is wrong to a burglar.

JUDGE: Why is that?

CHERRY: Because they take things, literally.

JUDGE: Stealing from others is property theft.

CHERRY: I didn't take a fence.

JUDGE: Enough jokes! Didn't your mother ever tell you that you could be anyone you wanted to be?

CHERRY: Your Honor, identity theft is a crime.

JUDGE: You're awfully annoying, you know that? This trial better not go on much longer.

CHERRY: Hopefully it's a briefcase.

JURY: [groaning] Oh dear God, she's terrible!

JUDGE: Order in the court!

My jokes refuse to land; the meager crowd has dispersed. Even Josiris has decided she's seen enough. Halfway through the act, she'd stubbed out her cigarette and gone back inside the store.

But it doesn't matter. The point of the piece is that I get to remake it every day. All new jokes, all new bits. Every day I'm put on trial. Sometimes I'm acquitted. This is one of those days, I think; I'm going to let myself off on good behavior.

The woman in the pink visor and cheap sunglasses gets up from curb, clapping enthusiastically.

"That was pretty good," she says. She's tacky and cute and exactly my type, old enough to be my mother. "Do you know any jokes about Florida?"

You can tell the same joke a dozen different ways and always land on the same punch line. As long as you still get a laugh, who cares?

Sometimes the very best surprise is that there's no surprise at all.

"Would you like to get a drink?" I ask. "My treat."

"Hell yeah, if you're paying."

"Yes. And I'll drive."

I put away my sign and shut my trunk. I throw my empty Big Gulp into the dumpster and the roosting pigeons fly out. Someone zooms past on the strip, stereo blasting a familiar song. I open the passenger-side door for the pink-visored woman and drive us both a fair way down the road. When I get to a local spot that I like, I hand her a ten-dollar bill and tell her to head inside first. The sun is starting to set and it's going to be happy hour soon. After a minute of watching the sky turn radio-active, I follow along after.

I'm just a clown walking into a bar.

Stop me if you've heard this one.

Acknowledgments

I want to start off by thanking the person who really made this book possible. And that is my wife, Kayla Kumari Upadhyaya. I know it's normally tradition to save your spouse for the end of the acknowledgments, but I can't help myself. She deserves top billing. Kayla: thank you for your endless support, for always reading my work, for listening to my bad jokes (and for always punching them up), for one thousand beautiful meals and a million laughs to go with them. You are so incredibly hot. I love you.

Thank you to my publisher, Riverhead Books, and everyone there who has worked tirelessly to champion this gay book about a birthday party clown. You guys really took a chance on this one! Thanks to my intrepid new editor, Alison Fairbrother. It's been a whirlwind, and you got right down to business. You believed in me and my work right from the start. I am so grateful. Thank you to Cal Morgan for putting me in such good hands.

I love my agent, Serene Hakim, and all the stars at Ayesha Pande Literary Agency.

Thank you to the Ragdale Foundation and all the other fellows at my residency. My time with you was invaluable; I rediscovered myself in your fields and flowers and haunted rooms. To all the ladybugs I met: you were lucky for me, I hope I was also lucky for you, too.

Thank you to *Literary Hub* and Jonny Diamond and the fact that you let me write a drunk advice column every other week. I can talk y'all into anything, it's really wild.

Thanks, beer. Thanks, BOGO Publix wine. Thanks, happy hour. Thanks, airport bar.

Thanks, Bravo.

But more seriously, thank you to my first reader and incredibly gifted friend, Jami Attenberg. I am forever awed by your genius brain. Thank you for always taking the time to talk to me about writing and one billion books (and, let's be honest, literary gossip). So many trips spent petting little dogs and drinking good (and bad) wine, stumbling around the beautiful streets at night, soaking in the damp air, cackling, making plans for our writing futures. I'm so lucky to have a friend (and mentor) like you!

My best friends Maria Rada and Serpent Bota. I love you both so dearly. You listened to me yap for a literal decade about my writing, uncomplaining, even when I was at my most boring (and I was boring A LOT). I could not have done any of this without you. Thank you for being there for me no matter how many times I forget to return your text messages. Or when I drunkenly tell you that I'll help raise your children (Maria, I don't think you should take me up on this). Or when I drink a whole bottle of wine and tell you a story you've already heard fifty times (Bota, bless you). Thank you for being my VIPs. My heart is your heart, you can have it anytime.

Vivian Lee and Willie Fitzgerald! You're both funnier than me and a thousand times more charming and cool. Frankly, it's annoying. Imagine . . . Dragons. No one else I'd rather be roasted by. TEETH TEETH forever.

Sarah Rose Etter, Carmen Maria Machado, Sam Irby. The Greatest. Eye Emoji. IYKYK.

I have so many friends that it's sickening. You are the reason I'm able to write. Tommy Pico (who officiated my wedding, truly an all-star who can do *anything*), Caroline Casey, Morgan Parker, Tara Atkinson, Frances Dinger, Kim Selling. Hannah Oliver Depp. Esmé Weijun Wang, Danielle Evans, Lyz Lenz, Matt Salesses, Manuel Gonzales, Tony Perez (and Tony's mom, Claire), Maris Kreizman and Josh Gondelman, Jason and Emily Diamond, Isaac Fitzgerald, Alex Chee and Dustin Schell, Sara Ortiz. Steph Opitz. Claire Landsbaum. Sabrina Imbler. Yashwina Canter, Sreshtha

Sen, Lille Allen, Tajja Isen, Isle McElroy. Elissa Washuta. Sally Neumann. Lupita Aquino.

My wife's friends are my friends! Becca, Timlin, Quiniva, Christina, Drew, Emma, Caroline, Jillian, Aly, Mariah, Melanie, Erin, Rayna, Paul.

My wife's family is my family! Elizabeth and Alok, my wonderful in-laws. Thank you to the Upadhyayas, the LaLondes, the Mosses. Meredith Shock. Lars and Niki. Baby Lola! Thank you most especially to my sister-in-law, Alex Upadhyaya, who took on our entire wedding and made it gorgeous. I can never thank you enough.

Thank you, *Autostraddle*!

Thank you, Tin House Workshop!

Thank you to every person who sent me a clown meme!

Lola Jane and Timmy Tomato.

My son, Mattie, who is basically my clone. I'm so proud of you, buddy.

I love all my Florida friends. You make me so proud to live here. T Kira Māhealani Madden (and Hannah Beresford, you are Florida by association), Laura van den Berg, Stef Rubino and Stacey, Lauren Groff, Dantiel W. Moniz, Ryan Rivas and Chelsea Simmons, Bobuq Sayed, Chris Alonso. James, Alicia, Kristopher, Alex, Ashley and Sophia, Jairo, Rob and Reuben, Daniel and Ben, Delano, Sarah. Heather, Alex, Andrea. Michellina. Leslie and Sarah. Erica, Molly, Gabbie, Vanessa. My sister, Rachel Anne. Margo. Karen Russell. Alissa Nutting. Lindsay Hunter. Greg and Holly Golden. The Vulgar Geniuses! Aloma Bowl and the Brooklyn South Bar. *Orlando Weekly* and Jessica Bryce Young. My 7-Eleven and all the cashiers, you know who you are. The Courtesy Bar, which is essentially our Cheers—everyone knows us by name; nothing brings me greater joy. Rollins College. Fidds. Stardust Video & Coffee. The Enzian and Eden Bar. Big Daddy's karaoke and too many Miller Lites. Lizards and snakes and too many fucking birds to count them all. Mosquitoes. I-4 traffic. Lakes and so much goddamn water and mildew. Humidity. The smell of the grass after the rain.

Florida, I'm obsessed with you. I can't ever get enough.

Now I'm going to thank Kayla, again. What? You didn't think I would? C'mon, I'm a wife guy.